Praise fo

"With the language of a poet and the precision of a journalist, Chadwick artfully unfolds an unforgettable tale of family, unspeakable grief, and the glory of the human capacity for forgiveness. Great storytelling is what she does, and we are the beneficiaries."

—David W. Berner, author of the *The Islander*

"This heartwarming, tender story of letting go and forgiveness is beautifully told. In its poetic descriptions of nature and of small-town life in the midst of change, *Mercy Town* comes fully alive."

—Céline Keating, author of *The Stark Beauty of Last Things*

"Chadwick has crafted a story that lingers in our hearts long after we have put the book down. This book will remind you that forgiveness—not just for others, but for yourself—heals the heart."

—*BookTrib*

"Nancy Chadwick takes us deep into the hearts of those whose lives are upended by others' mistakes and shows what mercy can mean to all."

—Penny Haw, author of *The Wilderness Between Us* and *The Invincible Miss Cust*

"The impressive blend of pacing, contemporary issues, and drama transforms *Mercy Town* into a thought-provoking novel that will appeal to fans of realistic fiction."

—*Readers' Favorite*, 5-star review

mercy town

mercy town

a novel

nancy chadwick

SHE WRITES PRESS

Copyright © 2025, Nancy Chadwick

All rights reserved. No part of this publication may be reproduced, stored in a retrieval system, or transmitted in any form or by any means, electronic, mechanical, photocopying, recording, or otherwise, except for brief quotations in reviews, educational works, or other uses permitted by copyright law.

Published in 2025 by
She Writes Press, an imprint of The Stable Book Group

32 Court Street, Suite 2109
Brooklyn, NY 11201
https://shewritespress.com

Library of Congress Control Number: 2025908957
Print ISBN: 978-1-64742-968-3
E-ISBN: 978-1-64742-969-0

Interior designer: Katherine Lloyd, The DESK

Printed in the United States

This is a work of fiction. Names, characters, places, and incidents are either products of the author's imagination or are used fictitiously. Any resemblance to actual persons, living or dead, is purely coincidental.

No part of this publication may be used to train generative artificial intelligence (AI) models. The publisher and author reserve all rights related to the use of this content in machine learning.

All company and product names mentioned in this book may be trademarks or registered trademarks of their respective owners. They are used for identification purposes only and do not imply endorsement or affiliation.

To the forgivers
And the heavy-hearted souls who seek mercy

The stars are not wanted now: put out every one;
Pack up the moon and dismantle the sun;
Pour away the ocean and sweep up the wood;
For nothing now can ever come to any good.

—W. H. Auden

march

I wasn't the only one whose life changed forever the minute the echo of a loud bang sliced its way through the spines of the spruce and the arms of the tamarack. The resonance was preceded by a soft click that was the talk of neither mature red-winged blackbirds nor young crows. Some people moved on from the aftershocks of that late afternoon spring day, and some didn't. For those who didn't, the hate grew over the years to a seeming point of no return. It defined them as something other than what I remembered them to be—kindhearted, forgiving. For others, they held their compassion inside, close to the heart, so as not to excite the ire of those who were opposed, sending the town of Waunasha into a frenzy of disunity that couldn't be touched because of its heat. It just wasn't right.

I grew up in Waunasha, a small rural town in north Wisconsin on the south side of the Loch River, where the frames of farmhouses dug deep into the earth that kept us fed and profiting. While I plodded ankle deep in sedge and rye grass anywhere in my backyard, the river slivered quietly yards ahead, behind a thicket of birches that sought their happy place near water and could be seen through pockets of space, their slender, wavy leaves

mercy town

in contrast with the hardy, larger leaves of their sugar maple neighbors. It was the bodies of trees in the old-growth forest that kept me and Bean safe during our walks as we asked them for their guidance and protection. With our every youthful step among the understory of Canadian wild ginger and wild geranium, we acknowledged their existence and their places upon the very earth where the trees for generations have sunk their footing.

The surrounding deep landscape held the Payne family close—my papa, Ellis; my mom, Carolyne; my younger brother, Bean; and me, Ret. Well, it's really Margaret, but Bean called me Ret because Margaret was just a mouthful of syllables, and using only one seemed to get to the point. In the middle of a clearing was our old white house. When I was tending to the front yard with Papa, keeping in motion with sweeping, wiping, and gathering of whatever had been discovered astray, he'd remind me that our home had remained in the family for three generations, with its painted black shutters and a front porch that got the most use during three seasons out of four. Ripples of smoke puffing from the chimney told our neighbors that we were at home, should we be needed.

On the north side of the river, a half dozen long-standing cabins appeared squat, dark, and soft like ink splotches, stained upon a clearing on a hill, surrounded by a mix of looming conifers and deciduous trees with nary a sunbeam intense enough to penetrate Dell Landing. This was the place Mr. Kipp had called home his whole life. Until one spring day, it wasn't. And that's where I found the true story.

thursday

The anticipation of an announcement one morning at the *West Prairie Journal* was enough to jump-start me out of bed. As I used to tell Bean, you just have to believe if you want something to come true. That day, as soon as my eyes focused on the ceiling fan, I believed I'd get the assignment to be the feature reporter for "About Town," the new section of the *West Prairie Journal.*

I had always called myself a writer, ever since I was a child and could read story books. Sometimes I didn't learn stories through the turning of pages, but through the words coming from Papa's mouth. In those days, storytelling began after supper, when the sun was settling herself down from her day's weariness. It was routine as any morning chore, like feeding the horses or mucking out their stalls. After supper, Bean and I would sit small on the floor and see him looking large as he rocked in his chair by the fireplace in cold months, or outside on the porch if it was warm enough. With his feet encased in old leather but with new soles, flat to the wooden floorboards, he'd rock, his heels falling into a rhythm. But before he would begin, he'd ask. "So, what makes for

mercy town

a good story?" Bean would pipe up, "One where I want to know what happens next." I told him, "One that makes you think." I'd listen to stories intently and then think that perhaps I could write one myself.

Visits to the Waunasha Public Library on weekends told me so. I'd run my finger down book spines, overcrowded and stacked high on shelves that were plotted like labyrinths. A need to write grew with each pull from the shelf and stroll through an aisle. I wrote short things about this and that through high school, and worked on the newspaper, the NASHA NEWS, as a lead reporter. I took every opportunity to submit my work to writing competitions at school, in my town, or even to the city paper, the *West Prairie Journal*. That's where I met Mr. Simpson, the editor. How I flooded him with submissions, from op-eds to hard news to features. I hoped one day he'd see my talent, or if not, at least my perseverance, and offer me a job when I finished school. Then one day in May during lunchtime, while Mom and I looked for a graduation dress at Fay Rhodes, a fancy ladies' dress shop in West Prairie, I spotted Mr. Simpson standing outside the newspaper office, in front of the open window of the Carmine's Taqueria food truck.

"Oh, yes, Miss Payne," he said, his cheeks plump with beef. "Of course I remember you." I wasn't sure if he was just saying that, or if he really did remember me. "Listen," he said, crouching lower as if about to tell a secret. His black-framed eyeglasses dangled from the front pocket of his shirt. The first two buttons were undone, and I could see coarse, curly salt-and-pepper hair poking through. "After you've finished school, and if you're still interested in writing, come talk to me."

"Still interested?" I exclaimed. "Yes, sir, I certainly am. Graduating in two weeks." I held my chin higher and my shoulders back. He stood upright, grabbed his eyeglasses, and told me to call him after I graduated. Well, I did. I got myself together, dressed

nancy chadwick

in a suit of navy gabardine and heels to match, and knocked on Mr. Simpson's door. And he let me in.

"Ya got time, Margaret. Relax," Jesse told me, drinking his morning coffee at the kitchen table while perusing the sports page in the *West Prairie Journal*. I paid him no attention while I buzzed around the kitchen like a bee finding its best landing spot.

I guess you could say I'm a morning person. As if poked with a shot of adrenaline, I was in high gear as soon as my feet hit the carpeted bedroom floor in the morning, multitasking while dancing around the kitchen. A bite of ham-and-cheese pastry and a gulp of orange juice, followed by a dainty sip of scalding black coffee, clean up, grab my bag and keys, and out the door I'd go. Whoops. Sometimes I'd forget to give my husband a kiss and caress on the cheek, so I'd backtrack a step or two to give him the attention he deserved.

"You hardly ate a thing, hon," he said, watching me flit around barefoot, shirt untucked, hair astray, while he sat buttering his toast with nary a wrinkle exposed from his button-down shirt to dress trousers. The tracks from the teeth of his comb were visible through his clean, coarse hair.

Jesse has a stomach that matches his frame—deep, cavernous, and never satisfied. He's solid, all right, and handsome, of hearty Irish stock from his father, Clay, mixed with a bit of German and Norwegian from his mother, Effie. I, on the other hand, had Mom's willowy frame, not to be confused with weakness. We could trace ourselves back to Grandma Carter, a steadfast homemaker, on my mother's side, and the penchant for storytelling from Papa's father, Albert, who started a newspaper in a small town somewhere in Alaska, I thought.

"It's enough for right now, thanks. The assignment for the first feature in the new section of the paper is being announced

mercy town

this morning, and, well, I hope . . . no, I *will* get this," I said with a fist pump. I believed the day to be full of promise as the sun rose this morning to break the spring chill.

"You'll get it. You've proven yourself at that paper."

With that shot of assurance, Jesse leaped from the kitchen table as if his legs were on springs, grabbed my waist, and enveloped my entire body with his. He was warm and smelled of evergreen. He gave me a fat kiss on the neck before I slipped away to the sink to rinse my coffee cup and breakfast dish. Bentley, our best beagle, was at my heels, begging for leftovers.

I looked through the window, no longer framed by frost, to the backyard. The air had softened with temperatures now above freezing. Yellow and purple crocus broke through the warmed flower beds that encircled the patio.

"Hey, ya know, I'm looking forward to our anniversary this June," he said, standing next to me at the sink, drying his coffee mug.

"That's summer, Jesse. I just can't think ahead right now. I'm too focused this morning. Sorry." I dried my hands and spun to scan all surfaces for my bag and laptop.

"Doesn't matter. It'll be here before you know it." He stopped me in full dance, grabbed my hand in his, the way he always did, and pulled me close.

When I was eighteen, I knew I wanted to marry Jesse. I remembered him as the older boy from Woods Mill, a larger town just south of Waunasha on the other side of the railroad tracks. Woods Mill was considered more sophisticated and wealthier than my side of the tracks, where the living was simpler and poorer. When we were kids, Bean and I would tell Mom that we were going on a scavenger hunt in the woods. This was code for a wander along the undesirable railroad tracks where we'd find just about anything: soda bottles, a Nike sneaker, a broken fishing pole, a woman's underwear. While Bean poked with a stick the remnants of humanity, my eyes were drawn to the bright colors of goldenrod and black-eyed Susans that rose from the dark of the detritus. Until my eyes came upon one Jesse Reed. He usually appeared to be searching for something he had lost, hanging his head and strolling along. Bean would stare at him, confused, like he was some special forager assigned by the county. I, however, would look at him as the one who didn't belong. He was dressed too nicely: clean denims, a tan button-down shirt that was always tucked in and held with a belt, stiff brown boots that looked as if they never saw the elements. We'd meet, chat a little about the finds he and Bean had, if any, and then I'd share my discoveries of new flowers coming up with the developing season. Bean would take the lead while Jesse and I followed. When it came time for Jesse to go home, he'd give me a nod and a wink, after his hungry eyes gave me the up and down, then walk backward before turning around to return to where he came from. I already wanted to see him again. By then, we could hear the five o'clock Great Northern Railroad's whistle traveling through with the breeze, telling us it was time to go home.

Breaking from Jesse's hold, I scanned the desk in the corner, a collection of daily living, pushing away unopened mail, unpaid bills, and lists scribbled on bits of paper, lots of them, some expired and some I had misplaced. Furthering my search, I rushed to check the time on the cuckoo clock ticking in the hall, before taking the stairs up two at a time to the guest bedroom. It was a spare in name only, as I had claimed it as a writing place on the day we moved in. It was a sufficiently cozy space for my imagination to blossom and my words to find their resting places on the page, yet insufficient for welcoming any guest. My habits in keeping tidy leave much to be desired. I pushed aside on the bed a box of old clothes ready for the needy, and clean laundry that required hanging, then scanned the tops of the dresser and bookcase. And there it was, on the desk. I slid the laptop into my bag, shifting the contents of a notebook, file folders, and loose paper so all would fit. Threading my arm through the straps, I glimpsed at petite framed pictures highlighted under a small lamp's dim light on the desk. They were of me and Bean, with Mom and Papa at our house in Waunasha, sitting under the arms of the black oak in the backyard, when each day seemed to be a copy of the previous one and the hum of routine from sunup to sundown was comforting. I touched them in prayer, remembering. When I yanked on a chair to push it back into place, a leg caught on something underneath the desk. I pushed harder, but the chair wouldn't budge. I bent down to have a look and remembered this dark place was where I had once stashed a box, one I had marked "private." Tipped on its side, it had spilled my treasures: photographs of me and little Bean, Billy the crow, a handknit scarf made by Grandma Carter. And that was all. I thought I had placed my journal here, the one with a last entry date of March 9, ten years ago, but it was not there. I had dropped it that day, somewhere in the mud, and camouflaged among the decayed leaves. When I had found it weeks later, near my sit spot, its stiff leather bindings were scratched from twigs sticking up like spikes from the spring defrost. I could not return to that place for quite some time until the promise of summer erased the spring days that had brought remembrances of Bean ten years ago.

That morning was a day of sure spring because Mom relocated her gardening caddy from its winter parking spot on the shelf in the shed to the front porch. As Bean had said every year when he'd see her with the tool tote in her hand, "It must be time now, huh, Ret?" When I'd tell him, "It is, Bean. Shall we go out and say hello to Mother Earth?" I thought every seam in his clothing would bust from excitement. After being cooped up in winter's hibernation, he was ready to greet another new life cycle of growing things. The slap of the screen door sounded like a starting gun, as if we were anticipating a race of some kind. Pop.

We were off. Mother yelled before we hit the last step of the porch stairs for Bean never to leave without his sister, and for me never to come back without my brother.

Our lively steps across the backyard increased as we noticed when connecting with the trail how Mother Earth had budded quickly that spring. Tree stumps and broken limbs interrupted the defrosting water's urgency to travel again. Bean's pace exploded ahead of mine. I guess he outgrew the guiding ways of his big sister. At first, I was glad to be alone, but I missed seeing the forest through his eyes; I'd come to depend on his interpretation of the world, as if I'd grown too old and the familiar too trite. But it was the stars, and the sun kissing the river, I told him . . .

And those were my last recorded thoughts of that morning before I heard the echo, the shot bleeding through the forest, jarring the birds to safety. I sprang from my spot, dropping my journal and leaving open the page of the day that had begun and ended in just one paragraph.

"Did you find your stuff?" Jesse yelled from the bottom of the stairs. I pushed its contents and my memories back under the desk until they were out of sight and in a tomb of darkness once again. I slipped on a pair of heels, tucked in my shirttail, and pulled back my hair, securing it with a clip, then checked myself in the full-length mirror that hung on the inside closet door. Staying with the usual rhythm of readying myself for work, I grabbed my work bag and rushed down the stairs. With my thoughts elsewhere, I said, "See ya," passing him, where he stood in front

mercy town

of an open refrigerator as if memorizing its contents. I grabbed the thermos of coffee waiting for me at the counter's edge by the door, where Jesse always leaves it for me on work mornings, and scratched Bentley behind the ears. "You be a good boy, now," I told him. With the vision of my journal and then seeing Jesse, I was reminded that I never did tell him the full story about Bean. And that was okay, for now.

The morning sun had risen higher, splashing pink and gold onto a bluing sky like a painter on his canvas. I gave a wave to Donny across the street, who was suitably dressed in tied brown shoes. He nodded and tipped the chapeau on his head. We appeared to be on the same schedule: he, picking up his newspaper from the driveway, me, getting into my car and leaving for work. The comforting familiarity of seeing a neighbor and keeping pace with my departure brought me back to the present. I tossed my tote into the car seat beside me before I slid into the driver's side. With one last check of my face in the rearview mirror for insufficient cleanliness or errant lipstick, I was ready. Putting the car into reverse, I heard, "Wait, Margaret . . . you forgot . . . your coat," as Jesse ran to the car. I rolled down the window, then took the raincoat he passed through the opening.

It was a difficult balance—tending to my husband and marriage while focusing on work. Time spent on assignments for the paper was time away from Jesse and what brought us together— long walks, poking the earth to search what lay at our feet and what we saw on the horizon. And I was reminded every day to always roll down a window to see what was on the outside.

"You going to be okay today?" he asked, reaching in and placing a soft, warm palm against my cheek.

"Sure am. I'll handle whatever comes my way just fine."

"I might be a little late. Reviewing plans for the Dell Landing project," he yelled as I rolled the window back up. I couldn't hear much of what he said; I figured if it was important, he knew to call me. I usually never got that involved in any of his real estate development projects, as they were too complicated even for a newspaper woman like me who asked questions all day. We waved at each other before Jesse went back inside.

Before pulling out, I locked my attention on our house, a home that Jesse and I had made. While I had been commuting from Waunasha into West Prairie to work for the paper just after high school, he had gone to the state college. We kept in touch with long, late-night phone chats and weekend visits, never wavering in our eagerness to see each other. Eventually, we had come full circle, with both of us ending up with jobs in the city. We married soon after and bought the house all in the same year. He held my hand while guiding me, blindfolded, from the car parked at the curb, up the sidewalk, and then stopping at the front door. I heard children shouting at their moms, dogs barking, a lawn mower. I itched to see.

"Ta-da," Jesse said, slipping the covering from my eyes.

"A house? Whose?"

"Ours, Margaret, all ours. I bought it for us, to live happily ever after. I know it needs work, but it *is* a classic, isn't it?" His smile was as big as that house.

My excitement overwhelmed my ability to speak. It was perfect.

When we held the keys, the thought of turning this old house into our home made that June day the happiest day of my life, well, except for marrying Jesse. We painted the house in oyster white, the front door in sky blue, and pulled overgrown bushes that had hidden the living room windows. We trimmed hedges and planted colors in the name of roses, coneflowers, and peonies. It may have had old bones, but it was new in heart and soul.

I stared at our new, old home before easing out of the driveway. I waved to Olivia, a new mom next door, as she walked with baby Jeffrey, who was tucked inside a fancy stroller. Arbor Lane

mercy town

rustled with the beginnings of the day when owners walked pulling dogs, middle-schoolers eagerly rode their bikes, and cleaned-up dads left for work. At the intersection, I stopped before making a left onto Fairfax that would take me into the city. I waved at old man Anthony, seeing his tie flapping over his shoulder as he rode his bike in the crosswalk. He gave me a nod as he headed to work as a geography teacher at Thornwood Elementary.

The traffic along Fairfax was neither rushed nor heavy but moving along at a refined pace. Virginal green, appearing to be pulled by the early sun, brought the promise that spring was on its way. I softened my grip on the steering wheel and dropped my shoulders when I eyed signs for BEDFORD SQUARE CITY CENTER. I signaled for the exit and chuckled each time I read it. I didn't really consider West Prairie a city, though neighboring towns referred to it as such. When I thought of a city, I envisioned skyscrapers and buildings of glass and steel that commanded entire blocks, high-rise apartment buildings, and offices of thousands of square feet. Of course, I drew this from early memories of when Papa would go to agricultural conferences in Chicago. West Prairie was really a village, self-contained with just the necessities of economic living: city newspaper, village hall, police, fire, and public works departments, a library, and a restaurant or two. I was content with this reminder that I had everything I needed at home in West Prairie and at work in Bedford Square.

I was usually one of the first in at the *West Prairie Journal* office, and that day was no exception; I was the lone car sliding into a space in an empty lot. I liked to walk into a quiet place where I could have time to myself, much like I had when I was a young girl and retreated into the woods with my journal to observe the natural world's behavior. Some days, those pages became heavy with my reflections, as no two observations would witness the same recording.

I had never been this nervous about any Monday morning staff meeting before. Though sometimes I'd get bored reporting the same old things—what had closed, what had recently opened, and what was under new ownership—I took Mr. Simpson's assignments in stride. But that morning's meeting was to be a lot different. Instead of our usual meeting of brainstorming for topics most important to the city and to its residents, Mr. Simpson was to announce the assignment for the new section of the paper. I broke into a sly grin, thinking how Lonnie and Clarissa would handle their pre-meeting emotions. He would be as cool as ever. He'd sit back in his chair, hands folded behind a horseshoe of brown fringe along the back of his head, exposing a paunch that would pop through the opening of his suit jacket. Clarissa, on the other hand, would prove herself as if it were her first day on the job. She had a competitive edge that was sharp, showing her piercing looks and pointed words when she felt slighted or overlooked. It had happened before and perhaps would happen again, as I was sure to get this assignment and Clarissa would not.

Stepping out of the car, I smoothed the horizontal waves of wrinkles on my skirt, as if this tidying would be cause for extra consideration by Mr. Simpson. Perhaps attention to detail was a qualifier and what he was looking for in a star feature writer. Straightened out and ready, I yanked the stubborn front door lettered in gold capital letters, WEST PRAIRIE JOURNAL. A card swipe got me through another set of doors. The closed-in air emitted overnight by electronic equipment was stirred as soon as I flipped switches for the overhead ceiling fans. The sound of fingers tapping keyboards would soon replace stillness and quiet when reporters dropped into their empty cubicles like sugar cubes into coffee cups. I dropped my bag, coat, and thermos on my desk and looked ahead, distracted by a light coming from the break room. The coffee machine was in full cycle with its sputtering, chiming in with the clicking of the overhead fan blades. The

mercy town

fragrance of fresh coffee and the chirping of Lonnie's youthful voice reached me.

"Coffee's on," he announced. He lumbered to his cubicle like any linebacker, shifting from side to side with each weighty step. Only he was no footballer, but short-legged and soft. And he never sat kindly. He'd push off his feet, just when his bottom hit the seat, gliding on the chair's rollers until he bumped into the front wall of my cubicle. Despite this repetitive slight irritation, we worked well together.

"You look like you're readying yourself for an important meeting or something," he whispered, winking.

"I suppose you could say that." I walked away to the break room. That's when I saw Clarissa entering, vying for space through the front door with multiple totes hanging from her bony shoulders and thin arms. Not a strand of platinum hair was out of place despite the heavy breeze that accompanied her. She was matchy-matchy from her red pumps to the red scarf around her neck. We had learned to ignore her entrances, never giving her the satisfaction of the attention she wanted.

On my way back to my desk, I saw Kirby, dressed in a white short-sleeved button-down shirt and checkered tie, making his way through the aisles with the stainless-steel mail cart. He tossed the bundles with precision on each desk, landing them just left of its center. It was near enough to grab yet set aside to not disturb a writer who was working. Lately, Clarissa's bundle had landed with a plunk. The drumbeat caught the attention of those nearby as they noted the intrusive sound. She gave the stack of fan mail a pat, which then put a smile on her face.

I sat across the aisle from her and couldn't help but be distracted by her opening each envelope with a monogrammed letter opener. She'd shake the paper, freeing the letter from its binds, then read it, audibly sighing with a reply, "Oh, gosh, so nice, such nice people." She turned each page face down upon the previous one, creating a neat stack she admired. It was a rhythm she got into, and one that had never changed since her first day at the newspaper thirty years ago when she invoked the start of a new column, "Metro Mix," that had never seen its stack of mail diminish.

She called to me from across the aisle. "Ya ready for the morning meeting, Margaret?" Her sarcastic undertone matched the smirk on her face.

"She thinks she's a shoo-in for the spring feature assignment," Lonnie said with a nod her way.

"Morning, Margaret . . . Clarissa . . . Lonnie," Mr. Simpson said, entering the floor and taking long strides up the aisle to his office. The positioning of his tortoiseshell glasses on his nose and not on top of his thicket of dark hair told me he was already focused on the morning's meeting. Up and down those glasses usually went, just like a child's swing.

"Good morning, Mr. Simpson," I told him with confidence.

"Good placement on your public transportation piece. You got good insight, Reed," he said, tapping the top of my cubicle with a soft fist. Mr. Simpson usually called me by my last name when there was a compliment involved. I didn't mind. It made me feel like I belonged to the journalist pack. I grabbed my edition, scanned the headlines as we do every morning, and paged to the Metro section. "Developer in talks with forest preserve's Dell Landing." Developer? I wondered if this had something to do with the new feature. My stomach cramped, and my mouth got dry. *Dell Landing? What would any developer want with that old, stagnant piece of property in small-town Waunasha?*

"Let's go, people, we have a paper to run and the spring feature assignment," Mr. Simpson shouted over the whirring of computer terminals. I dropped my paper in that instant. Clarissa was the first to file into the aisle, sliding her red skirt down her curvy hips. Then me, then Lonnie, who pulled up the rear, in a ritual as if we were in church exiting the pews.

mercy town

The editorial staff of nine hustled into the conference room, filling seats at the rectangular table for ten. The lighting was dull. The veneer table and the threadbare chairs created a picture of the paper's history that started in the forties; it would appear that neither the lighting fixtures nor the office furniture had been updated since. I stood to the right of Mr. Simpson, who took the helm, with Lonnie springing next to me, forever by my side. My coworkers' eyes darted to and from one another. We followed Mr. Simpson's lead with nervous energy by pulling up chairs closer to the table before opening notebooks, taking a sip of coffee, and placing pencil in hand, in that order. Mr. Simpson dallied with scanning pages in an open folder in front of him, pulling down his glasses to sit low on his nose, then looked up from the tops of its rims and eyed each of us before speaking. My chest expanded with a deep breath; my hands dampened. I second-guessed myself about sitting so close to Mr. Simpson and shifted in my chair just a smidgeon to my right, a bit farther away from him. Whispers hushed. We waited for him to begin.

"First off, good job, Clarissa, on the long public transportation piece. Letters are already coming in after the first part of the three-part series, as you have probably seen already. You put yourself in there, out on the streets, asking hard questions, and involving the community. It stirred a lot of community response. Well done." The room shifted in unison, unsure if it was lack of patience or boredom from hearing another round of Clarissa's praises from Mr. Simpson. We clapped to her success. I gave Clarissa, sitting at the opposite end to where Mr. Simpson was sitting, a hard-eyed stare as she dropped a red-stained lower lip. Her eyebrows jumped in surprise as if she didn't see this coming. I admired her quickness and covert aggression in getting the stories she wanted from those closed-lipped sources who had all the answers to her questions.

nancy chadwick

Lonnie leaned his shoulder into mine and whispered, "You're up next, Margaret." A clearing cough was heard before I caught a whispered "suck up" Clarissa's way.

Mr. Simpson cleared his throat and swung those eyeglasses back atop his head. His eyes, the color of tobacco, stared at us, and our wide-eyed faces returned the look.

"Now, about that inaugural spring feature . . . I've made my decision." His voice was clear, unlike the mumbly monotone he typically used when reciting the agenda at other morning staff meetings. "As you know, this is big for the *Journal* as we have, in the past, seen a jump in readership after running a feature. Our goal is to increase revenue, and with readership, advertisers come knocking. It's a win-win for all."

An overhead fluorescent light blinked as if on cue, building the anticipation.

"Mr. Simpson," Clarissa spoke as if she were on air in an interview. She waved a pair of fingers in the air, clutching a pen with the others. "I'm looking forward to offering my best to you and to this paper for the spring edition, as it represents the best talent pool in the state. I'm ready when you are." She folded her hands politely in front of her and pushed a clump of wayward strands away from her face. The gray from the overhead lights showed her true middle age, despite her attempts to appear younger with a heavily made-up face.

Coffee cups descended slowly from mouth to table. I couldn't stand it anymore. I prickled as if a million ants were crawling all over me, and I thought my heart couldn't pound any harder. And how it had gotten so hot in there? I opened the top button on my blouse to breathe easier. Was I having a panic attack?

"Well, doesn't that tell you who's grabbing for the top spot?" Lonnie whispered. I didn't mind Clarissa's unsolicited plug for herself. She *was* an excellent reporter, unlike anyone I'd ever seen. She had a knack for putting interviewees at ease, confiding as if they were her best friends.

"As you know, I've been in meetings with the board. We are on our toes to increase readership, and I'm happy to report that it is up by four percent." Mr. Simpson fiddled with the tie around his neck, then smoothed it flat down his chest. "Now, we're a small city paper here in competition with the digital world, and that may not sound like much, but we have loyalists who look for our big stories with their names and pictures in them. We're going on the offense." With that announcement, Mr. Simpson stood. He looked at each one of us, building the anticipation. "With that in mind, I'm announcing a new monthly section. We're calling it 'Around Town.' We aim to have stories about local businesses and the folks who are integral to them. There's a lot of development going on here in West Prairie, with new apartments, the filling of office space, and the opening of small businesses. We need to chat with the developers to get their perspectives. And then we need to hit the streets. Bringing in community involvement is key." His voice shifted, dropping an octave. The air became thick, and our impatience grew thinner. I buckled up, ridding myself of my lack of confidence.

"And that's why I've chosen Margaret," he gestured to me with an open hand, "as the first feature writer for 'Around Town.'"

Slouching staff straightened. Clarissa's pen rolled off the table. Lonnie gave a congratulatory clap or two before the others joined in. And I froze. After that intro, I thought Clarissa was the sure thing. But Mr. Simpson got me there.

"Margaret, the county has one neighboring town in particular that is seeing a jump in developer activity. Apparently, Waunasha is undergoing quite a transformation."

"Waunasha?" I repeated as if I hadn't heard him correctly. Or maybe it was to confirm I *had* heard him correctly.

Clarissa said from the other end of the table, "Don't look so disappointed. It's a happening town these days, thanks to the new development." It was as if she knew all about it, giving herself a one-up, and me a big zero.

"I'm sending you to Waunasha to bring us a story about their revitalization. Get resident reaction, developer plans, county input," he continued. "I trust you won't need me to direct you, as you will do just fine at finding the heart of the story."

The silence broke with an exuberant round of applause while Lonnie, with his hand on my shoulder, nearly shook it from my neck. "I told you, you got it, girl!" he said.

My mouth, which couldn't have gotten any drier, made me unable to talk. I wasn't even thinking that I had just received my first feature assignment; I had to go back to my hometown.

I remained seated while waiting for the staff to leave the room. And then I stood.

"Mr. Simpson, thank you so much for this. I am so grateful. I was thinking—"

"You're the one, Margaret. I trust you. You've proven yourself."

"But I think Clarissa would do a great job. She knows how to get information, dig deep, uncover a lot that I'm not sure—"

"You'll do a fine job, Margaret. Finish up the week here and make your way to Waunasha," he said.

Mr. Simpson gathered his folders and notepad and clutched them with one arm to his barrel chest. With the other hand, he picked up his coffee mug and left me alone in the room.

Despite the cooler air from exiting bodies, I was flushed, paralyzed, knowing I couldn't get out of it, yet I didn't want to. I shouldn't, as this was an opportunity I was waiting for—one to explore what had happened so long ago and what had changed the townspeople and my family forever.

I dashed out to find the ladies' room, unbuttoning my jacket to breathe a little easier. I needed a few minutes alone to balance

mercy town

my excitement at receiving the new assignment with what it meant for me. When I left Waunasha after high school graduation, it was as if that spring day were on repeat. The town couldn't stop talking about what happened. My mom and Papa couldn't talk about it at all. We were all torn apart because of the horrible accident, each of us handling it in our own ways. Mom acted as if nothing had happened, continuing with her job at the Supervalu and managing the house, and keeping her head down. Papa managed his way with anger in his steps and a bark to his conversation, staring his opponent down in any discussion like hunting a coyote in the middle of winter. And my way was to avoid it altogether and not go back home.

I turned on the cold water from the faucet with a heavy hand, as if it were more difficult to do than it really was. The stream ran through my fingers and into my palms before I splashed what remained on my face. Under the unforgiving fluorescent lighting, my reflection in the mirror revealed the fifteen-year-old girl I once knew. It took a tragedy to make people see who they really were. And what happened on that Sunday afternoon, on the promise of a spring day, had changed the lives of the Paynes. Going back to Waunasha was going back to that girl and to that accident.

"Well, hey, hey, aren't you the one who got the golden pencil," Clarissa cooed, sashaying through the squeaky swinging door, then stopping next to me. We studied one another through the streaked mirror.

"Well, I'm humble—"

"You know why he picked *you*, don't you?" she said, leaning in close to the mirror to further study her claret painted lips. "He likes you, Margaret. You have the city inside your rural girl-body. And people like that about you, Miss Country Giiiirl." I watched her place a sheet of tissue between her lips and press them together. "Oh, and ... congratulations." She fluffed the hair on the sides of her face before pirouetting out the door.

Well, then, she couldn't help but to editorialize now, could she? Didn't matter. I knew she'd have to tell me how she really felt.

I smoothed wrinkles and pulled taut the wayward collar of my jacket as if to dissolve the terrible memories that had been choking me. One cleansing breath from belly to sternum, and I was out the door and back to my desk.

The hum on the floor and the buzz of overhead lights were distractions that helped me to return to my place for the remaining day and not focus on the drama of the morning. Business as usual resumed. Clarissa and I ignored each other, while Lonnie gave me nods and salutes with two fingers in the conclusion of our conversations. Calvin and Jimmy in Transportation hovered over Cheryl's desk, where the three of them collaborated on an investigative piece on the lack of accountability with the City of West Prairie Department of Public Transportation. I got busy finishing a piece on Spring Break Spectaculars, poring over notes and cross-referencing on Internet searches.

"Hey, Sandy and Renee and I are going to The Birches after work to bend elbows. Want to come?" Lonnie said, sliding his chair in reverse and drinking an imaginary beer. He pushed a little too hard, and the cubicle wall jiggled.

"No, thanks anyway. I'm going to finish up here. You guys go ahead. I'm going straight home after this." I resumed typing.

"Are you sure? You, Sandy, and Renee are the good ones, so we all should have a great time."

Lonnie preferred to look upon the newspaper staff as either "the good ones" or the "not so good ones." He didn't like to refer to his coworkers as "bad" because he said there were no bad people, just people who did bad things. I agreed with him on this one. The good people truly cared about the stories they wrote. They were good writers, with their hearts and souls pumping through every piece. And Sandy and Renee, in Arts and Entertainment, really were good writers. It's not just about the reporting of a new art exhibition in town or an indie concert at the rec center, but the expression of the artist and the meaning of their work. And the not so good ones? Well, I hate to say it, but Clarissa wrote what people wanted to read. She knew what emptied newsstands. And for that, Mr. Simpson gave her a long lead. He trusted her. And the stacks of mail rolling in on the morning cart proved it. I don't like it when people talk about me, so I don't speak about others in an unflattering light.

"Yeah, I'm sure," I said, waving him away.

My gaze stuck to the computer screen so he wouldn't be able to see me not as happy as I should be about getting the new assignment, but concerned about what the assignment meant. I realized I was keeping secrets from the *West Prairie Journal*—that Waunasha was home, that my little brother died there ten years ago in an accidental shooting. It made me think of when I got my first assignment covering City Hall, which didn't go well. The assignment was fine, but not so much for me as the writer. I didn't see it. Instead of seeing a pair of the mayor's close staff members a little too close, an overreach followed by a cover-up, driven by a reelection, I portrayed the staff as admirable for going beyond their call of duty. Who wouldn't want the mayor's staff to make him look good? I was blind and naive to think that they were part of the solution of good functioning government and not the problem with running West Prairie. Mr. Simpson scrapped the piece; I was mortified. From that point on, I vowed I would always find the real story.

I needed to grow thick skin. But it was awfully hard to come by after what the Paynes had gone through.

"Okay, what's up? I sure can tell something is bothering you." Lonnie moved closer to my cubicle. "Here you get the first feature story of the first new section of the paper, and you're not happy? It's your chance, Margaret."

"Chance for what?"

"To show them, you know, that you command respect, and to be treated equally."

"I didn't know that I hadn't been doing that already." I tackled papers willy-nilly and shoved them into an accordion folder. "Do you mind? I've got to finish this," I huffed, looking at him beneath the tops of my eyelids.

I hadn't meant to cut him off, but any more talk would be fodder for continued conversation, and I wanted to end it so he would leave.

The hours circled quickly, and cubicles had emptied. I, too, was ready to go home; it was after 6:00 p.m. I filed my last story about the installation of new village officers and closed my "pendings" on my desk before leaving for home . . . and Waunasha.

"Last call, Margaret. We're heading over. If you change your mind, and I hope you do, stop by, just for a quick one," he said, slipping his arms through his jacket and pulling open the knot of his tie.

"Thanks, Lonnie, but I'm going to spend this evening with my husband."

"Gotcha there," he said, winking with a two-finger salute.

Out of the corner of my eye, I saw Clarissa was packing up. I chuckled, knowing that she included herself in every after-work outing, regardless of receiving an invitation or not. She wanted to be the first one at the bar and at everything, really, making it known that she was always the one who first thought of these social outings. Anything to attract kudos from coworkers.

Lonnie walked me out and into the parking lot. It was already dark, and the chill of the evening was refreshing, though a nip of frost was settling in. Clarissa had revved her white Chevy Malibu, then waved a billowing, white-sleeved arm from an open window. The gust of chilly wind blew her stiff hair sideways

mercy town

before she hit the gas, leaving exhaust plumes and the parking lot behind.

"We'll be there till around eight, if you change your mind," he yelled before he squeezed into his Corolla.

The night's navy blue calmed my anxious self, and the crisp quiet settled my raw nerves as I pulled out of the parking lot and headed home on Arbor Lane.

Every passing day, the horizon held its rim of light longer, not ready just yet for the evening hours to fall into darkness. I clutched the steering wheel tighter, then cracked the passenger and driver's side windows for air. Wafts of camphor from fir trees slipped through. This was my decompression time, when I left behind thoughts of work to make room for the sights and sounds and smells of the natural world I learned to connect with, growing up in Waunasha.

I had driven this same route for many years now, one that had felt automatic, as if I weren't aware of how I got to pulling into the driveway. This assignment was giving reason for me to return to Waunasha, where matters had never really settled. I replayed Mr. Simpson's announcement, and all I heard was "Margaret," "Waunasha," "feature story." And the only images that popped into view were Bean's and Mr. Kipp's faces, stars, and the sun kissing the river.

I pulled into the driveway and turned off the ignition. And then I sat. Rain tapped the windshield and made the asphalt shine. Muted light bled from the front porch lights. I trudged up the front steps, arms wrapped around my belongings and checked the mailbox. Jesse must be home, as the box was empty. The new flagstone path from the front sidewalk to the back yard led me to the side door. A quick check of the flower beds along the way showed the daffodils and crocuses seemed to have sprouted bigger heads since this morning.

I yanked open the door and entered a fully lit kitchen in a

French country style with powder blue walls, white curtains, and a cream wood table. Jesse was standing in the center of the room, wearing my apron over an open-collared, tieless shirt. I dropped my things on the chair tucked under a nearby desk, a traditional depository of all things: bills to be paid, mail, keys, chargers, scissors, note paper, sunglasses. And then I had a good look at him. The apron didn't completely cover his torso, as it did mine; the straps around his waist were wrapped with little remaining yardage. He gave me a good look too, with arms out like a T, as if showing himself off in all his glory. I laughed and became flushed with happiness at seeing him.

"Hi, honey, you must have left early." He gave me a wink. Leaving the paper on time was really leaving late.

"You funny, Jess."

He continued to chop tomatoes, peppers, onions, and basil for a spaghetti sauce with precision like any honed chef. Then he turned down the flame spiking under a pot of boiling water. I pulled out a chair and slumped over the kitchen table, hoping he would notice my desperate need for a drink to quench my thirst and calm the drama of the day. Instead, I inhaled the scents of a pending supper that made my mouth less dry. Jesse was so involved in supper-making that he didn't notice my quiet demeanor, that of a wife who was facing a return home to visit the young girl and sister she once was to Bean.

I unraveled the apron from his middle and took over cooking duties. Not that I thought he wasn't doing a good job and needed to be removed from a dangerous situation—open flame on the stove, large sharp chopping knife—but because cooking is therapy for me, detaching me from work. It redirects my concentration to chopping, making mounds, dumping all ingredients into a hot pan and then getting lost in a rhythm of stirring.

"I got this. Let me, please. Now go, shoo, have some time for yourself. I'll call when supper's ready."

mercy town

Only the therapy wasn't working. My nervous hands plunked a pair of pork chops into a sizzling frying pan next to the simmering veggie pot. My concentration hadn't quite made it to what I was doing, and the next thing I knew, the chops were on the floor, next to an upturned hot frypan. "Oh, nooooo," I yelled before kneeling in a heap, clearing strands of loose hair from my teary eyes. Jesse came dashing up from the basement.

"Honey . . . oh . . . what happened?"

"Too hot . . . I just dropped . . . a little burned. It's okay," I said, shaking my head.

He raced to prepare a cold, wet towel to wrap around my hand.

"I'm okay, just clumsy, rushing as usual."

I was crying and sweating, and I couldn't see because all the hair I had knotted that morning fell from the top of my head. Jesse picked up the chops and pan from the floor while I remained kneeling, feeling helpless and useless. I wanted to confide in him about what happened at work, not just that I got the first assignment of the new feature, but that because of it, I had to go back home to Waunasha. I had to go back in time. I couldn't say it.

Jesse helped me up from the floor and pulled a chair out for me to sit. I was a heavy lump, and grateful for the respite. He took command and cleaned up the mess I had made. At the table, he talked about his day, the meetings, oh, the meetings, he told me. "You got to wonder how anything gets done if we're always meeting." It was okay that he was going on about himself. I wanted to listen. I didn't want to talk. At least not then, anyway. I wasn't ready.

Despite the vegetarian supper, without the pork chops, it was tasty. Our conversation rolled out in typical question-and-answer style:

Him: Do you want to do laundry on Saturday?

Me: Sure. Can you ask if Pete and Sandy want to go out for a pizza that evening?

Him: That's a great idea. How about drinks first here?

Me: Sounds good.

When our eating and conversation ended, I washed dishes and Jesse commanded his usual post of drying them. He was a man who focused easily and concentrated well on any task. I wished I had that in me now. I let the security of routine guide me: eating, conversing, then cleaning up. Perhaps I owed it to the day of mixed emotions: joy and impending fear. While he chattered about his new development project—cabins, clearing, woods, Dell Landing—things that didn't register with me, my reflection in the window above the sink took my attention beyond into a black backdrop where the fence that divided our yard from the next had disappeared into the night's darkness. "Great," I said, every few sentences. I didn't pay his words much attention.

Jesse went downstairs into the basement, where he usually put in a couple of hours of work. It's his office, really, and man cave, dressed in deep browns and black, surrounded by tan walls and piled carpet. He had all he could ever need: television, couch, desk, treadmill. I was always welcome there; he invited me frequently. But tonight, I politely declined, as I had my work to tackle. I shut off the kitchen lights and went upstairs.

It was getting late, as the moon's beacon of light seeped through a window in the guest bedroom that doubled as my writing place. While I prepared notes for the assignment, I heard him rummaging in the kitchen. He was on time with his pre-bed ritual of setting out the coffeepot, coffee and mugs, and perhaps a stack of bagged bagels and a jar of peanut butter. His footsteps got louder; I heard him in the bedroom. After he spent a few minutes in the bathroom, I heard a flush and the thud of the toilet seat. I welcomed my burst of laughter, smiling as I thought of his mom, Effie, a tidy woman of politeness and etiquette, who taught her son good bathroom manners from the start. His travels settled, and I knew he had gotten into bed. And then it was quiet.

mercy town

I shut off the computer and desk lamp and went into our bedroom. Jesse had fallen asleep with the nightstand light on and a book about making it in real estate splayed open on his chest. He was just dozing, not sleeping deeply yet, as the book wasn't rising sharply from his breathing.

A lively wind had strengthened and changed directions, finding a path through the cracks around the window, making the drafts of air chilly. I changed quickly into long sweatpants and a T-shirt, then tiptoed to his side of the bed to click off the light after gently removing the book from his chest and setting it on the nightstand. Supine, I listened to the winds force their way through the sugar maple leaves, whose silhouettes were like giant snowflakes fluttering on the ceiling.

The trilling of a nearby owl, who was heard but seldom seen, was the last thing I remembered before I fell into a hypnotic state. Moonlight faded and handed itself over to a soft rain tapping the slider window that reached across most of the wall. My breath turned deep and quick. I ran with heavy feet through dim light into the woods, my face sticky with sweat, and hair obscuring the path of layers of decayed leaves and defrosting undergrowth. I willed my sprint to be lighter so I could run faster along the path to find him. A tree limb banged into the window. The sound echoed, carrying the reverberation through the forest. I couldn't breathe. I yelled for him, but the only sounds that were clear were the breaking of thin ice and the trickling of water. Beeean?

I awoke with wide eyes and sat up. Elbows on my knees, I held my head where it felt heavy. I reassured myself that I wasn't there, but at home, in bed, with Jesse.

"Hey, you're having a bad dream. Margaret, it's okay. Just a bad dream." He propped himself up and rubbed my shoulder. I hugged my bent legs and curled into a ball.

"Yeah, I sure did. Must have been the spring storm out there."

We lay back down. My heart felt as if it were exploding into his hand that had settled on my chest. His touch was calming, and his body, wedged close to mine, brought me back to sleep. The storm outside had calmed, though the one I felt inside was just starting.

friday

The next morning, the sun had barely altered the room's lighting as gray clouds covered any promise of seeing a rising sun. I had slept through Jesse's showering and dressing. Usually, he's my alarm clock. After he launches out of bed like a rocket, I know it's time for me to rise. This morning, I didn't rush out of bed. Instead, flashes of the night's dream, running, panicked, losing Bean, sparked. I tried to shake them with deep breathing and long stretches of my limbs, but it was as if I'd been swept back years ago when Waunasha had suffered its biggest tragic accident. Bean and I had started out that day on . . .

"Margaret, you better get moving," he yelled from the bottom of the stairs, jolting me out of my narration.

"Yep, I'm up," I shouted back, pushing the covers aside and stepping onto the cotton comfort of an area rug.

After reviving in the shower's streams of warmth, letting slip down the drain my dream and my memories of that day, I pulled on a black skirt and tucked in a white cotton button-down shirt, then fastened a silver necklace patterned in a chain with a heart and diamond sitting in its middle, a gift from Jesse for our first wedding anniversary. A pair of earrings in my lobes and a watch

30

clasped on my wrist made me feel ready for the day. I grabbed my heels and hurried downstairs. Jesse already had coffee made and eggs scrambled, and an English muffin toasted, ready for plating. He handed me a glass of orange juice while I stood in front of the open refrigerator door, not quite knowing what I was looking for.

"How are ya feeling this morning? That was quite a bad dream you had." Jesse, clean shaven and smelling like Irish Spring soap, looked away from me so as not to make a big fuss over it. I knew he was prodding me to describe what was going on in my mind. But for now, I just wanted to forget it.

Sitting at the kitchen table and running my fingers over the pine's wood grain reminded me of being at home in the kitchen with my mother and helping her bake breads and pies. It was Grandma Carter's way of teaching tradition in the home that was carried down from her daughter to me. Making food from the hands of labor was all love and what home was about. This table had become a center for domestic work, conversation, and family unity, all of which I was lucky to have had as part of my growing up.

He joined me at the table, where he moved slower than I. I couldn't nibble on the toast or scoop up the eggs fast enough. We chewed in silence while I contemplated getting to the office, and he watched me in anticipation of any talk that I might start.

"Thanks for breakfast; it was a good start to my day," I told him, an affirmation more for my benefit than his. Jesse was big on beginning our days together at the kitchen table, even if it was only for a short time. These insignificant gestures meant much, though at times I failed to acknowledge that to him. Being married took a lot of conscious thoughts and actions. It wasn't just me anymore: it was having a partner, a confidant, a best friend who deserved consideration. And then I remembered that I never did tell him about getting the first feature assignment for the new section. He must have figured I didn't get it, or remnants of the night's dream were overshadowing my news.

"I got to get going," I told him, dropping my dirty dishes into the sink. "I'll see you later tonight." I grabbed my tote and a coat hanging near the door. After pushing my arms through the coat sleeves, I turned to look at him before pulling the doorknob shut. I left him looking clean and pressed, standing at the kitchen sink full of dirty dishes. I wanted to stay awhile in the comfort of home and the familiarity of scene with him, but I had to move ahead and wrap things up at work to start my new assignment in Waunasha. "Have a good day," was what I think he said, after I shut the door.

While I meandered in my car down Arbor Lane on my way to work, I thought of the many neighbors Jesse and I had come to know. My head swayed from left to right as I passed neighbors' houses, reciting who lived in them, as the sites offered comfort of home, and good long-time friends as a part of our places to be. When I came to the end of Arbor, like a T, at Fairfax, I sighed, as this drive was just like any other that would lead me into the city. Turning onto Fairfax, I met traffic that got me nowhere fast. I took a lighter hold of the steering wheel, and I understood there wasn't much I could do about it but go with the flow and resign myself to walking in the door later than expected.

Slower traffic sped up my mind's dialogue, remembering yesterday's meeting when I told Mr. Simpson that maybe Clarissa should have been assigned the new feature. I hit a fist against the wheel and then tapped my head. What did I just say? A reframed understanding came to mind: this would be the biggest opportunity for me to show management that my skills and experience were not limited to reporting on a new local business in town. I talked myself through to confidence I regretted not having shown yesterday. But, as they say, tomorrow is a new day, a fresh start. And this was my new day.

nancy chadwick

During my pep talk with myself, I had passed my exit, Bedford Square, City Center. I took the next exit, which gave me a chance to see outside the central business district.

I soon reached the square. It's a welcoming place with beautiful landscaping year-round: seasonal flowers planted in pots on the ground and suspended from light posts, winterscapes of ice carvings, and Italian lights strung up around door frames, and I thought that when sometimes you take a step back, and come at things from a different direction, it can give you a new perspective. Cars hadn't yet filled the street parking just yet, as businesses were not open. But an old brownstone building, etched with *West Prairie Journal* on its face, was.

I turned into the parking lot off Bedford Drive and passed the last building of a row of short-storied ones, from department stores to hardware stores to flower and coffee shops. I smiled, feeling a sense of belonging to this bustling, yet cozy city-like town where young and old strolled with smiles on their faces and kindness in their hearts.

Driving to the rear lot, where employees must park, I pulled into my usual space in the middle of the first row. As usually one of the first ones in, I wanted to leave the spots nearest the door for Mr. Simpson and his higher-ups. I peeked in the rearview mirror at a face without makeup, then rummaged through my purse and found blush and lipstick to cover up my pallor; a swipe of color on the cheeks and a dab or two on the lips was better than no color at all. I closed my car door with my elbow and directed my gaze upward. The sun shone in earnest; it was a new day, and I assured myself that it would all work out. I continued this confidence, repeating it like a mantra. I thought if I put it out into the world, it *would* work out. Thoughts of Bean made me smile when he said how I just had to believe if I wanted something to come true.

The newsroom would soon be in motion with scurrying bodies arriving and settling in after trips to the breakroom for a coffee

mercy town

fill-up. Lonnie had arrived before me. He would tell you how he and I were always the first ones in. Usually, I flipped switches for the overhead lights, fans, and copy machine before checking the thermostat and secretly lowering it. The cooler air was an elixir to combat sleepiness, foggy minds, and the dullness of words we might experience during a stuffy afternoon. This morning, there was no flip switching, as Lonnie had beaten me to it. The coffee pot had been cleaned, left dirty from the previous day, and a new pot was dripping. The ceiling fans stirred the air, with the smell of coffee making its way to me from the front of the floor.

"Mornin', Lonnie. Thanks for doing my duties. Sorry I'm late."

Lonnie glanced at his watch. "Nah . . . you're not that late . . . I'm early. I just caught all the green lights on the way here."

Lonnie also lived in West Prairie, on the other side of town, where he had raised two boys who were now off and married with lives of their own. It took him longer to get to work as he had a set of railroad tracks to cross, and he'd be damned if he ever arrived too late to catch the gates down and the train slowly passing.

"I have to get going on that piece on the anniversary of the West Prairie Chamber of Commerce," I told him, filling my thermos with more coffee. Mr. Simpson had given me their press release two days ago with the schedule of events, and he wanted me to get it in the paper ASAP.

Lonnie poured powdered creamer into his mug and stirred the dark brown mixture to turn to tan. "Simpson gave the interview with the president of the Chamber to Clarissa. Did you know that? Apparently, Simpson knew Clarissa likes to talk to people in high places." I liked to think Clarissa thought of herself as being in a high place here. Actually, I thought I could learn a thing or two from her about self-confidence, as it never seemed to wear thin on her.

"I'll drink to that," I told him, raising my thermos to his mug. "I could use a few quotes from her piece in mine."

We filed back to our workstations. Cubicles were now filled with reporters who were working on either their keyboards or their phones. I sighed in appreciation. This was exactly where I wanted to be. My newfound calm seemed to diminish the drama I had experienced the previous day.

The morning hours passed quickly. Lunchtime was approaching.

"Okay, spill it. Tell me you're not mad at me," he said, gliding backwards in his chair and stopping at my cubicle. I ignored him. He waited until I responded.

"What? No, Lonnie, I'm not mad at you or anyone else. I'm just . . . busy." I glanced at him, then resumed typing.

"Planning on your drive back to Waunasha? Are you getting your interviews lined up? When do you leave?"

"Oh, the questions. Stop already, Lonnie." I waved an open hand near his face. He appeared to be more excited about the road trip than I felt.

I got up and walked across the aisle to Clarissa's desk, where either I caught her doing something she wasn't supposed to be doing or she was looking at something she didn't want me to see. She closed the computer screen and covered some photographs with an empty folder before laying her forearms on top of it all.

"Yes?" Clarissa said. She stiffened her seated posture and turned a staid face to me. I stepped closer to her and crossed my arms, waiting for an explanation for her secretive behavior. Working for the *West Prairie Journal* was all our business, and there shouldn't be any secrets kept among us. Throwing suspicion on a journalist could be damaging, as I remembered Mr. Simpson once had pointed out during my first week of working at the paper. He told us if he ever caught any reporter doing something he or she wasn't supposed to be doing, and they knew they shouldn't be doing something if they had to hide it, they would be out the door so fast their keyboard would still be warm. "We

mercy town

work as a team, who have each other's backs and who collaborate for the good of the paper," he told us.

"How can I help you, Margaret?"

"Just seeing when your piece on Mr. Abel is ready. I need some of your quotes to finish my story."

"It's done and already filed with the boss. Use whatever you need."

I walked back to my desk and continued to eye Clarissa from across the aisle. She opened her laptop and waited for the black screen to light up. I thought what she was reading was personal, as she was leaning into what may have been small print. If it was business, she'd be reading from her desktop computer.

I eyed her actions, sitting back in her chair, staring at some photograph. I couldn't stand it; my curiosity made me get up and take the long way around to see Rae Ann about something or other. From walking behind Clarissa, I could see she had a page from a *Nasha News* article, Waunasha's local paper. "One dead in accidental shooting. Victim identified," read the large print. The photo next to the article was all too familiar. It was taken at the Clark County Fair, where Ellis Payne stood strong with Mom and had an arm around Bean in front of the John Deere for sale. A PAYNE GARAGE sign hung above them and the farm equipment Ellis was selling at the fair. I had taken the photo and submitted it to the *Nasha News* as an advertisement for Papa's business. Times were good then; Papa kept very busy. The smiles on the Paynes' faces were as wide and long as those summer days. "Bean Payne, 12, was shot and killed, allegedly by Mr. Kipp, who claimed the incident to be a 'mistake' and an 'awful accident,'" read the opening paragraph. I was too stiff to move.

"Hey, Clarissa, are you coming with us for my birthday lunch? The more the merrier," Lonnie shouted over the aisle while putting on his jacket. Clarissa, at first, didn't hear him, but then, as if knocked out of a trance, she replied.

"Um, yep, I'm coming," Clarissa mumbled. She sat back and shut the laptop, staring into the distance.

"Ya coming, too, Margaret?" he said.

I snapped out of my eavesdropping stance and took long strides to my desk.

"We're going to The Birches," he informed me. He looked as if he was itching to leave as he was running an index finger around his tight shirt collar as if to loosen the constraint.

"I'll be there. You go on ahead. I just want to finish something up," I mumbled.

I really didn't want to go, but I felt obligated. There was never a birthday lunch I hadn't attended; I attributed my participation to fostering work morale.

"Don't take too long, Margaret." Clarissa smiled demurely. She walked out the front door with Lonnie following. "It'll be a chance for you and me to get to know each other better, outside of work."

I looked at her with narrowed eyes. After working here all these years, what did she want to know that she already didn't? I wondered what she was up to. There usually was a double meaning behind what Clarissa said. And she thought I didn't know what she had read in that newsclip.

The Birches was within walking distance of the office. Under the bright noon sun, I walked past The Drip coffee house, the place to go for *real* coffee, West Prairie State Bank, Ace Hardware, and Millie's deli before reaching the front window where The Birches was etched in white script on a green awning. It had become the paper's gathering place over the years, at least since I'd been working there, whether for birthday lunches like this one, happy hour, or suppers with coworkers and their spouses.

mercy town

I was standing just inside the doorway, and my eyes needed to adjust to the darkness before I could search for where everyone was sitting. A long table in the back was where Rae Ann, wearing her spring-blue cardigan, was seated comfortably with Calvin and Jimmy to her right; they were wearing rolled-up sleeves and leaning into one another and making conversation among the others. I took attendance and learned most were there, seated, except for Clarissa and Lonnie. I wondered where they were. Because they had left the office before anyone else, they should have been the first ones here.

The chatter around the table did not break while I had a good look around the place. And when I did, there they were, Clarissa and Lonnie, sitting on the last two stools at the end of a fully occupied, shiny-topped bar. They were facing each other, leaning in, with their knees touching, talking discreetly. I moved near them, hiding behind a pillar and below a speaker. I strained to hear their conversation, but the Righteous Brothers were belting it out too loud for me to hear them.

The song finally ended.

Clarissa talked with her hands firmly in her lap. "So how much do you really know about Margaret?"

Lonnie's expression was fixed, and he listened intently as if she was about to divulge a secret. "I'm not sure what you mean. I know she's not from here. Started working at the paper right out of high school when she moved from some small town—"

"So small, it's hard to believe she went from Waunasha to West Prairie with no previous newspaper experience." Clarissa invited a pause with a sip of her Bloody Mary, disguised as a Virgin Mary, and with the obligatory veggie skewer. "She doesn't talk much. But she talks to *you*, Lonnie," she said, pointing an index finger lightly into his chest. "What *does* she say to you?" Clarissa cocked her head, then slurped from her goblet. She wiggled on the bar seat to better balance herself.

nancy chadwick

"It's just small talk . . . working on the house on weekends with Jesse and on her assignments during the week. I don't pry." Lonnie took three sips from his glass of iced tea and lowered his head. "Ya know, I don't want to seem too personal, especially in these days. I don't want to be accused of getting to know the ladies just a little too much." One side of his mouth curled up.

"Oh, c'mon, Lonnie, you're harmless." Clarissa slapped him on the knee, then busted into a high-pitched laugh. "Well, I've got something that might interest you," she said, moving so close to Lonnie's face I thought she was going to kiss him. "There's something more to that girl," she said, mouthing each word for the drama of it.

This conversation was going on too long. I popped from behind the pillar. "Hey, Lonnie, what are you sitting here for? We're all seated over there waiting for you." They looked at me in sync as I pointed over my shoulder to the back room where a table of twelve was filled except for three seats. I was glad to have surprised them, silencing their secret conversation.

"Club soda and lime, please." I waved to Bobbie behind the bar as she stood idle, watching the closed captioning on the mid-day news airing above her head.

"Y'all ready to order some lunch?" Bobbie asked, pushing the button for soda with one hand while plucking a lime wedge from a cup with the other.

"Yep, we are, Bobbie. We'll be over there . . . at our usual table, when you get a chance," I told her, then gave the pair an inquisitive stare.

I couldn't hear much of their conversation as the clanking of dirty dishes and glasses muffled most of the words. But what I did hear was enough. They sure didn't want me to know what they were talking about, given the abrupt ending to their conversation when I interrupted. I grabbed my drink from Bobbie and went to our table.

mercy town

I was still thinking about what I had interrupted at the bar while I sat among my coworkers trying to drop in on any conversation. I felt awkward, and I wanted to go home, but I couldn't dash out; it would be too soon.

Bobbie followed Clarissa and Lonnie to the table.

"Hey, hey, the birthday boy has finally arrived," someone at the table audience yelled. Clarissa sat next to me, and I shifted a little to the left, giving me space away from her. It didn't make a difference as she leaned in to compensate for the space I had created.

After we hushed our commotion, Bobbie opened a small notepad and took a pen from her apron pocket. We went around the table and gave our orders as Bobbie took notes.

"Ya know, Margaret, I'm genuinely happy for you about getting the assignment," Clarissa said. "I can't say I wasn't surprised, though, since you're the newer kid on the block, and, well, I've been around . . . the paper, that is, for a while." I stared across the table at Calvin and Jimmy, inviting myself to drop in on their animated chatter.

"I was wondering, Margaret," Clarissa continued, swiveling in the seat to face me. "After all these years working together, I don't really know much about you . . . and I'd like to. Did you go to school around here? Is this your first paper?"

"Community college . . . not around here . . . wrote articles, submitted 'em." I believed the more Clarissa knew about me, the more fired up she'd get to keep asking me questions.

The table raised their glasses. Rae Ann toasted, "To Lonnie, happy birthday to the most dependable coworker and friend, always ready to jump in for the team." Rae Ann had said this at every birthday lunch since he took the helm from the first editor-in-chief when he was in his thirties. Twenty-five years later, Lonnie never tired of reading the *Journal*'s headlines each morning. Clarissa and I joined the glass-raising. "To Lonnie, happy birthday."

"Now, as I was saying . . ." Clarissa lowered her voice.

"Oh, Clarissa. It's Lonnie's birthday, and well, there's cake to be cut." I gave her my best cheery demeanor to change the subject.

Clarissa backed off and turned to face the table. I hadn't looked at her, but I could hear her sigh in defeat. I was relieved, for the moment, but suspected that she would not stop there, wanting to know more about my past and how I ended up in West Prairie working at the journal.

For the few remaining hours of the afternoon at the office, I contemplated my pending drive to Waunasha. It wasn't that I didn't want to go home to see my parents, whom I hadn't seen in . . . well, a very long time. It was being forced to step back in time. I had come so far, personally and professionally. But quickly, I realized that the memories were still painful and raw. My heart still ached for Bean and that day.

saturday

It was the weekend, and I welcomed a respite to focus on my home and on Jesse before packing and leaving for Waunasha tomorrow. A hardy spring thaw was yet to come. I anticipated bursts of green popping from the flower beds and watching cracks draw on the defrosting earth. I was also excited for this day as in the evening, Jesse and I made supper together, just the two of us, for ourselves. We fell into a rhythm in the kitchen; then when seated, we acknowledged what a good team we made, a partnership we relied on no matter what.

This made me think of Mom and Papa. Mom was the primary meal-maker in the kitchen, tending to preparation by moving from counter to table and then back again, while Papa sat in the front room, ready to spring into action at her request to pull down a mixing bowl out of her reach, open the stubborn tight lid of a mason jar, or to feed Chip early as he was getting under her feet. Until being summoned, he'd read, or if it was winter, he'd pull up to the fireplace and gaze into the blazing wood releasing its fury into the chimney. How their lives now appeared to have separated, each to themselves, with their own lists of to-dos and chores and schedules. That wasn't how Jesse and I were. We handled together what we needed to do.

The direct sun beamed through the kitchen windows as I wiped the counters after breakfast. He scurried into the kitchen, wearing nothing but a pair of shorts and a hooded sweatshirt. A chill rushed through me just seeing him underdressed for a frosty spring morning.

"Going for a run. I'll see ya," he said, pushing earbuds into his ears and plunking a knit cap on his head.

"I'm off soon to Perkins to get supper and a few other things. Going to try again with the pork chops. Maybe you can grill them this time?"

"You're a funny one," he said, giving me a kiss. "And I'm looking forward to tonight."

He glided next to me and clutched my waist, pulling me close. I wrapped my arms around his neck, then ran my hands along his square, unshaven jaws before giving him a quick kiss.

I completed my grocery list and gave Bentley a reassuring pat on the head before grabbing a coat and pulling on a pair of short boots. Almost forgetting the list, I turned around and swiped it from the counter, then left the house and jumped into the car. As I pulled out, I thought about how I was happiest at home, making our life the best it could be.

The drive was typical for Saturday morning traffic in West Prairie as cars spilled onto the streets quickly and moved in sync. I could only think most people were headed to attend to their usual errands to the bank or the hardware store or to get a haircut, and others were going to Perkins, a family-owned-for-generations grocery store. The Paynes loved Perkins. Mom would drive us from Waunasha there to shop for groceries when we were kids because it was a general store in a small town where you could get anything you needed in one spot, from groceries to pharmacy

mercy town

items to a new pair of Wrangler jeans, unlike a big box store that lacks the customer service Perkins is known for. When Bean and I were little, a day spent at Perkins was like an adventure. After all, everything was bigger in the city. Going to Perkins each month to stock up was Mom's delight, as she had never seen so many choices in the baking aisle. When she would ask during our Saturday morning breakfast who wanted to go for a ride to Perkins, we ate, cleaned up, and got to the door faster than she could put on lipstick and grab her purse. When we arrived at the store, we'd gaze at the aisles, the longest the Payne kids had ever seen, so long in fact, they had to splice them, breaking them in half with a center aisle. Mom would grab our hands and slap them on the sides of a cart as if she were gluing the skins to the metal to prevent us from straying.

When I arrived at Perkins, I was reminded of how nothing had changed. The grocery carts still stuck together when I tried to pull one out from the row of them nestled into one another. With a hard yank, I won the fight, then triumphantly zipped through the open sliding doors. List in hand, I sliced through the middle of the aisles, reading the signs above to find the ones that matched what was on my list. I took a sharp turn to the produce section, stopping at a stand of mounded Idahoes next to a pile of Vidalia onions.

"Ret? Ret Payne, is that you?" was coming from somewhere on the other side of the stand. It startled me to hear that name as I tried to recall who might know me in West Prairie from when I was growing up in Waunasha.

I gave the woman behind the voice a glance. She appeared to be about Mom's age. Her salt-and-pepper hair was pulled back tight, uncovering a face of age spots yet with just a few wrinkles. She was dressed in the usual Saturday best for farm-working women: jeans, olive-green chamois work shirt, and thick leather work shoes.

"I'm sorry, I don't . . ."

"Oh, Ret, it's Mrs. Jenkins. June Jenkins. Your mom and I are good friends, going back to when you and Bean were very little. Your mom helped me with my two, Bud and Kenny." I remembered neither Mrs. Jenkins nor any of my mom's friends coming around and being with Bean and me. "Maybe you remember them? And I helped her with you and Bean . . . oh . . ."

Mrs. Jenkins covered her mouth, her eyes widening. She then scurried along with her grocery cart to my side of the stand.

"I'm sorry . . . I didn't mean to remind you of your brother . . ." she whispered. "My, how grown up you are now," she continued, changing the subject. "I hear you got yourself married. Congratulations. And to a tall, dark, handsome fella too, working in real estate. So how long you been livin' here now?"

I took a step back and focused my attention on selecting a couple of potatoes. "Just a few years now."

She resumed picking away at the onions, having a difficult time getting the job done as she examined each one closely while trying to carry on a conversation. "Do you get a chance to get back home? To see your folks?"

"No, not too much. Busy with work."

I pushed my cart to a wall of packaged mushrooms, carrots, and celery, hoping the discussion would find its natural ending. Peppering me with questions ignited an anxiety I thought had gone away, at least for the weekend, when I didn't have to think about going back to Waunasha just yet. "It was nice to you, Mrs. Jenkins. I really have to get going."

And with those parting words, I wheeled off to the checkout, through the door, and into my car without remembering how I got there.

As I drove home, I contemplated the run-in with Mrs. Jenkins. Returning to Waunasha wasn't about going on location for the article. It was about going home, a place I had put behind

mercy town

me after I had moved to West Prairie and married Jesse. I had wanted to flee then, much like that day after Bean was brought to the hospital, and I realized now that I still wanted to run away.

When I pulled into the driveway at home, I sat staring at the house, the front door, his Volvo parked in the garage. The scene was not homey. Coming from a home meant the garage wasn't used for cars, but for storage, packed with accumulated stuff one will never use, boxes like tombs, of memories. I looked forward to the many years Jesse and I had ahead of us, to accumulate boxes and store them in the garage instead of our cars.

"Hey . . . hello, Margaret?" he called, waving a hand from inside the garage, snapping me out of my contemplation. "I'll be right there to grab the grocery bags," he yelled.

I waved and told him, "I'm fine. No need. Be right in."

I hoisted the full bags onto the counter and settled my purse and keys on the kitchen table. Bentley rushed to me, and his cold nose gave my ankles and feet a thorough check.

"How was Perkins?" he asked, diving into the full bags and unpacking them, setting each item on the counter.

I wasn't paying much attention to his questions or anything else as I put in the refrigerator the multi-surface kitchen cleaning spray and new dishcloths I had bought.

"Honey, you okay? I don't think those need to be refrigerated," he said. He took the items from my hands.

"Yep, I'm fine. Whew, kind of crazy at Perkins, but then, when is it not on a Saturday this late in the morning?"

"C'mon, let's sit outside for a while before lunch. It's warming up fast."

Jesse had always known when I had something on my mind. He also knew that I wouldn't share until the time and place were right. And here he was, suggesting this was the right time and place. Still, I had put off the news long enough, and I knew I had to tell him. I had to leave for Waunasha tomorrow.

He grabbed a ratty sweatshirt hanging on the inside door-knob, then poured the last of what was in the coffeepot into our mugs. He took my hand, and together, we walked through the sliding door, letting Bentley out first. Jesse unfolded a pair of lawn chairs tucked under the eaves by the doors while I wrapped my cardigan more tightly around me in the hint of a cool breeze. Bentley took off, letting his beagle nose guide his travels.

We didn't talk, at first. The quiet pause he understood my taking was when I wanted to tell him something that was on my mind.

"I got the assignment, Jesse," I said.

"That's fantastic, honey, congratulations. I knew you would." He beamed, leaning forward and patting my knees.

"But I have to go back to Waunasha for the article."

"That's great. I'm so glad for you. You haven't been home in a while now. You can visit your parents, get your mom's home cooking, see your horses and Chip and Billy, maybe help your papa in the barn."

"Jesse, it's not that simple. . ."

My words trailed as I tried to get used to the thought of being home, seeing Bolt and Quincy, Chip, the best dog ever, and Billy, the crow. I had moved forward with my life, but I was afraid time had stood still in Waunasha. The wounds were still there, covered in a scab of sadness and tragedy.

"This will be a chance to make things right for yourself." He pulled me closer to him. My gaze shifted from Bentley's antics to his eyes. "This is your chance to have closure. You can see for yourself how the town has moved on. I'm sure it's not what it used to be," he said.

I sat taller in my chair. "And how do you know this?"

"Um . . . I . . . don't, really, but, you know, as they say, time heals all wounds."

mercy town

I was too far into my drama to notice that he was hiding something. I could usually tell he was holding something back when he looked not at me but far off into the distance, unfocused.

"Yes. You need to see Waunasha for yourself: the people, old friends and family, your home."

"This isn't a personal reunion, Jesse. I've got an assignment."

"When do you leave?"

"Tomorrow."

"Well, then, you better start packing."

"And I've got the rest of the day to be with you."

I stood, but he pulled me back down onto his lap. Our faces nearly touched. For those few moments, life was good.

"C'mon, let's have lunch, and then the afternoon is all yours," he said, holding the door open for Bentley and me.

After we ate, grazing on leftover cheese, ham, and strawberries from the day before, I deep cleaned the kitchen, as any spring cleaning would have called for. Given all that my pending departure suggested, I had better things to do, but keeping my hands busy was my way of thinking things through. When I called this chore completed, I stood with my hands on my hips, admiring my handiwork and the resulting shine in the sunlit room.

The old wood pinged and popped with my plodding steps upstairs. Before I could think about packing, I plunked down on the bed and acknowledged the stillness that had been my friend growing up. The quiet and I had always been in tandem when I strolled from my house to the Loch River, with the rustle of oak leaves and the crunch of pine needles underfoot. My journal would be along for the ride, slipped inside the front pocket of my coat. Bean always followed close at my heels. Soon, I'd see my sit spot, just off the trail. It was a special place I had found, surrounded by native forest magic, in air that could be heavy during humid summer days or dry during a frigid winter, or in wind that could be calm under a night sky or ferocious during a

July thunderstorm. I would rest on the old fallen log, and Bean would take off up the path as if it were his first time exploring the Loch River. For me, it was a private time to connect with Mother Nature, to observe movement and sound and smell. I was not alone, for I heard the heartbeats of the trees. I wondered if my spot was still there now or if it had been displaced. By now, it would surely be broken and decayed.

I pulled down from the closet shelf a duffel bag and a smaller suitcase, where I packed jeans, shirts, a couple of sweaters, and a light jacket. I hung a suit shrouded in plastic on the doorknob to take with me, just in case. And I didn't forget my outdoor trail shoes, leather kicks I hadn't worn since I left Waunasha. The dried mud and bits of hay remained stuck to the soles, the heels telling a story of my land-working days with Papa and long walks in early spring with Bean into the woods. It seemed so long ago, yet it was as if it had happened yesterday.

While searching the closet for more, I dragged out a misshapen box tucked away on the floor in the corner. Resting on the floor, I considered its contents and thought of releasing the old memories kept there. I wasn't exactly sure if I was ready to visit the girl I once was, but I reasoned it was part of preparing myself for returning home. Upon opening the lid, scents of dampness, of pine, of Bolt and Quincy, of Chip, of home, were released. Enclosed in the box were remnants of my girlhood: a sweet-sixteen gold chain ID bracelet, a tarnished watch face with a crumbly red leather band, photos from days playing in the backyard with Bean, a packet of sunflower seeds I had never planted.

And a silver necklace. Dangling from it was a slate-blue stone. Papa had it made for me one birthday as a connection to Bean when we used to skip stones together along the Loch River. I held the shiny pebble, heavy for its size, tight in my hand, and worked it like rubbing a genie from a bottle. With eyes closed, I thought about when it was just me and Bean in our own world. The stone awakened the genie, letting a spirit free. When I opened my eyes, a book with the gold inscription *My Journal* painted under hardened mud, its pages dried and shriveled, was staring at me. It was my last journal because after that day, I hadn't written a thing in it ever again. I held the book; its once auburn leather wore the color and texture of the earth. I gently fanned the pages, and a photo slipped out onto my lap. Tears clouded the faded-colored image. Bean had just turned twelve. How delighted he was to be sitting under the black oak as we celebrated his birthday the same way the Paynes always did—joining in with the wonders of Mother Nature as she sang praises of another year of life gone by and welcomed another year ahead. How clearly I could hear Bean's laughter; how vividly I could see him stuffing his mouth with birthday cake. I heard his voice and then silence. "Oh, Bean, I miss you!" I whispered. I dried my face, folded the box's flaps, and slid it back into the closet. I held the journal, with the photo of Bean between the pages, and my necklace, and found a place for it in my tote bag, safe with me.

I couldn't sleep that night. The dialogue in my head spun faster than I could keep track of as my eyes darted back and forth on the ceiling. I looked at Jesse, who appeared to be in a deep sleep, his chest rising and falling with full breaths. He could fall into such a state faster than anyone I had ever known, besides maybe Papa. Once he got rocking in his chair in front of a warm fire on a cold night, or on the front porch during a cool evening after a hot day, he'd nod off peacefully in the safety of home and hearth, with puppy Chip tugging at the edges of the braided rug. Even Billy the crow couldn't wake him with the tapping of his beak on the front window or porch railing, demanding attention.

Tears released like rose petals down my cheeks. I realized I would soon be in my familiar place, with the security of home, but it would feel wrong. Bean would not be there. I wanted Waunasha to be just as I had remembered, but I knew it had changed. For me to change too, I would have to leave Bean behind. But I just couldn't let Bean leave me again.

The rivers flow not past but through us, thrilling, tingling, vibrating every fiber and cell of the substance of our bodies, making them glide and sing.

—John Muir

sunday

When I awoke, the bedroom was aglow with light. I felt a little sprightly myself—excited to see Mom and Papa—as I skipped downstairs to the kitchen. Soon, the water pipes banged like pots and pans, a sure sign that Jesse was in the shower. I carefully lay bacon strips in a hot cast-iron pan, watching the strips sizzle and shrink, and shifting from one foot to the other before making a pancake batter and a fresh pot of coffee, too. I would leave for Waunasha later that morning, and I wanted it to be a good one.

"Well, aren't you the early riser," Jesse said, placing a kiss on my cheek, looking fresh from the shower with his uncombed, wavy hair. He was dressed in his standard Sunday lounging attire, gray sweatpants and a white hoodie with "Northland College" labeled on his chest. He fell hard for this one, considered it a playground where he explored the Apostle Islands and national forest, once taking classes there in the environment and sustainability. It was one of his happy places that we made a point to return to for a visit.

"I thought maybe after breakfast, we could take a quick walk. Spring is itching to bust open, and I thought we'd encourage it

mercy town

with a conversation with Mother Nature, maybe poking her in the arm," I said.

"Yep. Let's do it," he said, grabbing a plate.

We sat at the kitchen table and, with little conversation, quickly filled our stomachs. My thoughts were ahead as I was eager to get on the road to Waunasha. We cleaned our plates, pulled on light jackets and rubber boots, and opened the door to a welcoming spring day. Robins were back in town; their big singing voices told us so. He held my hand tightly as we strolled through the neighborhood, admiring the change from a dull gray winter into a burgeoning, colorful palette. More crocuses seemed to have appeared overnight.

"Are you ready for this, Margaret?" he asked, grasping my hand even more tightly.

"I am more than ready for spring to arrive. There's a lot of work to do in the yard."

"I'm not talking about that. You know what I mean," he said, nudging my side.

I waved to Marsha ahead in black tights and a pink jacket, who was flexing her legs and plugging her ears with buds, ready to take off on a run. "Not so sure. Perhaps fear is disguised as nervous excitement. Fear of the unknown. But I've got a job to do, and that has been my focus . . . and to write a damn good piece."

"But can you do both? Face the unknown and be objective in pulling together the piece?"

I didn't answer him because I didn't have an answer.

"Ya got a good drivin' day. Clear and crisp."

"Yes. It is a good day," I said, more in assurance for myself.

We circled a two-block radius and returned home. When I walked into the kitchen, I checked the time and saw that it was earlier than I thought. No use in standing around here, with nothing else to do but wait for the appointed hour. I went upstairs to make sure I had all that I needed. With one final survey of the room, my eyes stopped at the photos on the desk of me and Papa and Mom and Bean standing tall on the first porch step in the front of the house. It was a budding spring day then, just after Mom had planted pink petunias in the flower pots and settled them near the front door. I went downstairs satisfied I had everything I needed.

"Here, let me fill your coffee thermos," he said. "You have everything? Enough clothes? Your laptop?"

I studied the heap on the floor next to the door and did a mental checklist—suitcase, backpack, tote bag stuffed with laptop, folders, notebook, and journal. It wasn't much, but then it was only Waunasha and the simplicity of living for a few days. I scooped up my backpack and tote, and Jesse grabbed my suitcase in one hand with the thermos in the other while I slid on a pair of old Nikes. We filed through the door and walked around the front of the house to the driveway where my VW was parked. He tossed my things into the back seat and waited until I settled in the front seat before he handed me my thermos.

I rolled down the window.

"You'll do great, Margaret. This will be good for you. Say hello to your folks for me, and please call me when you get there." He gave me a meaningful kiss, then waved while I pulled out of the driveway and drove down Arbor Lane. Jesse and my home got smaller and smaller in my rearview mirror, and then I no longer saw them.

There's something to be said for driving alone for hours. There's no one there but yourself to carry on a conversation with. Like when I would plop down at my favorite spot by the Loch River. I started coming to that spot when I was maybe twelve, as soon as my mom would let me head out into the woods to the river by myself. She had confidence in my ability to be alone, to find my way there and back. I had learned this practice since I could walk and would toddle with Papa to the river. I was confident

mercy town

that I would always find my way home because of that clear, well-worn path from my sit spot to the house.

After a couple hours' drive, I left the city limits of West Prairie and was on the county road, awaiting the exit to the two-lane road Highway 30 into the county of Amherst, where the road sliced through the forests of birch, spruce and fir.

Halfway there, I took a break and pulled off the empty road to where Margo's Dining was lit in orange neon. The counter was open. Jeanine, as the name tagged to her white uniform called her, poured a short glass of water and dropped it in front of me. "Coffee?" she asked. Her voice was deadpan and deeper than I expected to come from the delicate face of an older woman.

"Mmm. Yes, please. And I'll have a ham and cheese on rye, but please hold the french fries. And a vanilla shake too." I surprised myself by asking for a shake, as I hadn't had one since Bean and I were young, and Papa would take us into town for lunch on Saturday afternoons. It brought back happy memories of when Papa spent time with us as if we were the only two people in his world.

I nibbled slowly while looking at the small television screen suspended from the wall behind the counter. I hadn't recognized the images being broadcast of downtown Waunasha. Main Street appeared cleaner and more updated than I had remembered. I couldn't tell why the town was in the news, but I reasoned it wasn't something too concerning as the reporter was all smiles and hand gestures to Main Street behind her. I finished my sandwich and took to-go what remained of my milkshake, slurping more of its melted vanilla cream before getting back into the car.

The last stretch of road bisected a forest of birch and spruce. Their tops became obscured as the skies turned overcast and hung low, and the calm air shifted to breezy gusts. I turned on the car radio and twisted the dial through static until I heard a man's urgent voice announcing, "Use caution when driving.

Skies will darken quickly as a fast-approaching storm will likely bring heavy winds, topping gusts at forty to fifty miles per hour, followed by heavy rains for most of the area. Watch for possible flooding in low-lying areas. Stay tuned for updates as they become available." When the report had ended, a calm female voice returned to the airwaves in song.

I switched on my headlights as late afternoon appeared more like evening. A quick flip of the windshield wipers cleared the suddenly pelting rain. I gripped the steering wheel more tightly and slowed, grateful for no traffic ahead or trailing behind. The battering drops turned to sleet as the assaulting precipitation was mesmerizing. Though I had slowed the car in caution, Mother Nature's fury had sped up. It was difficult now to decipher the road from its sides as the winds drove the rain sideways and blurred any road boundaries I had relied on.

"We break into this programming for an updated weather advisory . . ."

That was the last thing I remembered.

I awakened off the side of the road, and to a steady drizzle. My car teetered in an unforgiving ditch. Putting the gearshift in reverse and then back into drive, I tried to free the wheels, but the ground was too saturated and slick with mud. The wheels spun, and I went nowhere. I didn't know where I was as I couldn't make out any distinctive landscape features that could have oriented me.

In the blacked-out night, I felt for my phone in my bag and checked the time. It was nine o'clock. I should have been home two hours ago. I tried calling 911, but service was spotty as the storm's aftermath had left her mark. Staring ahead, I saw that there was no one coming down the road who I could flag for help. I sat and closed my eyes to find calm.

The tap on the window startled me. The noise became louder and was accompanied by bright white-and-blue lights flashing in my rearview mirror. I lowered the window.

mercy town

"I'm Officer Rudy. Are you all right, miss?"

"I . . . I . . . can't get out of the ditch. I'm stuck," I told the police officer. I could see his face only when the lights flashed on him. His body loomed large under his neon yellow poncho that flapped in the angry wind.

"Where are you headed?"

"The Payne homestead. I should be almost there, right?" I said, shielding my eyes from the bright light of his flashlight and the blowing rain.

"You're about five miles out. Come with me. I'll give you a ride."

I was relieved to learn that I was close to home. I quickly grabbed my backpack and wrapped my coat around me more tightly, pulling up the hood. The nice officer grabbed my suitcase and carried it like it was a small grocery sack. We hurried to the squad car, and I slid into the back seat.

"I'm so glad you were driving by and saw me. Don't know what I would have done."

"I'm on these roads come every storm. You're not the only one that gets sidelined like that during bad weather."

"I'm the first left after Woods Mill Road, the Paynes'," I told him, bleary and shivering. All I wanted to do was lie down and sleep away this nightmare. I caught him eyeing me in his rear-view mirror.

"Hey, are you . . . Ellis's? . . . Is that you, Ret?"

"Yes, I'm Margaret."

"Well, I'll be. Welcome back, Miss Ret. Your folks will sure be glad to see you, and you them, I'm sure.

"How do you know who I am?"

"Your father and I have known each other since we were in high school together and have kept in touch on and off. I left the police force in Madison to get back to a simpler life. He'd show me pictures of you and your brother and when he bought his business. I returned just after the accident with your brother."

nancy chadwick

"I don't remember much after that day," I mumbled, staring out the window, then focusing on beading raindrops.

"Let me tell ya, things sure have changed around here since you've been gone. How long has it been now? No matter. Main Street has seen some revitalization, they call it, thanks to a fancy developer. And that includes the land out by the river at Dell Landing. This will all be new to you. Here we are, Miss Ret. Looks like your folks have kept the lights on for you."

The officer pulled off onto the dirt road. He was just about to park the car where the house sat at the end, when Papa's silhouette appeared in the open front doorway. He always planted himself there when he was expecting trouble. Mom strained to look around his shoulder, as she was too short to see over much of anything. I stepped out of the car and thanked the officer while he carried my belongings and settled them on the porch.

He tipped his hat and waved to Papa. "All's good, Mr. Payne. She's just fine. A little shaken and tired. If you need anything, just call."

I ran to Papa and hugged him snugly, but he didn't move. When returning from anywhere, he usually hugged me so tight around the shoulders that my arms became numb. And I reached for Mom. Her body was warm and comforting. I was home. He looked too tired and soggy to figure out what that was all about. We all filed into the house.

"What happened? We expected you hours ago. We couldn't get ahold of you. The storm. The wind. The rain . . . We thought maybe you weren't coming. I'm so glad you're here." She rattled on desperately. She hugged me again, clinging, tears heavy in her eyes. Papa looked down at me as if I had just broken curfew. I dropped to the couch, exhausted. Chip, an old dog now with white in his snout, jumped up to greet me after a good sniff and realizing who I was. The end of my day was nothing like it had started. I sent Jesse a quick text to tell him I was home and that I'd call tomorrow.

mercy town

"I'm fine now. It's late. You two go on up to bed. I'm just going to sit here awhile." While I succumbed to the couch's softness and clinging to Chip, I heard Mom and Papa talking upstairs, but my groggy state kept me from following the conversation. With an arm over the back of the couch, I turned to look out through the picture window. The rain had stopped and seemed to have calmed the air of Mother Nature's hysteria. I had forgotten how thick black the night truly could be out here. The outside appeared to have no end. My reflection in the window was all that showed. I pulled up Mom's coverlet, smiling at the knowledge that she had set it out for me. When we were young, Bean and I would fight for the one Mom had made him, pulling it out of its shape as it was not big enough to cover the both of us. She understood what was happening and had made another one especially for me.

I woke a few hours later, exactly as I had lain. I sat up and at first felt I had been displaced. I thought I was still in my car in the ditch, but Mom's coverlet was tucked around me tightly, and the smell of old Chip and the sound of his snoring on the floor next to me brought me to the present. Logically, I understood I had grown up and moved on, made a new home with someone, yet the smell and feel of this room, this house, reminded me of the earlier years. It was as if my home had stood still.

Sunrise hadn't made her way to the horizon yet. The drama of the night before was still deep in my bones. I fumbled in my bag for the old journal I had placed there and resettled on the couch. The moon was a beacon, casting enough light to thumb through a few pages. Optimism and the courage to find my way were spread among the pages, hopefully out of Waunasha and into a place I could call mine. The photo of me and Bean slipped from the book; I studied it. Bean was twelve then, full of spirited wanderlust, of discovering the undiscovered. I smiled, thinking I had a little bit of Bean in me. I unzipped a small pocket inside the bag and pulled out the necklace, carefully hooking it around my neck. A lot was waiting for me to uncover, to find the buried and bring it to light. I slid the photo back into the journal, held it and my stone close to my chest, and fell back asleep until dawn.

monday

I woke to a filtered sun sitting on the pines. There was a soft tapping on the window. I rolled onto my left side and peered over the couch's back to answer the call. Was that Billy? Billy the crow was Bean's shadow. Bean found him one day flat out on the side of the barn. He picked Billy up, careful not to disturb his muddled wings, cradled him in both hands, and laid him in a basket of fresh hay. He cared for that crow every day, picking him up and gently blowing his warm, moist breath into Billy's face. Every time he did this, Billy's heart would slow, and his chest would settle. And then one day, when Bean walked into the barn, Billy perked up and hopped over to Bean in greeting, then started in with a cacophony of caws and shrieks. Billy tried to fly but didn't get very far, just a lot of hops and stops. Bean told him it would take time and that he had to be patient. From then on, Billy would tap on the front window, calling for Bean and looking for a handout of whatever was left over from supper. "Mr. Kipp tells me black crows are a sign of good fortune," Bean once told me. I never did pay much attention at the time to what he said, but now I found this to be a telltale of perhaps some connection with Mr. Kipp.

After Bean was gone, Billy didn't come around. Did he know Bean wasn't at home but in a different place? I would take a handful of peanuts out to the barn anyway and call and call for him, but he knew I wasn't Bean. And then one day, a different crow started tapping on the window. Upon further inspection, I knew it wasn't Billy because the old Billy had one wing that was crimped on the end. And this new Billy had the longest, sleekest wings held tight to his body. When I saw him, I knew it was Bean telling us he was okay. And so, we named him New Billy.

I leaned in the kitchen doorway and watched Mom get busy with breakfast making, but not before she filled a plastic cup with a scoopful of peanuts.

"How did you sleep?" she asked, handing the cup to me. Her face was tight, her movements quick. She was dressed in her usual denim capris and checkered button-down shirt.

"Restlessly. But I'm home now and looking forward to settling in quickly." I gave a good stretch to every limb, and a deep inhale. It was good to be home.

"Good. Take your time."

She greeted me as though I was part of her routine, a piece of her schedule, just as was feeding New Billy at first sight of him.

"I'm sorry I worried you and Papa last night. I was lucky that Officer Rudy was driving by. He figured out who I was . . . and I didn't know he and Papa knew each other."

She quickly readied the coffeepot, filled the toaster, and cracked a few eggs into a bowl.

"Mom, are you listening to me?"

"Yes, I am. I'm sorry, but we were so worried about you. I just hate to think . . . If something ever happened to you . . . I don't know . . ."

Her hands trembled when she tried to fish out the bread from the toaster.

mercy town

"Mom, it's okay. I'm here now, and we're going to have a good day. We'll talk later tonight."

I realized I was still holding New Billy's cup; I scurried outside to the porch. New Billy stiffened as we eyed each other, meeting for the first time. I placed a few nuts on top of the railing and stepped back. And when I did, he hopped up and nabbed one, all the while with eyes locked on me. His head tilted left, then right, as I whispered, "It's me, Bean. I've come back home."

New Billy squawked and hopped along the railing as if he was happy to have recognized an old friend. Chip, old now with graying throughout his muzzle and a fading golden coat, slowly loped through the screen door he pushed with his nose, then lifted his snoot to catch a scent of the intruder. Chip didn't mind him, though. Maybe he was just saying hello as his tail wagged in greeting. "I'll see you both later," I told them, then hurried back inside.

Rushing up the stairs to get ready for the day, I was stopped by Papa. I could tell from the corner of my eye that he had been watching me from the bottom stair while I talked to New Billy out on the porch.

"Good morning, Papa. I just met the new one. He's smart all right, warmed up to me quickly. Didn't seem to be bothered by Chip when he stuck his nose up on the railing."

"Uh-huh," was all he said before he went out the door. This was the first time I had a good look at him—in daylight and when I was rested. Papa looked tired. I had never seen such shadows under his eyes before. A beefy frame had once filled out his denims, work shirt, and canvas jacket, but now his clothes hung on him. I gave Mom, who was standing between the kitchen and the front room, one of those "What's up with him?" looks. His enthusiasm to see me and to start the day was not as I had remembered. Papa wouldn't think of starting his day without acknowledging his wife and kids with a touch of some kind.

"Your papa will be back," was all she said before plugging more slices of bread into the toaster. In the meantime, I watched him walk to the barn with New Billy fluttering behind.

A shower, together with a night of good sleep, revitalized me. Circumnavigating my girlhood bedroom while dressing in comfy jeans and a sweater, I realized the room hadn't changed. While filing a few things into my dresser, pictures of my first pony, Raisin, and me, the four of us in happy days when Papa first bought the house, were still hanging above it. I was four, I think, and Bean had just turned one in those pictures. Papa would balance me on his shoulders and Bean on a hip while telling us, "This is your home, where you will take root and grow." No one would have admitted how much work the new Payne house needed, as my folks were optimists, always looking for the power in positivity. A new roof and front porch, a coat of paint in "Snowbound," and a sidewalk in leftover construction stone made the house look postcard perfect. With Bean standing next to me and Mom and Papa together behind us, we were a family in strength and connection and surely spirit.

I pulled out a chair from under an old desk, a heavy thing, handmade from carved pine and ash, that had never been moved from this spot since its first day. Papa had bought it at a flea market and refinished it to darker heartwood, positioning it so that I could sit by the window overlooking the black oak in the backyard. My bed, draped in Grandma Carter's handmade quilt, never saw so much secret time of reading books and writing stories as it did a few years before.

"Breakfast, Ret," she called. I finished getting settled, then went downstairs and into the kitchen.

Chip, already under the table, was the first in. Mom was sitting in her usual place and nibbling on her breakfast. While I

mercy town

buttered toast and scooped scrambled eggs onto a plate, I noticed the kitchen had remained untouched; shiny red apples as canisters filled with flour and sugar and ground coffee were lined up on the counter. A sand timer as an oak tree with the sand running up and down its trunk, sat in the corner on the stove where it belonged. Everything had a home. A softness brushed my ankle. "That's Sophie, from Mrs. Henkley's cat's litter," she said.

The sight of something new and out of place made me grin. I sprinkled a few kitten treats into my hand and bent down to greet my new friend. "Isn't Papa coming in for breakfast?"

"He'll be in when he's ready. He probably hasn't finished all his chores."

When he's ready? I'd never known Papa to be only on *his* time. "He's usually pacing around here underfoot, impatient for you to get the meal made." I brought my filled plate to the table and quickly spread thick Mom's strawberry jam on a piece of toast. Sophie meowed on the windowsill in the front room, watching Papa chop wood outside. I slowed to eat and sip coffee, then studied Mom's face. Once a picture of soft youth—pink cheeks, wild strawberry blonde mane, and a figure Papa couldn't seem to get enough of—is now with fleshy spotted skin, a body that had softened from its once sturdy frame, and hair tamed from her face into a braid that showed a pallor. But my parents were always a team, and now it seemed she was feeling the effects of Papa carrying baggage for so long.

"I'm happy you're here, honey, and that you took time off work to visit and come home for a while," she said, covering my hand on the table with hers. The reassurance was warm and reminiscent of when we all held hands in the backyard under the black oak, spinning round and round its thick base. But I sensed the consolation was all mine, and this gesture was out of routine or obligation to her child. At first, I thought to tell her that I was in Waunasha because of a job assignment, but I held back, reasoning it wasn't the right time. I'd let the moment be with just Mom and me.

The morning passed quickly. Ice patches on the walkway cracked from slow warming as the spring sun reached higher in the sky. I never waited for Papa to come in for breakfast. Instead, I sprang upstairs and got ready for my first workday on my new assignment.

My girlhood room, once with a place for everything and everything in its place, looked rather disheveled. Last night's wet clothes were in a heap. My bag was turned upside down, with files, a reporter's notebook, pencils, my camera, and my laptop spilling out. In haste, I tidied, making my old homework desk a place for work. I grabbed jeans and sweaters and flannel shirts from the bed and hung them in the closet. Touching each piece of clothing was a reminder of where I had come from. I was back in the past, reliving days of cleaning out the horse stalls, feeding the chickens, and brushing Bolt, running my hands down his powerful legs, my fingers through his coat, still thick from winter and black like a moonless night. My connection to the Payne homestead ran deep, from the hens to the goats, to Bolt and Quincy. They kept us going because of the reciprocal relationship we had with them. They provided for us, and we gave them care in return. Being here was a reminder of that interconnection and a reawakening of my soul.

My, how the black oak had grown! I now noticed this because its canopy had filled most of my view when I looked out the window. I gazed at it below, recalling as if it were just yesterday when Papa tied the ends of two pieces of rope to a mighty branch, and to the other ends a piece of sanded thick wood with knots under it to make a seat for a real swing that was mine. When Bean came along, Papa hung another swing next to it, and together Bean and I let our spirits soar and our laughter fly. We would swing during a winter's snowfall or summer's downpour. It didn't matter when,

mercy town

as long as we were together, dreaming big with every high kick of our heels. Now the landscape had claimed her space, showing her years with wild grass, weeds, and bumpy terrain. The swing remained hanging but with a broken rope dangling from the limb.

Papa's heavy booted heels on the floor below announced he was in for breakfast and reminded me I had to ask him for a ride to go pick up my car. I hesitated to approach him, as our "good morning" wasn't much of one.

Papa wasn't there when I went into the kitchen, but his dirty dishes were. It used to be Mom would say, "You can tell your father his breakfast is ready now." And I couldn't forget to say, "now." If I did, Papa thought that he'd have some grace period because it wasn't really ready then. It was just something she would say, knowing it would take time for Papa to get to a break. Mom had always had a sense of timing and urgency, which had kept the family in line and running like one of his farm machines. Now Papa didn't need reminding, as he had been and gone already.

I opened the kitchen side door and saw in the distance that the shed door was open. The shed had held its age well, as it was a fine example of his woodworking and handyman skills over the years. Many times, Bean and I had watched Papa meticulously plot and then construct a place to house all the "what-nots," as Mom called them, the leftovers of what didn't belong in the barn or the house. I thought about how I had once never hesitated to approach Papa to ask him for anything. Now, my heart sped up, and I wanted to retreat.

The dark, musty space held remnants of childhood: old ice skates and a red sled, muck boots and raincoats, soccer balls and footballs, Mom's gardening tools, and Papa's work equipment. Mom's and Papa's belongings were separate on one wall, mine and Bean's together on another. He was concentrating on fixing something at his workbench, hunched over, studying the thick, rusty pieces of metal as he worked it with his bumpy fingers, with half of a middle finger missing on his left hand from a tractor accident. He wore a faded canvas coat, flannel lined in red plaid, a work coat that always hung on the rack by the back door, along with his army-green "Payne's Garage" baseball cap.

"Hey, Papa. Found you." I gave him a little playful nudge with my elbow as I stood next to him at the worktable. A couple of small drawers slid open in a chest of many, filled with bits of metal and situated to his right within arm's reach. Empty baby food jars, some filled with nails and screws, were lined up in a row on his worktable. This room hadn't changed at all. Dust, rust, and cobwebs told me so.

"Yes?" he said, turning his head my way.

"Can you give me a lift past the Dreyers' place to get my car? I might need your help to get it out of the ditch."

He continued to work on the metal mechanism of some sort, squirting a dose of WD40, then moving the arm of a crank back and forth. "Yep. Let's go, then." He wiped his fingers clean on a ratty red rag.

"Great! I just need to get my bag, and I'll meet you back at the truck."

I grabbed my bag just inside the kitchen doorway and yelled to Mom, who was somewhere in the house, that Papa was going to give me a lift to get my car.

"Oh, there you are," I said when she appeared in the kitchen. "Papa sure isn't talking these days—at least not to me, anyway. Has he been like this for a while?"

She stiffened. "Oh, he'll be all right. You don't need to worry." She went over to the desk by the door, rummaging through errant mail and slips of paper as if she was trying to find something she had misplaced.

"But I do worry. He's a changed man. I thought it would be just a matter of time, after the accident, before he'd come around. But he looks as if he's still living in the past. I see it in his face."

mercy town

I stepped closer to Mom. Behind her reassuring eyes, and smoothing over any roughness in the house, of tragedy, of the unmentionable, was a woman who may not have gotten over that day.

"You go on now, dear. Take care of whatever it is you need to do." She waved me off.

But I didn't move. Avoidance was easy; confrontation took effort.

"Mom, I haven't told you the real reason I'm back."

She cocked her head and tightened her grip on the dish towel hanging through the tie of her apron.

"It's because my editor asked me to do a story on Waunasha. I'll be here for a couple of weeks, doing interviews and reacquainting myself with home." She appeared to look through me. "... Mom, did you hear what I said?"

"Of course I did, dear. Well then, there's a lot here for you to catch up on." She gave up on finding whatever it was she was looking for and got busy putting away breakfast dishes.

I waved goodbye and shut the door behind me. That was not my mom. She would have asked why Waunasha, and what was there about it that commanded a newspaper article, but she smiled curtly and dismissed the conversation. My being home, Waunasha being back in the paper, and maybe old news about the accident could only remind her again that Bean was no longer with us.

I sat with Papa in the front seat of Old Red, an affectionate term for the pickup that had been around as long as I could remember. Papa would often refer to the truck, saying, "C'mon now, Old Red is taking us for a drive," when he would direct us to climb into it. We'd pull ourselves up and onto the back bench seat void of proper springs, and wait for a ride into town, giggling in anticipation of a bouncy one.

During the silent ride, I had a look around the inside of Old Red: the bench seat upholstery worn thin, cakes of mud on the floor. And then there were the dark red spots, now dried, on the back seat peeking from a plaid wool blanket spread across. Papa had laid Bean on the back seat, where his breath was halted and his jeans and coat were blood soaked, before rushing him to the medical center in West Prairie. Seemed Bean was still riding right along with Papa, though the blanket was hiding the memory.

"It's not too far, Papa. Just around the bend after the sycamores, on the left."

Papa spotted my car, then did a U-turn to park on the shoulder behind it. He jumped out of the truck and stood next to my car, waiting for me while I dug for my car keys. I pulled the set from my bag, then tossed it to him. He got in, started the car, and eased it from the ditch onto the asphalt quickly, as the ground had dried, providing stability.

"Oh, Papa, you did it! Thanks so much! I'm so glad the car is okay."

I pulled up on my toes and raised my arms to wrap them around his rounded shoulders in a tight hug, but I couldn't feel his arms around me. I quickly broke from the embrace.

"I'll be in town for most of the day. Tell Mom I'll be back by suppertime."

I searched his eyes for any connection, emotion, or pride that he had helped his daughter and made her happy. But his eyes were tired, his face troubled. I waved to him from my open window as I sped away.

Back on the two-lane road into town, the sky had cleared, and the sun was warming the car and me. Spring was fighting for its arrival. Buds popped from the sugar maples, and the forest floor was tinged with green life. I peered into the woods, taking advantage of their nakedness to see any signs of occupancy in the homes of neighbors. The familiarity made me feel I was at home again.

mercy town

I wondered what had happened to my parents. Mom's uncharacteristic response to why I was really back at Waunasha, and Papa's lack of affection, made me think of the disparity between now and the past.

I thought of this once-routine drive when Bean and I were little, with Papa at the wheel, Bean by his side, and me and Mom in the back seat. Papa didn't work on Sundays, so after church, he'd take us into town for some "family time," as he called it. It was a quick ride from Cavalry Baptist to Central Street, where we could get just about anything we wanted. Ice cream? The Fizz and Frost Soda Shop had it all, from root beer floats to banana splits. Mervin's mercantile had just about every piece of clothing in denim and camo you'd ever want. And who needed the Sears catalog when you could get things right away at Mervin's? How we all had grown. How times had changed.

I guess you could say Waunasha looked like an upside-down triangle. At the triangle's base ran the Loch River. Across the river to the north were the cabins at Dell Landing. They had been there for . . . forever. The Landing had always been known as the place where generations of Indigenous people lived and worked undisturbed, and where Mr. Kipp had lived all his life. Except for the smoke curls from the stoves unfurling in the sky, we didn't see the residents; they kept to themselves, taking care of the land, and the land taking care of them.

Downtown Main Street ran northeast to southwest on one side of the triangle, and on the other side, about five miles south, was our house, situated among a half dozen neighbors in clearings of spruce, fir, and maples. Plotted low were flowering ephemerals. You had to be quick to spot them in early spring, or they'd be gone in a flash. There was always something new growing, as no two springs popped the same.

Well, that was a new sign, I noticed ahead. DOWNTOWN WAUNASHA WELCOMES YOU was carved large in hickory in between two short pine poles. *I bet Mr. Kipp did that*, I thought. In the lower right corner, a birch tree, his trademark, was carved into it. Waunashans could see his woodworking scattered around town as carved benches in front of The Creamery, where you could sit while eating an ice cream cone, or inside Jack's café, where he made a few sets of chairs and tables. Conifers and large, empty terra-cotta pots adorned the front of the sign, waiting for the spring to signal their return to life, while a raised bed was outlined in rocks. I thought, *What a fancy new attraction for downtown!*

I continued my navigation, slowly reading signs and seeing who was still there and who had closed. No building was higher than two stories, and the wider sidewalks on either side of the street ran continuously through downtown. No painted lines marked parking spots; parking was where you made it. It was that kind of town that could be defined only by the community that lived there.

Neena's had remained in its original location. Established in 1957, the steel plaque said. The bones of it were the same, and upon further examination, so was the front window. NEENA'S was lit up in white and below it, flashing in pink neon, OPEN. The window was as tall as it was wide, and there was never a day when you looked out it from a booth inside that errant bird poop or smudges of grape jelly obstructed your view. Neena's once longtime window washer, simply known as "the window washer" would ride his bike, balancing a bucket, a mop, and squirt bottles between his hands. You could always rely on him, as if he knew just how long a clean window would stay clean and when it was time for a visit.

I recalled high school days there, sitting at the counter after school with my best friends, Nora and Evie. It was a place to look adult, but not to act that way because soon Harry and Ben would walk through the door. They appeared to always be

mercy town

together, hanging out wherever I was, and always late for home-room, despite living near town. They were on the wrestling team, a place for student athletes who couldn't make it on the hockey team, who begged for a place to be . . . somewhere. We'd do any-thing to get their attention, and then, when we got it, we'd do everything we could to get them to leave us alone. I gave a good laugh at that memory, as things seemed so simple back then.

I pulled into a parking spot a few doors down from the diner. Neena's wasn't as busy as it used to be at this time when male landowners in Waunasha came to congregate, drink black coffee, and have a platter of eggs, bacon, thick slices of toast and a mound of potato cubes. If Bean and I were ready for school early, which wasn't very often, Papa would drop us off there before school, and we shared in the delight of pancakes. The speed with which the men ate theirs made me and Bean stare impolitely. We didn't care, and neither did they. The lights were aglow inside, and I was ready to have myself a stack of those pillowy pancakes.

The bells jingled overhead, announcing my entry. I slid into an open booth with a view of Main Street and not much foot traffic. Inside, a foursome of older men was dressed uniformly: canvas overalls with a plaid shirt underneath, big boots planted underneath the table, and dirty caps pushed up a little above the brows. I smiled at the fact that a slice of life I had come to know remained at Neena's.

I pulled out a notebook and wrote questions—the who, what, when, where, why, and how—that I needed to find the answers to.

"Coffee?" she asked, dropping a short glass of water in front of me.

"Yes . . . please." Without looking at the face behind the voice, I turned over a coffee cup and placed it back on the saucer. She filled the coffee to the rim without a splash or a drip.

"Ready?" Dressed in a short black skirt and white but-ton-down shirt, she glanced at me without making eye contact.

"Yes, thanks. The Apple Betty pancakes, please, with plenty of syrup."

"Well, I haven't heard them called that in a long time. Are you from . . ."

We looked at each other. I recognized the ponytail of red hair pulled back, making visible a face with freckly dots and ice-blue eyes. "Amber? Amber Fielding, is that you? Oh, my, you haven't changed a bit."

"Ret? Ret Payne? I haven't seen you in . . . got to be ten, twelve years now."

We created such a ruckus that the four musketeers at the nearby table stopped laughing and had a look at the commotion.

"I *am* back in town." It was all the information I wanted to offer, as it was all too complicated.

"Oh, you got yourself married, didn't you? That ring shines brighter than anything else in here." When she smiled, a single dimple appeared on her face.

"Yep. Me and Jesse. Been living in West Prairie." I splayed my left-handed fingers wide and wiggled my ring finger.

"Well, we just got to catch up. I want to know all about married life and living way away from *this* place."

She nodded her head and hightailed it to the kitchen window, where she clipped the note with my order to the carousel, then picked up the foursome's food. She winked at me after dropping off their plates between big, eager hands already grasping forks and knives.

Amber and I were friends in high school. Our dreams brought us together. I wanted to be a writer of stories, of life, and the forest, and the Loch River. She just wanted to get out of Waunasha, whether through marriage or on her own. When we were in high school, Amber and I, and whoever she was going steady with, and maybe one of his friends, would stop at the diner after school to get root beer floats. It could never be just us girls. She contended

mercy town

having male companionship brought out the best in women. Not sure how she came up with that, but I always wanted to tell her that women are fully capable of being companions to themselves and to each other. Since Amber was a wife and soon thereafter, a mom after high school, she was never without companionship. She figured once she got out, the world would tell her what would be next for her. Well, she got the husband, and two kids, but not the out-of-Waunasha part.

"I knew you'd make it out of here, Ret," she told me, sitting just on the edge of the booth for a quick get up. "Kids?" she asked.

"Um, no. Jesse and I are full speed ahead in our careers. He works for a developer, and I'm a writer for the *West Prairie Journal*."

"The *Journal*?" she exclaimed. "I just knew all the writing you did in high school would pay off," she said, poking a pencil point in the air. "So, what do you think of it around here?" Her eyes grew wide, and she continued. "Old Waunasha has moved up with the times, including that fancy welcome sign stuck in a plot of old, gnarly earth. The Supervalu got remodeled. Had to bring their refrigeration up to code with new lighting so you could see better how the prices have gone up. There're now two banks in town, Waunasha State Bank being the newest, as some distinguished-looking guy with a lot of bucks bought it a couple of years ago. The S&L is still here, as us ordinary folks still deposit our paychecks and open savings accounts. But if you're a business owner or farmer and need a mortgage or a loan, then you'd have to go to First National in West Prairie." Amber paused at the ringing of the overhead bells. "Those bankers again, dressed in dark suits and striped ties . . . gotta run."

I wondered how she knew they were bankers. You'd see Mr. Findley at the S&L dressed only in tan slacks and a brown sport coat, his tie usually askew. I thought of the new Waunasha State Bank where Bean and I had opened our first accounts. It seemed

nancy chadwick

to anchor the end of Main Street with its white steeple that provided a place of orientation. Papa would drive us there when he thought we had too much money lying around from doing odd jobs. "Got to keep track of your finances," he'd say. "Don't keep your money lying around when it could be in the bank making interest."

"And did you hear yet about the planned new development, on Dell Landing?" Amber said, swishing back to my table to warm my coffee. "They want to put in a road to replace the little bridge and build cabins for the rich people to come over and 'recreate,' as they call it. Can you imagine that? Well, Waunasha's not made for their slicing and dicing to accommodate a rich person's dreams."

That's where Mr. Kipp lived. He was born on Dell Landing, as were generations before him, and he was as much a part of it as were the trees planted there hundreds of years ago. He knew the land better than anyone else. They couldn't just come in and wipe it all out. My hand shook with upset, spilling coffee from my cup.

"Look, I got to be honest with you. We're all divided here, Ret. After the accident . . ." she said, looking away and wiping her cheek. "No one ever saw Mr. Kipp. The only way we knew he was alive was the smoke coming from his chimney and a light in his front window. Someone said they saw him once near the little bridge, just staring out over the river to the skies, his nose up high as if he was smelling something. Some leave him be, believing it was truly an accident"—she lowered her voice to a hush—"and others . . . don't. They see him as a killing person, plain and simple, and believe he should have been arrested. I'm so sorry, Ret, about what happened. No one has forgotten about Bean. You know that, don't you? Such a spirit he was—he was contagious in this town."

I slipped lower in the Naugahyde booth, bowing my head as I felt the weight of what I had stepped into. I folded my hands in

mercy town

prayer to God that He might grant me grace in facing the challenges I had ahead. And then I wanted to hide, but I couldn't. I was angry as I wanted to forgive and move on, and I wanted the whole town to do that, too. But no one had. Including Mom and Papa. The accident pulled a thread loose in the fabric of Waunasha. "Amber, it's okay. It's time for me to explore more of my hometown."

"Gotcha there. I'll see ya again soon?"

I paid my bill, leaving it on the table along with a good tip.

It was time to feed my need for a distraction, as I didn't feel in a hurry to get on with the demands of my assignment. I made a few notes while seated in the car: *Town divided. We haven't forgotten. Killing or accident? Bean's spirit.* I remembered what Amber had said about a new road replacing the little bridge, right through the settlement. *What will happen to Mr. Kipp?*

I eased out of the parking space and drove slowly. Mervin's was on the right, in the middle of Main Street. I remembered it once had a dark brown stained exterior that looked like an oversized cabin, deep in the mountains and not a place for sporting goods. Papa would groan that it was where men gathered on a Saturday morning to "tell each other what they needed." Mr. Bruce was always eyeing a new fishing pole, and his fishing buddy, Mr. Cal, gave him every reason he could think of to get one. And he'd repeat the same reasons every Saturday, as if they were new ones and the best ones yet. Papa rarely stepped into that store, as he didn't want to get stopped by the "know-it-alls" who'd corner him and tell him what they thought he needed to know.

If Papa was in a good mood, which seemed to coincide with Saturday mornings—the mornings after I'd hear a lot of commotion and giggling going on in his and Mom's room—he'd take us out to the Oak Tree Inn. It was the only place for lodging back then. The Inn's restaurant was in the front, where it would benefit most from local foot traffic. For Bean and me, it was a special

nancy chadwick

place where Papa wanted to make us all happy. Mom said she could only be happy if her kids were happy.

I slowed to search for the Inn, set back from the road. The restaurant was gone, replaced by an expanded Carlisle Inn with a few cottages added to the back, taking up the entire block now. And with such a new grand front porch. Major and Marjorie's was where Major gave the men haircuts and Marjorie the ladies a wash and set. It was one space, divided in half by a couple from West Prairie who had opened it. The Paynes never set foot in there, as Papa said we didn't need others to do what we could do for ourselves. And there was another new sign: the Pen and Quill—a bookstore! I made a mental note to stop in this week.

The children remained on spring break. Otherwise, I would have seen a steady pace of younger ones, backpacks firmly secured, scurrying in and out of the public library doors. They didn't have far to access the library, as Tallwood Elementary was just east of there.

I continued my reacquainting and saw Cavalry Baptist Church's steeple. *Now, that's a sight that's never changed,* I thought. The white church, always looking as if it had a fresh coat of paint, anchored the end of Main. The cemetery fit snugly among the gentle gardens and flowering shrubs.

I came at the end of Main to the town's Plaza, where a fountain and memorial were displayed in honor of the founder of Waunasha, a military man who used his brave and tenacious spirit to build a town along the river. I circled the Plaza and headed back through town, noting the library and post office, and village hall. All appeared to have received face lifts in facades and square footage.

I zigzagged around blocks, noting new coffee shops, and pulled in front of one, the Coffee Grind. As with most establishments in town, I expected a bell to ring overhead when the front door opened, and the Coffee Grind was no exception. A

mercy town

bit of the old tradition had been carried forth to newer times. I ordered, then looked around, noticing how the place could easily have been found in West Prairie with a young barista behind the counter, artwork on the walls, classical music carrying soft notes, and the aroma of brewed coffee. But I wasn't there. I was back home in Waunasha, where, for the first time, I was finding it difficult to start a writing assignment. This morning's drive back in time had clouded my judgment and brought personal emotions into my professional work. My past had caught up to the present.

After the Coffee Grind experience, I moved on, getting in my car and rolling down the windows, tasting the crisp air, and smelling the scent of damp wood. Dim sunlight cast low shadows on the trees, splashing silhouettes of pine on my face. I drove past the Plaza and soon gripped the wheel, knowing I was nearing the trail, the one that led to the path to the little bridge. Clouds hung low, preventing me from seeing the illusion I was once treated to, the one I just had to tell Bean to see when the sun kissed the river.

I got off at South Hill Road, about three miles from the Plaza and downtown Waunasha. The Loch River was in sight, its side seams sewn tight with river birches and swamp oaks. Fisher Gate, a gravel area, was a perfect spot to park, listen to the conversation of growing things, and visit the latent memories of the past. I plucked a camera from my bag and swung its strap across my body, changed out of my shoes and into gum boots. A soulful walk along the river awaited me, with a destination I had in mind but kept myself open to stopping short of it. Among the undergrowth and emerging trilliums and ferns, familiarity told me I belonged.

The little bridge was up ahead. Following a bend and then an S curve, I came to my sit spot for a rest and a good look around. How the sight of it brought me joy! It was where I retreated to observe, to listen, to connect. My fifteen-year-old self had once met the peace of the forest and the quiet of the moments, with scribbles in my notebook about the trees talking their stories and carrying their energy underground to encourage new growth. It was also where I swore Bean to secrecy, to never reveal the special place. The old log, now more decayed and softer, would still be able and willing to meet me for a respite.

A chill from compacted leaf beds wrapped around my ankles. Though I was alone, I never felt lonely. I continued along the mucky path, remembering the magic and smiles and laughter that had once filled the hours for Bean and me, and the anticipation of reaching the little bridge at just the right moment. I thought returning here might be a good idea for me. Maybe laying eyes on a place that meant so much to Bean and me would suggest that I'd feel his presence, like seeing him in the breezes, a spirit threading through the trees and brushing my face. Instead, I felt a heaviness draw down me like a window shade.

I eyed the little bridge, some hundred yards ahead, then debated just how far I really needed to go . . . or wanted to. I followed the river, noting the squawking mallards, the jostling squirrels, and an occasional cardinal and sparrow jiggling the brush to settle.

My thoughts were deep when I heard a noise. *Pop. Pop.* A defiant sound broke the air like a gunshot. I heard it again. Instinctively, I stopped and hunkered down as if something was coming at me from overhead. A cold sweat blasted through me, and my heart took off in my chest. I ran, tearing through straggly vines hanging from tree limbs and dodging decaying tree stumps.

The wide body of an old oak offered its sturdy back to lean against. A crow above continued cawing. I was close enough to see a clearing, surrounded by a thicket of conifers on the other side of the river, where vacation cabins were known to outsiders but were a settlement of Indigenous people to us. Mr. Kipp's cabin was front and center of all of them and of Dell Landing, where gray smoke pushed through his cabin's chimney and a warm light

mercy town

was aglow in one of only two windows. Inside, a man's figure sat, and a tail of jet-black hair appeared inked to his back. He was smoking a pipe, pulling it from his mouth and patting tobacco in its bowl before striking a match, its red flame glowing. He rocked back and forth, and back and forth. Then halted. He turned to have a look out the window. I dropped low and hid behind a dogwood. Next thing I saw, he was standing in the doorway, then took an echoing step onto the porch. He didn't appear as I had remembered, tall and looming, but soft and blurred, dressed in dark denim jeans and a chestnut suede coat. He stared deep into the woods with a shotgun threaded through his arm, and I swore he could see or smell, or both, that someone was nearby.

"Who are you?" he bellowed. "Show your face." I waited for him to retreat inside before retracing my steps and escaping back to the car. My quick breath was heavy with fear. I didn't want to think what would happen if Mr. Kipp found me. The car was in sight; I broke into a run. I couldn't yank off my boots fast enough and swing them onto the floor of the backseat, before dropping into the front seat and gassing it out of there with nothing but flying gravel in my rearview mirror. I watched my speed along South Hill Road, as you never knew when a deer would dart in front of you. When I got to the two-lane, I sped up, letting the rush of cold air from an open window calm my nervous heat. I wasn't sure if the popping sound was real, or if my memory was playing tricks on me.

I couldn't help but think about the sound that day: the squeezing of the shotgun trigger, the propulsion of a bullet cutting the chill of the air. It was the sound that changed our lives forever.

That image of Mr. Kipp standing on his front porch, as if commanding attention, stayed in my mind as I drove all the way home. Some might have found him frightful, but Bean and I had considered him nothing but a gentle giant. I put that encounter behind me as I neared home.

The lights were on in the front room, and the warm blush from inside was inviting. I was eager to be reunited with Mom and Papa again. I had missed them, remembering the anticipation of home at the end of the road. I would hear his booming voice declare, "Here she is!" and Mom, upon opening the door, would usher me into the kitchen for an after-school snack with Bean, who was sitting and already had a head start.

"Hi, Mom . . . oh, let me help you," I told her, dropping my bag inside, then hurrying to her as she reached for a casserole dish on a top shelf in the cupboard.

"Thank you, dear. I didn't expect you home for lunch."

"Me neither."

She was already making one of our favorites for supper, chicken pot pie. I already knew what to do in preparation, so I jumped in to help with the chopping. A pot pie was always Mom's go-to to soothe any anxiety the Paynes might be experiencing. For anything from a costly repair to Papa's tractor to Mom's tireless work on the church's fundraiser, a pot pie would be in order.

"There's soup on the stove already warmed and rolls in the oven, too."

I took a bowl from the sideboard and poured a couple ladles full of potato soup into it. "I went to Neena's. I was happy that it was still there. I was afraid someone might have bought that old, stale diner and redeveloped it into an upscale place with bright lights and tablecloths . . . just for breakfast. Amber was working. You remember her? Amber Fielding, now Davis. Apparently, there's a whole lot going on in Waunasha, not only with development, but also with what you can't see."

"Is that right?" She didn't pay much attention to what I had said. Her attention was on whacking a chicken into parts, as if taking out a whole day's frustrations.

I sat to eat. "Yep. And I'm thinking there's a bit of what I can't see going on here in this house."

mercy town

She kept busy with her chicken parts, placing them into a large pot of simmering water, not responding to my comment.

A car approaching the house caught my attention in the kitchen window. I knew when we had a visitor in the dry months as I could see the first billows of dirt recoiling from the road, or in wet months, hear rubber tires splashing through puddles. Papa appeared from the barn, plunked a pitchfork into the ground, and waited. He always had exceptional hearing. He could detect the drone of log-hauling trucks on the interstate miles away before they rolled past the house. I waited too, my eyes darting from Papa to the empty road.

Mom paid no attention to the outside but focused on her prep work. "C'mon, stop staring and help me with this, please."

With my fingers, I worked pats of butter and dribbled cream onto a mound of flour. I heard a car door slam and looked out the front room window. Next thing I knew, Sheriff Cooley was talking to Papa. I didn't like how Papa was standing, with his hands on his hips, kind of defensive. And the sheriff was patting the air, near Papa's chest, as if to calm him. I wanted to preempt any emotional upheaval, so I grabbed a towel, wiped the mess from my fingers, and out the door I went.

"Well, hello there, Sheriff." I smiled, trying to be friendly to deflect any tension I might have stepped into.

"You can go right back in there, Ret. This is none of your concern," Papa said. His solid face told me he was serious. I instantly felt like that young girl again, like when the county once had come around looking for some kind of permit. Well, I wasn't that child who Papa must protect. I had a sense of responsibility for my folks and a need to protect them from any troubles the sheriff might be presenting.

I didn't budge.

"Now would you know who that might have been, Mr. Payne, hmm?" The sheriff narrowed his eyes at Papa. "Someone was getting a little too close to Mr. Kipp's place earlier today. Said someone had been traipsing again through his land. Told me he was suspicious."

"No, Sheriff." Papa took a step closer, as if ready to take on a challenge.

"Said he called out to whoever was there, but no one answered."

"Well, then maybe he was just imagining it."

"Sheriff," I said, "maybe Mr. Kipp was reacting to the rustling from the birthing of a white-tailed fawn. It *can* happen this early. Or maybe there were some foragers looking for mushrooms and dandelion greens, and he thought they were getting just a little too close to him and his place."

I didn't want to admit that I was the guilty one, so I offered an explanation in place of a confession. I didn't want anyone to know I had been near Mr. Kipp's place, lest that news ignite more ire than was already apparent. It didn't matter, anyway. I defended Mr. Kipp because he was defending himself and his home.

"Well, Mr. Payne, I just hope it wasn't someone looking for trouble, needling him and all, as that person would have to answer to me on a charge of harassment and trespassing."

Sheriff Cooley never took his eyes off Papa, who stood rigid with a frozen face. The sheriff slid into the squad car and started the engine.

Gravel popped from the acceleration of tires as the sheriff drove down Rustic Road. Papa offered no reaction; he remained silent.

Sheriff Cooley's visit didn't surprise me. The town understood Papa's anger; they thought it was justified. But anger can make people do bad things. And just maybe, the Sheriff thought it was Papa who had gone over to Mr. Kipp's to do a bad thing to him.

"C'mon, let's get inside," I told Papa, slipping my arm through his. He stared at his feet as they met the earth.

mercy town

Papa and I had just opened the kitchen door when Mom announced, "You two get cleaned up. Lunch is ready." She used to direct Bean and me as soon as we'd stumble through the door from outside. She'd say this every time, like a broken record, and as if we needed reminding. I think it was teaching us to ready ourselves with cleanliness before coming to the table and giving thanks before God and family, as if it would bring us closer to Him.

I surveyed the table to see if anything else was needed. All appeared to be in order. The ceramic lazy Susan was still turning after all these years and corralling the condiments that would have prevented Papa from getting up from the table to go to the refrigerator or pantry. Cotton placemats, my favorite ones with the red cardinal in the lower right, were at each setting, and Grandma Carter's everyday unmatched utensils accompanied their sides. I didn't call attention to a lone placemat on the table. It was where Bean used to sit. I didn't say a word about it, though I wondered why a setting continued to be made for Bean.

Papa sat at one end of the table, and I sat to his left, where I could look out the wide window to a panoramic backyard and carry my thoughts into the woods. With oven-mitted hands, Mom sat down the steamy soup pot on the table, then grabbed a basket of homemade buns on the counter.

"Let us pray," she said, bowing her head.

Mom and Papa reached for my palms on the table. Then they placed their other hands on Bean's placemat, as if connecting to Bean's space, reining him into the Payne circle. Mom awaited words from Papa, whose head remained bowed, but they didn't come. Finally, she spoke up. "Heavenly Father, bless us for these gifts of food from thy bounty, and grant us strength and continued health for which we serve in your name. Amen." And so, we ate in silence. But that didn't stop me from looking into the forest canopies, awash in bright sunlight that set the backyard into a spotlighted stage. When Bean and I were young, sitting in our places at the table, we could see the oak in full proportion, but now, after all the years of oak maturity, the window had cut off my view of the tree's top.

"That black oak sure has risen high and full," I commented. "And wasn't there a swing that Papa hung over the first limb? Bean and I chased each other till the sun dipped below the pines at night, and only after Billy crowed."

The memory made me smile and chuckle when I thought of Billy. But Mom and Papa looked as though they found no delight in the memory I shared, remaining silent, occupied with stabbing bits of potato floating in the thick soup.

"I'd look out to see if that swing had any sway in it. If it did, I knew I could thread the laundry on the line to dry in the breeze," Mom piped up.

"And the time Bean was on the swing and caught up in a bedsheet flapping on the line just a little too close." I laughed in the delight of remembering. "He jumped off and looked like a ghost, already dressed for Halloween. I think he liked—"

"That's enough." Papa pounded a fist on the table, upsetting the knives and forks. "No more talk of what was."

Mom lowered her head and stared into her soup bowl as if ashamed. I stared at him and didn't know if I should leave it alone or say something.

"It's okay, Papa, to remember things." I told him softly, reaching for that fist as if my touch would soften the tension. "These are good memories. Bean will always be with us and . . ."

He sprang up and shoved the chair behind him with the backs of his knees. He dropped his bowl and spoon into the sink, then plodded into the front room to stoke the fires before resting in the rocker.

I leaned Mom's way. "The anger he has, Mom. Have you two talked about what happened . . . at all?"

mercy town

She shook her head, then got up to wash the dishes while I remained seated and finished eating, succumbing to the comfort of food, a prayer to the good Lord, and my papa's pain.

Papa fell into a rhythm of rocking. This motion calmed him; his face was more relaxed and the palms of his hands open to rest on the arms of the rocker.

I cleaned my dishes and sat a while on the window seat in the front room, near enough to just be with him, yet keeping my distance so as not to bother him.

Mom strolled into the room and sat to resume reading *Shotgun Lovesongs* on the couch. I gave Papa a kiss and told him we'd talk later. I went upstairs to my bedroom.

The room was lit only by a candlestick lamp on my desk. I plunked down there in a chair and felt overgrown, tucked underneath a space where I was in command of a long desk and three drawers that held important, if not secret, things. Researching old *Nasha News* clips was not enough of a distraction, so I put down the paper. I was tired and felt drained after wearing the shoes of my young-girl self and tracing the steps of that fateful day.

I thought about calling Jesse, or maybe not; I wasn't in the mood to talk. But I called him anyway, more out of obligation. Our chat was short, with the usual small talk of how things were going. He was busy with new plans for a development . . . somewhere . . . I tried but found it difficult to follow him. As for me, it was just too complicated to tell him about my walk along the Loch River and seeing Mr. Kipp from a distance. Besides, I wasn't sure about what to make of it all just yet, seeing Mr. Kipp again, and still feeling the air pulse with the shot that broke it.

I lay down for a catnap and stared at the ceiling, where shadows danced from the light of a moving sun. My eyes darted from the far wall to the dresser mirror, unleashing a fear that for so long had remained buried, and now seemed to have been reborn.

nancy chadwick

I was a world away from West Prairie and seeing an underlying change below the surface of the facelifting of Waunasha. And then I fell into a restless sleep.

When I woke, most of the afternoon was gone. Papa would still be working at Payne's Garage, and I heard Mom banging in the kitchen downstairs. I closed my folder and joined her in preparing dinner.

tuesday

The next morning, the sun and I rose like warriors, ready to face the day with whatever would come our way. After an awakening shower, I slipped on a pair of jeans, button-down shirt and blazer, kind of business casual as I expected a day of interviews—cold calls, really. But after yesterday's uncharacteristic outburst by Papa at lunch, Mom's staid face, and the silence in the house, I couldn't let wondering what might happen next to distract me from having a productive day. I slipped on flat shoes as I knew I'd be walking through downtown, then gathered my laptop, files, a notebook, and my camera and rushed down the stairs. She had breakfast waiting, as she always had every morning for the past twenty-five years.

"Where's Papa? Has he eaten already?"

"Well, good morning to you, too." She pulled from the toaster rye bread slices and stacked them on a plate, buttering each.

I clipped back my wayward hair while rushing to Mom's side and gave her a squeeze before taking over the buttering duties. "Thanks for breakfast. I'm kind of in a hurry to get started."

Standing at the kitchen sink, only her head turned, and not her body, to watch me pull a glass from the cupboard and carry it to the refrigerator for a pour of milk. "Milk? I thought all women your age drank coffee now."

"Oh, I do. I'll get some in town at one of those new coffee houses. I'm eager to visit the new businesses downtown."

I fidgeted while seated at the table, taking bites of egg and toast until my plate was clean. Mom stared from the kitchen sink out the window to the black oak. I couldn't tell what she was thinking just from her face or body language, as she was as stiff and still as the emerging snowdrops from under the trees. I could ask, but sometimes I think thoughts should remain private.

"So, where *is* Papa?"

"In the shed."

"What's he working on these days?"

"Lord only knows."

She threw the dish towel to the counter, then shook her head. I met her at the sink with my empty plate, washing and rinsing, perhaps taking too much time. I pondered how to say what was on my mind without upsetting her. "Papa's been like this for a while now, huh? Kind of disconnected and closed. He used to be such a talker, telling stories and asking for updates on old Ben Roger's health and making offers of help to Bobby Mann and his failing fence." There wasn't a pocket of this town that didn't need some bit of conversation or commentary.

"Well, dear, that was then. Times have changed." She paused, then sighed. "And so have we."

Mom walked out of the kitchen to the back porch, where she lifted the lid of a tub of birdseed, scooped a cup, and poured it into the birdfeeder.

"I'm headed into town for a while. I'll see you around supper-time," I told her, sticking my head out from the partially opened door. I wasn't sure she heard me. Perhaps she, too, remembered those early days, when her two young ones burst with the prospect of spring and birth.

mercy town

I swung around the counter for the door. When I pulled my coat hanging there, Mom's appointment book went sliding off the counter, spilling envelopes onto the floor. I reached for the book and collected the wayward pieces, glancing to read the front of the envelopes. *Was this the mail I picked up the other day? And then some? Wisconsin Natural Gas, Farleys Fleet, Prairie Clinic, West Prairie State Bank.* I let this go, for now, put back the book where it was, and tucked the mail inside its pages.

I tossed my bag and coat inside the car, then glanced at the barn and shed for signs of occupancy—a light, an open door, escaping sawdust—to let me know where Papa was hiding. The swinging of a lone light bulb inside the shed led me to him.

Papa was dressed for the day in his usual Lee denims, plaid flannel shirt, and canvas barn jacket. The red cap on his head with PAYNE's in white on the front, dirty gloves on his hands, and Wolverines on his feet was a picture of a farm equipment repair shop owner.

The shed's interior was just as I had remembered. Its two by fours, though weathered, still held strong the small structure. Pops and creaks were part of its bones.

"You sure are eating breakfast early these days," I remarked, nudging him for conversation. But he didn't take the suggestion. He jimmied stubborn bolts to loosen them from a bundle of greasy metal parts. "Papa, we need to talk. You've said little to me since I've been back, and I'm worried there might be something weighing heavy on your mind. I thought it would be good if—"

"You don't need to know what's on my mind, Ret. You've got a job to do, and best you be on your way to do it." He moved from me to the other end of the worktable and positioned a ladder adjacent to his workbench. He climbed the first two rungs and reached for an army green toolbox, a hand-me-down from his papa, looking old from its many well-used years. When he pulled down a crate of rusty parts, a cardboard box came tumbling down with it. Papa tried to grab it, but it slid from his control. The box's tucked flaps flew open, and its contents spilled onto the floor.

I stared at the container as if an alien had landed splat on the floorboards. Papa stared at it too, paralyzed. How a single box and its plunk could snap us both into the past. A pair of Bean's ice-skating pants, his old winter jacket, and hat and mittens made by Grandma Carter were released from their folds. My stare poured through Bean's things as if willing him to also appear from the box. Misshapen outerwear that once clothed Bean sparked a memory of him toddling to him and wrapping his arms around his slender legs while reaching for my hand. But the clothes remained dormant, lifeless. We used to wait, anticipating just the right time in early winter, when Papa thought a section of the "back forty," as he had jokingly called it, was ready to flood. Though come spring with all the rains, Papa must contend not only with flooding but also with the rink's slow melting. Papa rushed to stuff Bean's things back into the box, collecting them by the handful. He secured the flaps quickly as if putting air back into a balloon that had become lifeless, as if to keep Bean whole, contained, remembered, secured.

I squatted to meet Papa, trying to slow him down by taking Bean's clothes from his grasp. "Ridding ourselves of old things, Papa, does not mean breaking our connections to them or to the people who possessed them," I told him. "Bean is not confined to a single, closed box. He is and always will be with us." I placed a hand on his as he secured the last flap.

I didn't expect him to say anything; I just wanted him to hear me. And I think he did. His budding tears spoke. It was the first sign of connection we had with each other since I'd been back.

I helped him put the box back on the shelf, then told him I was leaving for the day but would be back by suppertime. When

mercy town

I gave him a hug and a peck on the cheek, he wrapped one arm around me. It was a start.

While driving down Rustic Road into town, I thought about what happened in the shed. *There's got to be a way to sort through this and to move on while keeping Bean in our hearts and our memories. Letting go of loved ones has its own timetable, I suppose.* Perhaps the guilt becomes too much when letting go would be forgetting them, I realized. But Bean was a Payne, and being a Payne was in our DNA. The Paynes had been a part of Waunasha for five generations; at least that's what Papa always told us. Could have been even further back. But for now, Mom and Papa must give themselves permission to heal.

Mother Earth was trying her darnedest to warm us and to give life to the trees as the sun split the clouds. I wished for sun. It always seemed to make people happier and friendlier. *We sure could use a dose of that*, I thought.

My first stop was at Neena's to see Amber. There was a lot I could learn from her about this town, as she never missed the beat of its heart and the people who kept it pumping. Old habits didn't seem to die.

I pulled the car in front and walked in with the door chimes following. After a quick survey of my fellow diners, I took the same seat as I had on my first visit, in a booth near the window with a view of Main Street.

"Hey there, Ret. What can I get you?" Amber said, making her way to me with a coffeepot in one hand and a small plate of rye toast in the other. She looked as she always had, dimples like parentheses to enclose her perky smile, and a full hourglass figure any mom would envy.

"Hi Amber. Just a coffee, please, with room." I pulled out a reporter's notebook, special for this assignment, and made a

96

to-do list of calls to make and places to go. I was grateful for this morning's workspace, and I also needed Amber to help me fill in a few unknowns.

"How's it been since you've been back? Culture shock after living in the city for a while now?" she said, pouring coffee and setting the plate down on the table. If you were a regular at Neena's, you always had the rye toast.

"No, not really."

"Then what's up?" Amber set down the coffeepot. "It sure is too early in the morning to have so much on your mind already."

"Just trying to stay focused on what all needs to happen."

"And what exactly needs to happen?" Amber leaned in over the table and looked deep into my face as if to draw out the answer.

"I need to talk to a few of the locals, the old and the new ones. Can you steer me toward some of the new businesses?"

"Well, for starters, the Supervalu has a new owner. Bobby senior sold it to a chain grocer just last year. The agreement was to not change the name on the outside, but the inside would be up for grabs. Grover Hopkins is still village manager, yet Emerson Clem is getting popular. Looks like the young one is looking to unseat the older Mr. Grover in the election next year. You remember Emerson? Hard to forget him. He was in our class. Led the senior walkout right before graduation. Thought the valedictorian should be appointed by vote of most popular rather than awarded by high academic achievement," she said, chuckling and shaking her head. "I'm sure you can find Manager Hopkins at Village Hall, and Emerson getting his nose in Waunasha's economic development and underfoot with Mr. Hopkins. Make sure you get on over on the east side, too. You'll be amazed how Main Street here has become almost an afterthought."

"Thanks, Amber. I'll catch up with you again soon."

"Ya know Ret, sometimes it's hard to move forward when the past still has a hold on you," she said, picking up the coffeepot

mercy town

and heading to a table of rough-looking men, unshaven and dressed in baggy denims and dirty shirts. Just as I was about to call the village manager's office, the men, about Papa's age, were walking to the door. We exchanged inquisitive looks as if we both were seeing someone new. And I bet they had the same daily special, right down to the rye toast, as they were sure to be regulars. As they walked out, a pair of gentlemen strolled in. In stark contrast to the pair who left, they wore well-tailored dark suits, dark tie shoes, and matching short haircuts, clutching leather cases under their arms. They slid into a booth in front of me and lay their cases, engraved with ECCOSTAR in gold lettering, on the table. That word—Jesse's employer—popped like a firecracker.

I leaned to my left a little to catch their attention. "Excuse me, but by any chance are you two the developers working on the revitalization of downtown?"

The pair exchanged looks and hesitated to speak.

Finally, one of them said, "Why, yes, we are. Henry Banks and Joseph Long at your service, ma'am. You live around here?"

"I do, well, used to. I'm a reporter for the *West Prairie Journal*, and I'm back to do a story. And I hear there's some new development in the works for Dell Landing. I think I might want to talk to you about it."

The pair shifted. As friendly as they seemed to be, they had become tongue-tied. "Well, miss, we're from corporate, and I'm not sure we can discuss such plans as they are, well, plans. Nothing is signed off on yet."

How did they even know what my questions were?

The pair contradicted all things Waunasha. The previous pair could have been around since the establishment of this town, when the land was worked by Indigenous hands, when life was simple, when all Waunashans knew one other, and we claimed our spots for generations. And the dark suits that followed through the door were the opening of Waunasha's future, one that was unknown.

I knew I would get nowhere with those two, so I packed up my work, met Amber at the cash register, and paid my bill.

"I'll see you soon," I told her.

"Hey, Ret. I've known you a long time. I sure can see you wanting to do the right thing of forgiving Mr. Kipp, but the power of your anger towards him still has its hold on you. You'll work it out just fine. I know you will." Her smile reassured me.

I settled in the car and became absorbed with the busyness of Main Street. Front doors were unlocking, and soon the first customers of the day strolled in. As much as I needed to drive to the Village Hall and meet with Mr. Hopkins, I wanted to go to the Loch River for a wander among the memories and a silent chat with Bean. My sudden brush with memories and a need to connect with my brother was about seeking an affirmation from Bean, who was sure to tell me not to worry and to do what I needed to do. I wondered if Waunasha was torn too, between living in the past with anger toward Mr. Kipp, and wanting to move forward. Were we feeling guilty because we shouldn't leave the past behind and forget what we lost, as if in disrespect? Because we were pulled to find ourselves once again in living our present lives as we were meant to?

A haze crept through the sunny skies. My ringing phone startled me back to the present.

"Margaret, Simpson here." Referring to himself by only his last name was something I had never gotten used to.

"Oh . . . Mr. Simpson . . . Good morning to you."

"You making progress? Seeing a lot of change over there? How are the folks handling it?"

"Well, Mr. Simpson, I've got interviews lined up at the Village Hall and I accidentally ran into a pair who are from the corporate developer's office. Yes, change is in the air here, and I'm working through my priorities."

mercy town

"Good to hear it, Margaret. Keep me posted, please. I'm looking forward to reading your good work."

Well, half of my update was true. I hadn't yet made it to Village Hall, but I understood the developers were in town. I told him of the progress he wanted to hear, but not the part of me wanting to digress to the Loch River.

Spits of rain hit the windshield. After confirming I had my boots and raincoat in the back seat, I pulled out from the parking spot. But I didn't turn off to the Village Hall. Instead, I kept driving toward home. Surely, an hour spent away from working on the story would not set me back. When the asphalt ended and a gravel path began in tandem with the Loch River, I parked. The rain became steady, and the dark sky had turned grayer.

With the engine off and the wipers intermittently clearing my view, I sat and felt pulled to the past like a vacuum. Admitting weakness for succumbing to flashbacks to the accident was putting my drive for doing my job in jeopardy. I feared not getting the right story, but I wondered what, if anything, was right anymore. Mom and Papa weren't right, and Waunasha certainly had changed.

The rain had let up, and I turned off my wipers. An aura cupped the clouds, readying the skies for clearing. I dressed in gum boots and a repellent coat before venturing out into the woods. Soft earth succumbed to my trudging feet.

After the accident, I couldn't go to the Loch River for at least a year because it had betrayed the trust I had in it and in Mother Earth. But now that I had returned, the spirit of a spring awakening, the memory of magic in summer's growth, and the falling of fall into slumber was all that was on my mind. It was a reconnecting to the heavens and to the strolling Loch River, and to trees I had good talks with. Ten years later, my sit spot, a tree log, a remnant in size, was large, still offering strength as a piece of a giving tree. Heads of spring flowers emerged, and there was a new softness to the bark of saplings. What had remained unchanged comforted me, yet I couldn't help but think that change was sure to come.

Gentle breezes switched to windy gusts in the waning light of the late afternoon. The shift was typical of spring up north. Dotted in the birthing landscape, flags of fluorescent orange waved across the river for my attention. I heeded the calling and trudged near the river's edge, where ribbons were attached to short stakes stuck in the ground. These were land markers, like the ones I had seen at the Pearsons' or the Gustafsons' when they were building onto their farmhouses. Only this was no home addition. This was something on a bigger scale. These must be the property markings for the new development of Dell Landing.

I followed the path to the little bridge and came upon a line of plotted stakes. Only these ribbons were fluorescent pink to designate the road that would replace the footbridge connecting Waunasha to Dell Landing. On the other side of the river, constellations of light illuminated cabin windows like fireflies on a late summer night. I squatted low so that no one would see me and think of me as an intruder, remembering that day when Sheriff Cooley came over, suggesting that Papa was involved in trespassing on Mr. Kipp's land. I never did confess that that trespasser was me and not him.

Mr. Kipp's cabin had no light in the window. Its appearance of unoccupancy puzzled me, and I was concerned that he would never let a light, either by fire or lamp, go unlit. To do so would rob the spirit of direction. "Keep the light," he would say, "and your spirit will always find its way home."

"What are you doing, here, miss?" The gravelly voice startled me. I reached for the ground before losing my balance.

I stood, legs like springs, then stiffened. His face, once strong with tight eyes and high cheekbones and a jawline that spoke of a warrior, was now soft with a map of lines on his skin.

mercy town

"Sorry . . . I . . . noticed all the stakes, the markings. Something going on here? Do you know what's happening?"

He explained that a couple of men, dressed in pressed khakis and stiff L.L.Bean plaid wool shirts, hardly looking like the land surveyors that they were, traipsed the woods with duck boots on their feet and clipboards in hands.

"I shouted to them that they were trespassing. But they remained mute when I asked them politely to remove themselves," he told me.

"Looks like something will soon be built here. Do you know what it is?"

"All's I know is we're being run out of here with no place to go. These trees'll be gone, land flattened," he said, gesturing with an open hand and sadness in his eyes.

I believed this man to be Mr. Kipp. But I argued with myself that no, it couldn't be him. It had been ten years. That night, I never got a good look at him because my eyes were locked on hands holding a shotgun and not a face. This old man, now with a gentle voice and kind eyes, could not have been the man who had accidentally shot my brother.

His stare lingered—as if he knew who I was.

On my way back to the car, I stopped at my secret spot to sit for a talk with myself and with all who would listen. I explored the skies with her slivers of blue appearing as if trying to escape from a gray seal. Dropping my head in prayer, I talked to the trees and asked them for guidance, pulling in all the energy that was emerging quickly. And in doing so, I was talking to Bean, too, invoking his name. He was in the trees, and the heavens and the earth. I asked him what I had gotten myself into and to please help me, as if he would answer right then and there. In his own way, and in his own time, I believed he would. For now, all I saw was a town that was quickly facing its new future.

The hum of the car's engine and rhythm of its wheels made me repeat, like a mantra, that the past needed to be reconciled first.

I pulled onto Rustic Road, relieved for now, as I awaited the turnoff to Woods Mill Road, where home would be at its dead end. I arrived early, before supper, and I considered taking Bolt out for a ride. We could be together to find freedom and peace of mind. Mother Nature gave us a sense of place when my own sense felt caught between back then and the future.

We ate supper in a hush only the Paynes knew, a silence that had been built in layers over the years and had worsened during my absence, until we finished. While I helped Mom wash dishes, the reflection of us in the window was a slice of ordinary life, yet it was proving to be far from usual. The backyard loomed without borders that defined our land, and invited imaginations to roam free.

The clean-up was completed. Mom turned off the kitchen light, and I wandered into the front room and kneeled on the couch in front of the window. Papa rocked in his chair and read the *Nasha News* by the bold amber light from the fireplace. This would signal the settling of the day into evening and the time for him to tell Bean and me one of his stories. When Papa was done speaking, he would say, "And that's our story for tonight." Bean would pull a cardboard box from under the couch and set up his toy railroad tracks, his small hands deftly keeping their alignment while he ushered them along the floor. Mom grabbed her sewing box near the couch and joined Papa in a chair near him to work on some mending by the light of a floor lamp. The aura inside our home against the ebony sky reminded me of the small light in the window of Mr. Kipp's cabin that sat like a star in the terrestrial night. I wondered how he was spending his evening.

mercy town

I went upstairs to my room and got busy typing up notes, which were made not in sentences, but in words: ECCOSTAR, suited men, Mr. Hopkins, the east side of Waunasha ... Mr. Kipp, the stakes. Since I'd been here, the days' events seemed to have run together as I noted how quickly the time was passing.

My phone rang, and it was Jesse.

"So, tell me, how was today?" His voice was chipper. I moved to a small stuffed chair by the window, tucking my legs underneath me in the comfy spot.

"Sorry I couldn't get into more of how things were going here." My voice softened as I recalled Mr. Kipp's emotion when he sounded threatened. I held the phone tight to my face as if I didn't want anyone else to hear my admission. Truth was, he and his land *were* threatened.

"It's okay. How's it really going? I can sure tell by the tone of your voice that there's something more going on than just the article."

"Waunasha is in a state. It's torn apart. Maybe I was so eager to move on and away from here that I didn't see how divided people were. Seems like the same thing is on everyone's mind, but no one is talking about it, including right here in this house."

"I'm sorry you're going through this. Have a talk with your folks, a real heart-to-heart."

I think he could have heard my heavy breath and sighs. "I went to the river today. Mr. Kipp caught me watching his place."

As soon as I mentioned his name, I realized I never did tell Jesse who Mr. Kipp really was. Jesse was my future, my moving forward. Being honest with him—that it wasn't just some hunter who accidentally shot Bean, but Mr. Kipp, on Dell Landing—meant bringing the past into the future I was building with my husband.

"Mr. Kipp?"

"Oh, he's one the residents on Dell Landing." I quickly changed the subject and mentioned Mom's quiet demeanor and

Papa's touchy ways. "I think I've had enough for one day. We'll talk soon, okay?"

"Margaret, everything will be just fine. It'll all work out. You'll see."

I hung up, reassured Jesse was and always had been there for me. *I know I'll need to talk to Mr. Kipp before I leave here. It's been too long and* . . . I was so caught up with Mr. Kipp on my mind, that I forgot to ask him about the two men from ECCOSTAR and about the stakes in the ground around Dell Landing. Tomorrow was another day I would be glad to greet.

I got ready for bed and typed a few last-minute notes about how the people of Waunasha were torn, how Main Street felt like their spirit was floating in and back out like the tide's ebb and flow. When I walked down Main Street, the once-friendly chatter and simple hellos when passing one another were absent. It wasn't as it once was. The accidental shooting left a festering wound that hadn't healed and closed among all Waunashans, not just with the Paynes. The town wasn't ready to move forward; I included myself in that, despite the landscape and ECCOSTAR saying it was time. I shut down the computer and read a few more newspaper clippings in the *Nasha News*, waiting for sleep to catch up with me.

In a deep sleep, a dream took over. I was defenseless, standing next to the river's flow where the water's anger was pulling me into her fury. I felt overpowered. And Mr. Kipp stood behind me, motionless. His heaviness was draped over my defenseless, cowered frame. And then I turned and looked over my shoulder. It was Bean. He had fallen onto a pile of decaying, wet leaves and remained there, listless. His breath pulsed in the cold fog. I knew he was alive, but I couldn't go to him, nor he to me. I pulled through heavy air as if every inch mattered. We were close, yet so far, beyond our reach of one another.

Until the weighty limbs of the hickory scraped my window, shaking me awake.

wednesday

Lonnie just had to tell me on the phone that morning what happened with Clarissa the other day back at the office. He said she was doing some of her own investigative work on the side. Said how she leaned so close to the computer screen, it was as if getting closer would make her read faster. She'd occasionally narrow her eyes and look down to reference something in her notes, then return to Internet searching. "I certainly thought she was up to something," he told me. "She clicked through screens of newspaper reports as if becoming one with the story. When I stood next to her with a file folder in my hand, she didn't hide what she was looking at. She told me to just leave it without taking her eyes off the computer." He then said he asked her what had gotten her so intrigued. Then she showed him something from the *Nasha News,* reading aloud a headline. "'Shooting of boy stuns small town.' And they ran a picture, too," he said.

Lonnie told me he wasn't getting it and that he didn't understand Clarissa's intent.

"And then she yelled at me, told me to look, poking with her finger at the photo."

He read back to me what he read in the newspaper. "'Ret Payne, 15, of Waunasha, with her brother, Bean, 12, before his accidental death on March 12,'" and then asked her right out why she needed to bring all this up, when it had happened ten years ago. He told her to leave it be. He said Clarissa just couldn't resist stopping at my desk when she got up to get more coffee. She nonchalantly snooped, checking out photos of my family, me at my high school graduation, and then my wedding.

Being subtle was not part of Clarissa's DNA. She never could help herself.

"Then what?" I snapped.

"She eyed a white corner of what looked like a card peeking from under your desk blotter, then gave that corner just enough of a pull to reveal a birthday card. She opened it, and a photo of a young boy slipped to the floor. She picked it up and held the card, then mouthed while reading the words inside. 'You're the best big sister I could ever have, Ret. Happy birthday, Love from Bean.'"

Lonnie told me that she said it changed everything.

"And just how does that 'change everything?'" I asked him.

"She put it all together—you, Waunasha, the shooting of your brother. We started arguing about it, how she thought it *did* change things, and I thought it hadn't changed a thing."

Lonnie admitted they started arguing because I hadn't previously disclosed that I was originally from Waunasha and was affected by what happened.

"She told me you should be pulled from the assignment because of this," he said, his tone low and quiet, as if afraid to tell me.

"What? How could she say that? Well, she could because I wasn't there." I jabbed the air with my finger. I was steaming. "And to have the audacity to be sneaking around my desk. Well, what did you say? And I know you would have said something." I

mercy town

held the phone tight to my mouth as if the words would be heard louder on the other end.

Lonnie, in my defense as always, admonished her for such thoughts. "I told her in no uncertain terms to let it go and to let you do the job our boss had assigned you."

But I knew Clarissa. I knew she persisted, like any good lawyer who argues a case. "She wasn't done. She jumped up, shook my arm, and said that's where the story is." Lonnie told me Clarissa believed the change in Waunasha wasn't one of development—it was the aftermath of a shooting, one that was personal for me. "She wanted to know what happened to the shooter, a . . . Mr. Kipp? Then she did an Internet search for his name. I told Clarissa to hold on, and that there was no story. The only story is the one that you were assigned," he continued. "I guess I pointed a finger at her while giving her an eye, telling her again to 'leave it alone,' before I walked away."

Since I started at the paper, Lonnie had been my chief defender, always telling it to me straight if ever I was veering off on a tangent for an assignment. During my first months there, he was my alarm clock, chiming in when deadlines were near and making sure I would make them. I wasn't used to working under the clock, as my writing had always been driven more by reflective thoughts than the timeliness of turning in factual statements.

Lonnie must have felt an obligation to let me know Clarissa was poking around in my personal history, but I wasn't sure what he wanted me to do. What could I have done this far away from the office? I was glad he told her to forget about it. But I knew she wouldn't. She was like my dog Chip with a new toy, prancing around to show everyone what he had. I trusted Lonnie to stand up for me should the need arise.

Now, I knew Clarissa well enough to know she'd jump at any opportunity to see me sink, as we always seemed in competition for column space. Clarissa usually played nicely, but she also worked smartly. She had her years and cozy relationships with the higher-ups as they tendered their work affairs and outside friendships with happy hours and barbecues. It made it appear that they considered the *West Prairie Journal* staff like family. And I understood that when a new one came along and tried to join such an establishment, they had to earn their way into the *Journal* family membership. But I had been at that paper for a few years when my inner security stopped me from being bothered by office politics. It was too distracting and time consuming. I loved what I did every day and had been lucky to have Mr. Simpson take a chance on me.

After a gray morning with spitting rain and ominous skies, the day had cleared with a sun invoking optimism, spurred by those spring showers that brought the flowers. Eventually, the sun would shine, and then everything would be all right. It was the middle of the week already, and urgency rushed through like a shot of adrenaline. I had to show more for myself by working with the county folks and the developers than sorting out my personal conflicts at the Payne household.

Before I left for downtown, Mom asked me if I could please mail the few envelopes stacked on the desk near the door. "Will do," I told her, grabbing the pack and slipping it into my bag. "I'll see you later today."

While driving into town, I noticed the tree shadows, once long and darkening, now were shorter and lighting my way. By the time I parked in front of Neena's, Main Street was spotlighted, offering warmth and that small-town feel I had grown up with. I parked there, reasoning I would stop for lunch after circling downtown on foot with a tote of files and a notebook slung over my shoulder, first stopping by the post office to mail Mom's envelopes.

mercy town

The old post office's face was as bright as ever, looking as if it had just been power washed and the window trim painted with a fresh coat of white paint, even though the sun hadn't yet made it to that side of the street. I stepped inside and found the mail slot, checking the front envelopes for stamps before pushing them into the box. All the addresses were familiar, except one, "Louis Archer, Attorney at Law." I wondered what Mom and Papa were doing corresponding with a lawyer. I studied the envelope, front and back. It felt light in my hands as if there was only a single piece of paper folded inside. I dropped the letters in the opening, remembering the name "Louis Archer."

The public library was a couple doors down from the post office, with a stationery and supply store and a card store in between. I popped into the library and recalled days and some nights I spent here, researching articles and checking out books. For old times' sake, I wandered the aisles of bookshelves, noticing the scent of old, dusty paper, and located the information desk, computer room, and the new additions of "quiet" rooms. Seems the library had updated its décor too, with new carpeting, study carrels, and desks. Even the checkout desk had a new counter and computer. For a small-town library, it was impressive.

A familiar woman, with now steel-gray hair pulled back into a bun, sat behind a computer at the circulation desk.

"Hello . . . Mrs. Thorngate?"

She looked up over the tops of her wire-rimmed eyeglasses before pulling them off her nose and letting the chain catch them to dangle on her chest. "Yes? May I help you?"

At first, she didn't recognize me, and for a moment, I thought I had the wrong person. But the chirpy voice of my teacher from high school English and Composition class confirmed it was her.

"It's Margaret . . . um, Ret Payne, Mrs. Thorngate. From senior year English and Composition."

"Well, I'll be." Her rosy lips matched her plump cheeks. Her smile made her eyes squint. She was just as I had remembered—inspiring and comforting, all rounded into a five-foot-two package of pleated skirts and cardigans. She knew which students were struggling and gave them attention, letting them know they weren't alone. I had my doubts in high school about writing as something I wanted to do with my life. But then an acceptance of a submission I had sent away long ago came through, just at the right time to wash away my uncertainties.

"Well, well, come back to enter more writing competitions, did you?" Her hazel eyes gleamed when she smiled.

She remembered. Mrs. Thorngate was my number one fan and promoter of me and my work, helping me to be the best writer I could be. She always urged me to submit to local and national writing competitions. A canvas bag with at least three books, a larger notebook, a few ballpoint pens and pencils, and a smaller, journal-like book would always be slung over her shoulder. At any one time, she'd stop and pull out some piece of paper from her bag and scribble a thought or two. She got me into that practice should an idea or inspiration strike me.

"I'm in Waunasha on assignment for the *West Prairie Journal*. A new feature, reporting on the revitalization of Waunasha and how it's turned into quite the attraction."

"Well, the only thing I know is the new development at Dell Landing and wiping out those old cabins that are in a good position to go up in flames during the next drought spell." She leaned her top half to the left of the computer screen, putting her in the aisle and us closer together. She whispered, "But Ret, what's really brewing is confronting that shooter. He's a stand-your-ground kind of guy, and no one is going to get him to move to make way for a new development. He's got that whole tribe up there in those cabins behind him." After she realized what she had said, she bowed her head in apology. "Sorry, I didn't mean to bring up an old wound."

mercy town

I touched her hand. "It's okay. It's okay to talk about . . . the accident. Seems like most do want to talk, yet it seems to raise the ire of those who want to leave well enough alone."

She took my hands in hers and held them gently. "No one has forgotten, I can tell you that much."

Her mouth opened as if she still had more to say. "Thank you, Mrs. Thorngate. Now, if you'll excuse me," I said, shifting from one foot to the other. "I've got a few errands to run for Mom before getting back to work, and you must have work to do yourself."

Her eyes softened, and she slunk back into her chair as if disappointed our chat would not continue. "Oh, of course, Ret. You get on, now. Thank you for stopping to say hello."

If there was one thing I had learned from living in Waunasha, it was how to end a conversation. One did not walk away from others unless all parties agreed to the chat's ending. It was all about sharing and connecting, as the town was one big clan of neighbors. I wanted to tell her I'd come by to see her again if I had time this week, but I didn't want to get her hopes up in case I couldn't make it. She was an original Waunashan who wanted to share her emotions and talk about the past. It was how we used to be, but were no longer.

I waved and smiled. "Maybe I'll see you again soon."

Mid-morning, Main Street became busy with housewives, young moms toting toddlers, and self-employed men from outlying farms who had come into town for provisions. It was the Waunasha I had grown up with and depended on for grounding and learning a thing or two about home, family, and community. I continued canvassing the retail establishments lining Main Street, passing a new hair salon, Rossi's, Italian, no doubt, and Fay Rhodes. I was glad to see it still was in business. Both store windows boasted lights, black and white, in remodeled contemporary glamour. It was good to see Main Street windows filled with commerce; I hadn't passed one empty storefront yet. And I still had the east side of Main Street to discover where ten years ago, there was nothing but double-wides and wild landscape.

Soon, the land became more occupied as Waunasha expanded her limits to two-story homes dressed in white wood and colored shutters and with garages in the back. Small businesses moved in, and then word got around that good money could be made by selling handmade goods of wood and wool, oil paintings, and jewelry. The east side became the artsy part of town, with enough elan to make it classy and sassy. Yes, Waunasha had come into its own. It had found a fork off the beaten path of Main Street and become a place for people to not just pass through on their way up north, but to stop and enjoy a little of Waunasha folk too.

I stopped at Neena's for lunch and to say hello to Amber, but it was her day off. I slid into what had become "my" booth and took in the diner smells of french fries and french dips. The early crowd, seated at shiny faux-wood tables for four, were the regulars, no doubt, similar-looking men I had seen my first time back here. They were sixty-somethings with expanded bellies and large, rough hands to steady themselves. A waitress doled out booster seats for toddlers as often as she poured coffee.

Amber's fill-in spun from the counter, ample hips swiping the end of it. Her white oxfords glided on the buffed tan linoleum. "Coffee for you?" she asked, setting down a trifold laminated menu at the end of my table.

"Hi there . . . Joan." I spied her name tag pinned to the left collar of her white blouse. On the opposite side was a yellow daffodil pin. She held a small notepad. "How about a Cobb salad and a piece of strawberry pie?"

"That's it? Salad and pie?" she asked, knowing the answer, as she had read it back from her notepad.

mercy town

I scanned the menu to find a quick something else, as Joan made me feel I hadn't ordered enough. "Yep, that'll do it." I closed the sticky menu and handed it to her.

"No soup or sandwich to go with, huh?" She raised her eyebrows.

"Just that, thanks."

She mumbled a little something, like "Well, that's a why bother," as she walked away, but I didn't mind her. She sure could have taken a note of cheer from the display of the daffodil on her shoulder.

I settled quickly, pulling out my notebook and pencil from my bag and turning pages in review of my schedule of who I was meeting when and where. I had called the county office first thing this morning, and someone named Gretchen had answered. Her succinct speech and enunciation said she had no time for friendliness, so I got to the point. "Hello. My name is Margaret Payne . . . um Reed from Waunasha, and I'm a reporter with the *West Prairie Journal.* I'd like to come by this afternoon to speak with Mr. Jennings about the development happening in Waunasha." I had hoped that slipping in that I was from Waunasha would help my chances of getting time with Mr. Jennings. I almost made the mistake of telling her I was from West Prairie, best known by Waunashans as the place where big-city folks showed off their money. She put me on hold, and while I listened to Carrie Underwood sing her number one hit, I prepared my interview strategy.

"Well, Ms. Reed? Mr. Jennings doesn't make it a habit of talking to reporters in his office, but since you are a local and your father did great work over the years with us here at the county, Mr. Jennings can give you time."

I chuckled at the thought of his "generosity." He *should* give me a few minutes of his time. In all the years Papa was devoted to the county, he worked hard to make sure citizens' needs were met. I had an hour before I needed to leave to get to the county building, which was plenty of time to finish my lunch.

Foreboding clouds accompanied me on my drive to the county building. But often, what appeared to be bad weather here could turn out to be good just an hour later. I thought ahead to my arrival, hoping Waunasha's village manager, Mr. Hopkins, whose main office was in the building too, would be available. Mr. Hopkins was up for reelection, and with a bit of luck, maybe I could have a chat with Mr. Clem, his rival, who I had learned would be a sure challenge for Mr. Hopkins. I owed Amber for filling me in on this one.

Straight highway driving put a consistent push on the freedom I always found when traveling to different parts of the state. For a while, I could let go of the town's feelings, and my own, about the accident that I was still carrying in my heart.

The sky had broken into pieces, and clouds floated like a flotilla on the Loch River. Traffic had slowed by the time I entered Clark County. I turned off for the business district. How it had dressed itself in modernization! From newly paved and striped roads, to parking garages, drive-ups, and drive-throughs, to banks and coffee shops. I had known this district to be right out of middle America, including the sound of country music guitar strumming through the only tavern's swinging doors, a general store that was indeed general, a small movie theater, and a post office with the government building, the oldest one, plunked like a concrete brick in the middle of the block. Clark County had caught up with the times. I could see WALMART in white letters in the distance, and by the looks of it, I'd be caught in its traffic.

The main county building had remained preserved, a relic from the 1950s, but its multiple additions, including the courthouse, might have meant a map was necessary to navigate the campus. Luckily, I saw the ENTRANCE sign right away and found

mercy town

the front door easily. Up three steps and through glass doors marked COUNTY OF CLARK in black letters.

The soles of my shoes squeaked on the buffed linoleum floor as I walked to the middle of a long hall where elevators pinged as doors opened and closed. I waved off the young woman sitting tall with bobbing ringlets of short, dark hair when she pointed to the directory hanging on a near wall. Fourth floor, Room 9, Doug Jennings, county commissioner. While I waited for the neon orange numbers to settle on *L*, one door opened, and two men exited. They looked alike, dressed in khaki slacks, white button-down shirts, and brown tie shoes on their big feet. Handlebar mustaches appeared to cut their faces in half. I eavesdropped on their conversation as they stood between me and the bouncy hair lady. I had learned from a recent photo in the *Nasha News* that Mr. Clem was the one with an untied shoelace.

"Ahem. Mr. Clem? May I have a word with you?" I said, intercepting his exit of the building. "Margaret Reed, *West Prairie Journal*, and I'd like to talk to you about a new development I hear is happening over on Dell Landing," I said in my best business voice. It echoed through the lobby.

Mr. Clem stopped and avoided eye contact. "There's really nothing going on over there. Where'd you get that notion?" His stride picked up as he searched for the revolving doors.

"Talk is my source, Mr. Clem. And Waunashans sure do know what they're talking about, as I am one of them. Besides, you're trying to unseat Mr. Hopkins for village manager, and finding you in this county building, I'd say that confirms something is going on."

I quickly stepped in front of him. "Look, we both know that eventually, the development will be confirmed. Depending on the deal the county struck with the developers and perhaps your involvement in the sweet end of the deal, it'll make news. Now,

nancy chadwick

why don't we have a sit-down and a friendly talk? The *Journal* will run this big story, and that's why I'm here."

I checked my watch and realized I should be sitting with Mr. Jennings upstairs. "I've got a meeting with Mr. Jennings now. I'd like to meet up with you afterward to get a statement from you about the new development. After all, you could be the one to sign off on this deal. Maybe the constituents ought to know your position." I put a hand on Mr. Clem's clenched shoulder.

"And I look forward to that meeting, Ms. Reed. Just call my office to schedule. Good day, now." With the tip of his head, he slipped through the revolving door.

I hustled back to the elevator banks and stabbed the button. With a *ping*, the doors opened on the spot. I exhaled, relieved. I didn't want him to think I had stood him up.

"Hold that, please," a strong male voice yelled. A short-sleeved, hairy arm reached in between the doors. "Thank you," he said.

I looked at the man with narrowed eyes. "Mr. Hopkins, by any chance?"

"Yes ma'am. Right here as you see me," he said, chuckling at his own humor.

"Margaret Reed with the *West Prairie Journal*. You must be joining me in Mr. Jennings's office, right?"

"Mmm, I didn't think . . ."

"Perhaps you didn't know you were meeting now with him . . . and with me. I'm so glad you're here."

Mr. Hopkins's head tilted back to watch the lighted numbers above travel from *L* to 4. He motioned me out first, and I sped up to find Mr. Jennings's office. The hall was quiet; I was wondering if it was some government holiday. The stiff closing of an office door echoed through the deep hall. I didn't need to check the names on the doors, as I was sure that was Mr. Jennings standing at the end of the hall.

mercy town

"Sorry for the delay, Mr. Jennings," I said, offering a shake of my hand. An unruly mustache, in contrast with his head of black hair, cut short in a straight line across the back of his neck, hid his upper lip. He appeared neatly dressed in a starched light blue shirt, and his khaki pants were free from wrinkles. "But I ran into one of your associates here."

I gestured to Mr. Hopkins, who was hanging back. "Mr. Hopkins appears to already be meeting with you." I gave Mr. Hopkins a supportive nudge to move closer. Mr. Jennings's brows lifted. "I hope you don't mind," I told him, grinning.

I took the lead and went into Mr. Jennings's office, followed by Mr. Hopkins, then Mr. Jennings.

With the looks of a government-issued space, the office had two standard black-seated chairs in front of a faux-wood desk aligning with a smudgy rectangular window. On the wall, to the right of the desk, framed certificates were hung among group photos of middle-aged white men who looked similar, with shiny bald heads and wearing thick-lensed eyeglasses. A pair of dark gray metal file cabinets were pushed together against a beige wall. A large painting of this very building from its first establishment hung above them.

I sat first, followed by Mr. Jennings behind his desk, then Mr. Hopkins, who sat beside me.

"I'll get right to it," I said, pulling from my tote bag a notebook and pen. "I understand there is a rather large development proposed for Dell Landing in Waunasha. It appears to be the talk of the town. Quite an undertaking, I hear. Can you tell me about it?"

I itched to get to why the county was striking a deal with a developer to raze the undisturbed land claimed by generations of Indigenous people. I was no attorney, but I sensed imminent lawsuits.

Mr. Jennings coughed and wiggled, drawing a forefinger along his neck, held tight inside the confines of his collared shirt. He leaned in and folded his hands on the desk. I sat on the edge of my seat and flipped to a clean new page in my notebook.

"Ms. Reed, the county has owned that land for as far back as it had started keeping records. We have an opportunity to bring dollars and notoriety to Waunasha. Folks outside the state will want to see what we're all about, and in this day and age, it may even trend on that social media as one of the top hidden gems, I think they call it, to experience year-round."

I deferred to the village manager. "Mr. Hopkins, what do your constituents think about this? You *are* up for reelection, aren't you?"

"What are you implying, Ms. Reed? That this is some stunt by me to gain political points?" Suddenly, Mr. Hopkins found his voice. "I can assure you that this deal is the best thing that has ever happened to Waunasha and to the county."

"Yes, and what about that deal? May I please see the terms?"

Both gentlemen shuffled their feet and looked into the distance. It was what they weren't saying that told me there was more to the deal that Waunashans weren't going to like.

The office suddenly felt heated and stuffy. The radiator underneath the window behind Mr. Jennings banged loudly.

"We're still in negotiations. Nothing has been finalized."

"Okay then, what *can* you tell me about it? How much is it worth? Surely you can tell me that, as it will be public knowledge once the signatures are in place. I mean the cost to replace the bridge, new cabins. But then . . ." I paused and looked up, as an idea had just popped into my mind. "There'd be another cost, one not in dollars, now, wouldn't there? There'd be the loss of old-growth forest and the creation of impervious areas where there were none, and by the way, that would have to affect the Loch River, right? And it would mean displacing those who currently occupy those cabins on Dell Landing. There's a whole lot to consider here . . . wouldn't you say?"

mercy town

I offered Mr. Jennings a first shot at telling me. And then I looked at Mr. Hopkins. He appeared to have lost his voice again. I figured he didn't want to say a thing, lest he lose votes. Making voters happy was in his self-interest, but not exactly the right thing to do for them and for Waunasha.

"The county owns that land, Ms. Reed," Mr. Jennings said, leaning back in his chair. He put his hands behind his head and turned up the corners of his mouth as if in a "gotcha" moment.

"No doubt about that, Mr. Jennings. But you've been around here long enough to know that we take care of our own, speaking up for those who feel they don't have a voice. And I'm not only talking about those folks who live in those cabins on the hill, but also about our forests, the spaces that have provided for us when we were in need, the Loch River."

The more I spoke, the deeper I dug myself into a complicated story, one that dealt with village politics and finances, unearthing things that might be done for reasons of greed and not because they were the right things to do.

"I will be talking with ECCOSTAR, and I am sure that they will speak highly of their new project. After all, that's why I'm here, to see just how this development and any previous others have had an impact on Waunashans' way of life, the town's growth, and its economy. By the way, what a lovely welcome sign put up at the entrance to town—the landscaping and woodwork. Would any of you know who was responsible for such fine handiwork?"

I looked at both staid faces. I had hoped my compliments and inquiry into who was responsible for the design and implementation of the welcome spot would disarm the gentlemen in their defensive stance.

"That would be the boys at Willston's Landscape Architects. They're a new bunch, young fellas who started a business recently. Seems like it took off, as they've been busy ever since they opened doing commercial and now some residential work."

nancy chadwick

"Well, I'll be sure to pass along my compliments," I said, stuffing my notebook and pen into my bag. "I'm on a deadline. Mr. Jennings, Mr. Hopkins," I said to each of them, offering a handshake in closing, "I'll be in touch again soon. I can show myself out. Thank you for your time, gentlemen."

It felt like the longest walk ever down the hall to the elevator and out the building's front door. My head spun all the way to the car. Keeping quiet on a deal that was supposed to show promise for Waunasha was sure to have major implications. And I thought I had pinpointed what those implications were. And those two men knew it too. If this deal held so much promise for Waunashans, why were they keeping the details so quiet?

As I had learned from Papa, when you've got a lot on your mind, get in the car and drive. And I did think about what my next move would be all the way back to Waunasha. I hadn't gotten answers, but maybe I had been asking the wrong questions. I needed to ask just the right questions.

By the time I made it back to Waunasha, the sun was showing itself with highlights of the many new signs on clean storefront doors. The pleasing weather was conducive to exploring the east side of town, where Amber had suggested. What had once been undeveloped land, overrun with magnolia and holly and lined with self-made walking paths through wild grass and waist-high weeds, was now home to the Clark County hardware store that had expanded into additional space. And I did not know who now owned Bud's Tractor Supply, but I'd ask Papa about this one as he certainly must know Bud's, given his Payne Garage business. Instead of Waunashans needing to drive the fifteen miles out for a fix, or for building supplies or a new tractor, the retailer had come to them. I made a note to visit Bud's tomorrow.

Back on Main Street, the new storefronts were articulated in wider windows, decorative facades, and fresh paint. The plaza at the end of Main was no exception. Power-washed cobblestone

mercy town

matched the earth's hues, and the granite and marble fountain of Big Wauna, in the name of the founding father who settled there, received a good shine too. The story had it that Bud Wilkins was big-boned with dreams of creating a town that was for and of a settlement of farmers and small business. Word got around, thanks to the Indigenous people who drove a hard bargain with Mr. Wilkins, eventually settling on the area of what was now Dell Landing in exchange for offering needed trade services to early settlers. When the town got together on the Plaza for holidays and special events, they commemorated Mr. Wilkins and his contribution to putting Waunasha on the map. But it was always with the Indigenous people in mind, who were the real first establishers of this town.

I followed an easy curve west onto South Avenue, where the Loch River was at my side. Papa might drive to aid his thinking, but sometimes I had my own way of seeking a clearer mind. The fresh, citrus scents of the pines, softening mud, and damp evergreen worked their way into the car. The familiarity and anticipation of my visit made me smile. In a half mile was the turnoff, by the birches, where the river was near, and mankind was but a distant memory.

I pulled into a gravel clearing and parked; I sat for a time. I thought of the simple connections here in what was turning out to be such a complicated place. When I realized I couldn't solve all the problems at that moment, I shook my head to rid myself of them and slipped on my boots and a jacket.

Then my phone rang.

"Hi there, Margaret. I wanted to get you before the dinner hour."

"Mr. Simpson . . . everything okay?" I hoped my voice was steady, as hearing his had startled me. I got back into the car to sit.

"I'm hoping you can tell me. I'm looking for an update. How's your work coming along? Are you finding enough for a solid story?"

"I've been at the county building, talking with the commissioner and village manager, and will interview business owners in the morning. It's taking a little longer than I expected. They're all busy folks, and it's hard to get even a few words with them." I hoped this sufficed and was a good enough reason that I had little to report.

"I'm getting a little concerned, Margaret. I trusted you were up to the task, but now, I'm not so sure. Is something going on over there? Something that is deterring you?"

"Not in the least, Mr. Simpson." I said each word emphatically. "I'm trying to be as thorough as I can. I won't let you down. It'll be a good story, maybe even my best one yet."

I thought about what I had said. My best story yet. I knew I had all the elements, but there were still a few missing pieces. Right then, I felt nothing was coming together.

Passing softly through the path of decayed leaves and leftovers from last fall, I followed the old trunks of mixed deciduous trees that led me to my sit spot. When I sat, I found it was as strong and solid as it had once been when it had lent me its limb for quiet and connection. Beyond the brush was the river where it rippled in the shape of a V, as if it were parting its ways. Must be the winter's tree debris lodged in the riverbed, creating the effect.

I thought of the elements of earth and sky, of trees and a river coming together in a rhythm that never appeared to be unbalanced. I suppose I came to be a writer not just because of all the time I had spent on this log, pouring my words into a journal, but also because I had learned to be an observer. The river's flow, the birds' conversation, the squirrels' dashing were stories in and of themselves, as the shape and movement of the natural world told me so. I thought of the story I had told Bean. If he got to the river at just the right time, he could see it sparkle like diamonds. Bean got to see the diamonds, all right, and the sun kissing the river

mercy town

was the last thing on earth he ever saw. For an hour or so, the pages got a heavy dose of my thoughts.

Being on my sit spot had disturbed a lot of memories I thought I had settled. The memories of Bean and me growing up and the accident had been reframed into a new context, a modern one, where the meaning of the Loch River had changed, but its ancestry had remained. I didn't know how to reconcile the opposing views. There wasn't much time to figure it out before I needed to return to my assignment and to my car to get the job done.

Before I pulled out from my parking space and headed home, I called Jesse.

"It's good to hear your voice, Jesse," I told him.

"Boy, can I detect something going on with you?"

"I had a meeting with the county commissioner and village manager. I poked them a little about what's going on with the new development I was hearing about on Dell Landing, but they didn't budge."

"Where are you now?"

"In my car. I just came from my sit spot. I guess I was feeling a need for the familiar, for a little comfort, ya know."

"Margaret, I need to tell you—"

"—I'm not sure what's going on or what I've gotten myself into. This seems big, Jesse. It's not just about a new development, but about not so good consequences. At least downtown Waunasha is shining bright, something I can write about."

"You get on home, Margaret. Enjoy your night. Look at the moon after supper, and I'll be looking at it too, thinking of you."

We hung up, and I realized I didn't let him tell me what he needed to. I never did ask him about his day.

thursday

My meeting with the county commissioner and village manager was just the start of poking through the mask of a development hiding behind the truth—the displacement of Indigenous people on Dell Landing. Some would gladly see Mr. Kipp lose his home, and after the accident, I was surely one of them. I wanted to be rid of him, as I knew any sight of him would reignite the pain in my heart. But after being here for a few days, and reacquainting myself with home, I understood the importance of being home, and I was sure Mr. Kipp felt the same way. Home is where you belong, your identity, a place where you can always find refuge. If I couldn't forgive, how could I expect anyone in this town to?

Sunlight woke me earlier each morning like an alarm clock, as I counted on it to brighten more than any gray day ever could. I dressed with a little more gusto, slipping on tan slacks and a white shirt and navy blazer. I figured I had meetings with a couple of suited men, so I should at least suit up a little myself.

In the kitchen, Mom was already frying up a pair of eggs while bread browned in the toaster. I grabbed a slice as soon as it popped from the slot and slabbed on a smear of peanut butter. "Where's Papa?" I mumbled with a stuck mouth.

mercy town

"Your papa left for Farley's about ten minutes ago."

I remembered Farley's fondly, as I loved going to the feed and garden store with him on Saturdays. There was always something I wanted to get: new gardening gloves, a jar of earthworms for Billy. "I didn't know he was still working there."

"He puts in as many hours as he can."

I fretted over Mom's and Papa's well-being and wondered just how long they could keep up the homestead by themselves with no hired hands. But it'd be when hell froze over before Papa hired anyone to manage things. He was his own man, born from Clay, a traveling salesman of finer household goods, and Effie, a telephone operator. Their youngest preferred having his two feet on solid ground and working with his hands. When Papa referenced his occupation as being in agriculture, he thought this gave him an elevated status when he would need to buy feed or farm equipment: only the best quality, and not any budget buy or sale item. Yes, Ellis Payne was all about perception and how others would see him and how he wanted to be treated. He might have been stuck in Waunasha, but he would always rise to the top and be looked up to and not down on.

I slid a sunny side up from the fry pan onto the second slice of toast and ate standing up. This had become a habit of mine in the morning as I reasoned I hadn't much time to sit; I was usually running late for work.

"Okay. I'll catch him there. Is there anything there I can pick up for you?"

"You know, they've moved since you left. They bought the Carlson place and converted the house and barn. Looks real nice. Lots of space to pull in and load up now. And no, I don't need a thing. Thanks just the same."

She sat at the table, already set for me and Papa . . . and Bean. She looked tired and ate as if it were an obligation and not out of hunger. I put my hand over hers. "I've got to run. We've got the weekend coming up, when we can fix a bigger breakfast and linger a little longer over a second cup of coffee. We'll get him to cook a slab of bacon, just as he always used to." She put her cup down and stared out the window. She smiled, as if recalling happier times when we all did just that. She and Papa would dance around the kitchen when preparing Sunday breakfasts. Bean and I would watch them giggling and getting in each other's way.

I cleaned my dishes and dashed upstairs to gather my bag. A fresh coat of lipstick and a slip on of loafers, and I was ready for business.

"Mom, I'll see you later tonight. I've got to run into town." I yelled loud enough for her to hear me, as I didn't know where she was in the house. They seemed to make themselves scarce, especially Papa. He slipped into and out of this house like any good mink traveling the Loch River. He didn't seem to stay put in one spot for very long.

I leaned into the morning and a green carpet was emerging as the grass appeared to be taking a stretch in growth. With windows down, the scent of cut grass pushed into the car. Daffodils and crocuses filled the flower beds with color. The drive into town was slow enough to help me ease into the day.

I reached the plaza and turned east. With the river on my left and a view obstructed by maples, I greeted the landscape in gratitude. Ten years ago, I never had a reason to go here; there were only homesteads sitting on wavy pastures and dirt roads squiggling through them as if connecting dots. Besides, my home was always on the west side of Main Street. Homesteads had since been bought by a new generation of remodelers and builders, of entrepreneurs and small business owners, expanding the village limits of Waunasha.

I pulled up next to Papa's truck in front of Farley's. The sign was as I had remembered, with large, white block letters against a chocolate-brown facade. I waved hello to Jason, who was no

mercy town

longer a teenager, posted as a cashier in the store's front. He was working a few hours for a few dollars to keep his folk band, the Sunrisers, touring local towns. His voice was deep now, and his face sculpted, grown up from a youthful appearance.

"Ya seen Papa?" I asked, walking past him as he checked out a young mom with a grabby toddler on her hip.

"Ret? Is that you? He's in the back, stocking," he said, distracted, pointing to his left.

The aisle was filled with everything anyone would want for birds: seed, suet, houses, and feeders. Papa was talking to someone I didn't recognize, not Jake Farley, the owner, but a younger man, dressed in too-nice denim pants and a clean navy-and-green plaid shirt. And his leather Wolverines were not broken in.

While the clean and tidy man continued to chat about feed orders, I went to look for the small jar of worms for New Billy. The place sure had changed. The once chalky cement floors were now buffed to a shine, to look as if they had been painted. New steel shelving had replaced wood framing. There were signs, too, sticking out from the end of each aisle, that helped you navigate to the correct turn.

"Ret? Ret Payne, is that you?"

I looked to see who had called my name.

"Mr. Shoots?"

"Whaddaya doing in town? Last I heard, you're living in West Prairie and are no longer Miss Payne. Everything okay with the folks?" He gave me a long look. Why did he think there was something wrong with Papa and Mom?

"Yep, we're all good."

I knew he was poking me to find out why I was back home.

I didn't feel I owed him an explanation. Giving Mr. Shoots any information meant feeding his loose lips. And Papa never paid any attention to gossip. When he would come home from the garage, sometimes I'd overhear him telling Mom about some of his regulars. "Every time Shoots comes into the repair shop, he's got a story about someone," he would say, starting right in on complaining to her about our closest neighbor and the only farmer within a couple of miles of us. Old Man Shoots would come into Papa's garage just to talk to him about a fussy piece of some farm equipment. "By the time he was done narrating the symptoms, I knew more than I cared to about Mr. Kipp," he would say. "And then Shoots would get into it about him, filling me in as if I was unfamiliar with the 'world back then.' And then he said that every time Mr. Kipp would hear something cracking the silence in the black of night, he'd grab his shotgun, yank open his front door, stand his ground, and aim down that barrel straight ahead. The door would ricochet off the wall and hit him in the backside so hard it startled him, and his gun went off." Shoots believed Mr. Kipp had a short fuse just like his gun. Once when his gun went off, the pellet went clear through the chicken coup and landed stuck in the wall. "Kipp was lucky he didn't kill all his chickens with one shot, though there were a lot of feathers left floating in the breeze," he would tell her, painting Mr. Kipp as being irresponsible with a gun, shooting willy-nilly first, then later asking questions. I had grown to have quite an impression of Mr. Kipp from that narration.

"Well, I'm sure your folks are happy to see you, as I am, too. You working in West Prairie?"

"Yep. At the *West Prairie Journal* in the city center in Bedford Square." I continued being more occupied with jars of worms than the conversation.

"Oh, you turned into a reporter, did ya? I knew you had the writing way about you, and I'm glad to see you're successful at it."

"I got to run, Mr. Shoots. It was good to see you." I quickly selected a jar and went to find Papa.

I had a feeling I had made a mistake, telling Mr. Shoots more information than I wanted to. Soon, the whole town would have

mercy town

a story about me he had spun—that I came home to stir up some controversial goings-on in Waunasha with my investigative reporting. I'd rather no one knew of any story just yet.

I paid for New Billy's worms and went to the back of the store to find Papa stacking shelves.

"Hi, Papa . . .Who was that man you were talking with?"

"The new owner. Bob Granger."

"New owner? What happened to Mr. Farley?"

"Moved out of Waunasha . . . with pockets full of cash."

"But Farley's been with the Taylor family for four generations. And you've partnered with him to make Payne's Garage what it is today. You've shared customers for decades," I said as if my pleading would change things. "Who are these new people anyway, and why would they want to buy an old feed and garden store?"

"Development."

"You mean it might no longer be here?"

"That's right."

"But aren't you angry?"

"Can't do much about . . . anything."

He stepped heavily away from me to check inventory against a list on a clipboard he was holding. He squinted and used an index finger to slide down a row of lines.

"Here, let me help you. You really need to get those eyes checked, Papa. Looks like you could use a pair of eyeglasses. How do you fix machines in the garage if you can't see well?"

"I got it, and there's no time to take care of that right now. I manage." He reached for the clipboard, but I held onto it.

Mr. Grainger stood by a pair of barn-sized wooden doors at the back wall. At the sound of a couple of loud horn honks, he slid them open, and a gust of wind and dust rolled in and stopped at our feet. He gave a hand signal for the truck driver to back in his truck, spewing exhaust in our faces, to unload sacks of grain.

nancy chadwick

"Papa, I know you're working. We're going to finish this conversation tonight, after supper. Okay?" I handed the clipboard back to him.

I paused before leaving him, waiting for an acknowledgment or some reply. I got neither. On my way out of the store, I waved to Jason at checkout and hustled into my car. Before I backed out, Mr. Shoots waved at me in the parking lot. He rushed to my car door, and I rolled down the window.

"Sorry to bother you, Ret, but I didn't want to say anything to you while your papa was in earshot."

"What? What is it, Mr. Shoots?"

"Well, I want you to know I mean nothing by telling you this, other than my concern for the town and its folks and how we're getting . . . or not really getting along."

"Mr. Shoots, get on with it."

"It seems . . . I think your Papa hasn't been right since the . . . since then, and especially since you left home. People are talking about how angry he is at Mr. Kipp, saying that he should be locked up and forgotten. I think that's the real reason he won't show his face in town or even outside his home, because of how some feel he's such an awful, contemptible, low-living human being. I hope maybe your visit, and you talking with your papa about things, will help him out some. I'd hate to see him lose his temper in the store over something petty."

"Has he lost his temper in the store before?"

"Well, no, but he is angry, you can tell. Just like seeing how the accident has turned some folks to anger and some to sympathy, and I'm sure your papa is not sympathetic to the man who . . ."

"Thank you, Mr. Shoots, for calling that to my attention."

And with those words, I rolled up the window and pulled out of my space, speeding up onto the road while he shouted, "I don't mean nothing mean-spirited," in the billowing dust.

mercy town

I left Farley's with nothing but Papa on my mind and a jar of earthworms in my hand.

That Mr. Shoots was something else, pushing buttons with his mere presence and his words. He should have been the one to make himself scarce in town, rather than Mr. Kipp, because of his air-stirring ways. The more I thought about it, the more worked up I got. I usually took his conversation for what it was worth, usually considering it of no value, but I agreed to the truth of his claim of a divided Waunasha that had never healed after the accident. My anger surged at the thought of him as a good-for-nothing who should be locked up forever. He was responsible for the division of this town and for creating a loss in the Payne family.

I returned to Main Street and slowly drove up and down each new street until new homes replaced storefronts and offices. I checked my rearview mirror for a police car following me, wondering if they thought me suspicious. A gray, low, nondescript building came up on the right. The storefront's large, dirty window obscured a handmade sign, ECCOSTAR REAL ESTATE DEVELOPER. I hit the brakes and swerved to parallel park. *This space was once occupied by Sharp's Sewing and Tailoring,* I thought. Mr. and Mrs. Sharp were quite old, even back in my girlhood days. I'd pass the expansive window that offered deep natural light to see Mrs. Sharp at the sewing machine, and Mr. Sharp fitting a gentleman for a new suit. They were snuggled deep among the shelves of bolts of wool and gabardine, cases of giant spools of threads, and racks of finished garments. It was a space big with memories from a time when providing neighbors with suits and mending was a way of life.

I jumped out of the car and gave the front door a good pull, setting off the subtle notes of chimes overhead. I noted how the tradition of door chimes seemed to have never been lost with the building of the new.

132

Nothing but the minimum to run an office was here: a pair of plastic chairs (at least they matched), a copy machine, and a counter clogged with a coffeepot and boxes of pastries. Folders and binders were strewn on a table behind the desks as if it were a credenza. Bluish-gray lighting from above didn't offer much clarity of who I was looking at, seated behind the desks.

"Hello, gentlemen. Margaret Payne from the *West Prairie Journal*," I said, getting their attention. They stood at the table with their backs to me. "I'm sorry to drop in like this, but I was driving by and noticed the sign. I remember when it was Sharp's Sewing and Tailoring," I said, pausing in reminiscence. "Anyway, would you possibly have some time now to meet? I am looking for information on one of your developments." I shook the hands of these men who stood about the same height and wore pale blue button-down shirts and navy ties. They even parted their dark hair on the same side.

"Oh, sure, please, have a seat," they said, extending their hands in unison. Brothers? Family business?

"John Henry here, and this is Todd."

"Please, Ms. Payne. C'mon back to the conference room."

Conference room? I laughed, thinking the Sharps had used the room where customers changed their clothes for fittings. We sat in the middle of a small square where a circular table stood, with four chairs surrounding it. The air was heavy and claustrophobic.

"Brothers?" I asked, pointing back and forth at them.

"Twins," they announced together. John Henry added, "We bought the family business from our father, James Burgess, and have been expanding ever since, opening this temporary office while a new development gets underway."

"And that's why I'm here. I'm doing a story on the development in Waunasha. I've been talking to new business owners and seeing a lot of changes around town over the past ten years or so. What I didn't know before I came here to do the story, and have since learned, is that there's a new proposed development for Dell Landing. I understand there's to be new cabins, a visitor center, a new park, and recreation, a year-round thing."

"We grew up in Woods Mill and would ride our bikes to Dell Landing. We loved the place, especially seeing those old cabins and talking to the Indians—" As soon as he said, "Woods Mill," I froze. Jesse grew up there. It was a small town. Everyone knew each other. All the kids went to the same lone school.

"Indigenous, you mean," I said..

"Um, yeah," the twins said, looking at each other. Todd said, "We wanted to make it accessible to everyone, so that they could experience what we did when we were younger and learn about our forests and living off the land."

"Jesse Reed. Ring a bell?" I said.

The two looked at each other.

"Payne. I don't remember Jesse having a sister."

Right then I remembered I had introduced myself with my maiden name. Sometimes I did that when I was on assignment. It was a slip-up, unconscious, maybe because when I was home, I felt like a Payne, always had and always would.

"He didn't. Doesn't. I'm his wife. And could you please tell me if he has anything to do with this project?"

I gripped the arms of the chair. Normally, Jesse would never tell me what he was working on, but I would have assumed he'd share if he was involved with the Dell Landing project. I was already mad about something I hoped wasn't true.

"Oh, yeah. With Jesse's experience in corporate, he fit right in with ECCOSTAR after they merged with Star Real Estate. Dell Landing is in his portfolio."

I had to move on with this meeting. Jesse's relationship with Dell Landing meant a whole new private discussion between him and me that I couldn't wait to have. My heartbeat surged, and the heat of the disclosure made me flush.

"Well, I understand your commitment to offering outdoor experiences, but I was wondering about the consequences of this development. The old trees and native growth will be cut down to make room for your proposed project. More importantly, you will displace people who for generations have lived on their land in the cabins and worked in those barns to produce goods to sell for their living and for Waunasha. Where will they go?"

"Ms. Payne, we're in charge of implementing the new development. I can't speak to your concerns as that would come under the jurisdiction of the county," John Henry said. He seemed to be the lead talker and Todd the nodder, in agreement.

"You mean it's not your problem, but theirs?"

No comment from the twins. This time, they didn't look at each other.

It seemed I had two confrontations ahead. One with Jesse and one with the county commissioner and village manager.

"Well, I'll be discussing the county's problem with the commissioner here shortly. But make no mistake, this project is by no means ready to be signed off on. There's still a lot more to be discussed and ironed out. You'll be hearing from me again soon. I promise."

I stood and offered a handshake. The twins popped to their feet.

"It's okay, I'll show myself out. Thank you for your time."

I raced to the front door, and into my car, not only for fresh air to cool the sweating I endured sitting in that airless breadbox, but also for escape from the heated topic. I rifled through my bag, looking for my phone. Adrenaline flushed my cheeks with heat. Restraint was a challenge; I didn't want to lose my cool, though I was screaming to tell them they just couldn't do this.

"Hey there, hon, how's it going? I didn't want to call you as I knew you'd be . . ." Jesse said.

"Hi, Jess . . . Um, Dell Landing. Tell me that's not one of your projects. I was out walking the trail along the creek the other day

mercy town

and saw a few stakes sticking up from the ground, with bright orange-and-pink strips waving in the wind. And then I ran into two suits coming into the diner, said they were from ECCOSTAR, and then I just got out of a meeting with twin brothers. Said Dell Landing was in your portfolio and . . ."

Anger and frustration kept me from getting the words out fast enough. I should have talked earlier to him about this, but the links in the story kept coming, and I had to keep up with the chain.

"Um, well, yes, Dell Landing is one of ECCOSTAR's projects. And I didn't mention it to you because I didn't want it to influence your article. It's all business, Mar—"

"*Business?* That may be so, but Waunasha is hurting. My papa is hurting, and his anger is flowing in and out of the community like Lake Superior on a day of gale force winds. We're divided here."

"I'm sorry, Margaret. But if you'd see how the project will benefit—"

"And what about Mr. Kipp? Where will he go? He and his people have been on that land for generations. That land provides for them. They make a living there."

"Mr. Kipp? Who's he?"

"He's the one *who shot Bean.*"

"Margaret, I didn't know . . . he was the one."

At this point, I knew my arguing would not make a difference, let alone stop everything until the town could come together.

"Maybe you should go talk to him. Clear the air. You two have an unspoken bond, you know. But only if you are ready to face it."

"Jesse, I can't talk to you about this. You're talking about too much change happening, and it's colliding with the rift here that still hasn't settled. You're pushing for Waunasha to move forward when the past hasn't been reconciled. I just can't think about . . . I don't know if I can . . . Goodbye."

I had lost control of the professional Margaret on assignment and of the personal, familiar Ret of Waunasha, so much so that I hung up on my husband. I questioned if I could write this article and do it the justice it deserved. But there was more that was going on there. Soft rain blurred the windshield. I slumped in the seat and breathed in thoughts of something good in the hopes it would purge my feeling of being overwhelmed. I wondered if this was more than I could handle.

When the same feelings would hit me in my preteen years and life was just too much, I'd rush from my bedroom down the stairs and out to the backyard and plop myself on the old swing under the black oak, where I'd find comfort. It would take me to places far and up as I pumped my legs back and forth, my heart lightening and the sun welcoming me. How carefree you could be on a swing, as if you had not a trouble in the world and needed only to enjoy the moment.

Eventually, Mom would corral Bean and me to the picnic table under the black oak, where we ate our bologna and cheese sandwiches and listen to her lessons about trees.

"We come together under this oak to remind ourselves of how connected we all are. Your grandpa Clay planted this tree almost . . ." Mom always paused here to recalculate the years, looking into the sky to do the math in the clouds. ". . . eighty years ago now. And it's still going strong, just like the Paynes have been doing for generations." Bean and I would sit up taller. "We respect this black oak," she'd say, giving its thick, craggy trunk a pat or two, "as it was thought the top branches extended so far into heaven that they reached God, and the roots dove so deep into an underworld that it would never lose its footing. We hold our faith in this old tree as it will always provide." I could tell by Bean's wrinkled brow that he didn't quite get how a tree could provide, but he took Mom's word for it. "You may not understand this now, but when you're older and gone from Waunasha, when you think of home,

mercy town

you'll remember this black oak." I couldn't imagine then living away from there. As long as the black oak provided and the wind chimes sang by the front door, I'd be at home.

I checked my watch and called Mr. Jennings to tell him about my meeting with the twins and that I had a few things to discuss with him. I was so fired up that I advised him I would see him early that afternoon to collect copies of the agendas and minutes from the planning and development meetings. I didn't give him time to reply as I told him I'd see him soon.

And then I took a much-needed lunch break.

A few businesspeople, some dressed in suits, others in dress slacks and button-down shirts, sat as singles at Neena's counter. I slipped in on the end, where it wasn't Amber pouring cups of coffee, but Joan.

"Hello," I said, giving her my best cheery self. Her eyes were locked onto my face. She wasn't wearing a daffodil pin this time, but a large letter *J*.

"Another Cobb and piece of pie for ya?" The pin lady was all monotone, with a face that showed boredom or maybe unhappiness.

"Oh, yes, that'd be great! Thanks . . . Joan." I offered all the kindness I could, hoping it would improve her grumpy spirit.

She moved effortlessly up and down the counter and among tables in the dining room. I thought about kindness and how sometimes a little dose of it could go a long way in showing care and empathy.

Anxious, I made the salad and pie disappear quickly from their plates then paid my bill and left for the county.

I slid into a parking spot in front of the stately county building, and before I elbowed the car door open, Mr. Simpson called.

"Margaret, have you got a minute? I wanted to catch you first thing before you might be headed out anywhere."

nancy chadwick

"Um . . . yes, Mr. Simpson. Is everything all right?" I held the phone closer to my ear.

"Oh, yes, Margaret. Just wanting to check on you and see how it's going. I'm eager to see what you've got."

"Mr. Simpson, I'm going to need more time. This is . . . there's a lot more to this story. I'm about ready to meet with the county folks. People don't move too fast around here, and I'm finding they sure don't want you to know their business." I told him any excuse I could think of to hold him off and to buy me more time. "After today's meeting, I can check in with you and let you know."

"Margaret, we're on a deadline. We're coming to the end of a week—"

"I'm trying, really I am. But this story has legs. That's all I can say for now."

"Just call me at the end of day, Margaret. And don't forget."

There wasn't much else I could do until I got my hands on the agendas and meeting minutes. But I knew I had owed him a call; I owed him an explanation of the complete story.

The black hands on the oversized clock in the lobby told me the county building would close soon, as government offices appeared to keep banker's hours. I hustled to the elevator and jabbed the button a few times, as if that would get its doors to open more quickly. The light above pinged 4, and I slid through a crack in the sluggish doors. At the end of the line of four closed doors, a light was coming from Mr. Jennings's office. I slowed my pace to catch my breath and collect myself.

Mr. Jennings was sitting at his desk and didn't bother to stand when I walked in. "Mr. Jennings. Glad to see you got my message."

"Ms. Payne. I'm afraid your request will have to wait until next week. Jodie, our documents and archives keeper, will need

mercy town

a couple of days. The office is downstairs on the first floor." He resumed reading the newspaper.

"Fine. I'll work directly with her. And is Mr. Hopkins in? I do need to speak with him."

"Just missed him," he said with a sly look, hooking one side of his mouth upward.

"I'll get to him. Thank you, Mr. Jennings."

I shook my head at his nonchalance, frustrated and angry at roadblocks to my investigation. I took my chances, hoping Jodie hadn't left for the day, and zoomed down the stairs to the lobby to find the documents room. The door was open.

"Hi. Are you Jodie?"

She jumped from her seat at a desk in front of a large computer screen, turning to me with wide eyes as if I were an intruder. Wearing a navy jumper over a white-collared blouse, she looked more like a student at a private school than a government employee.

I tapped my fingers on the counter and as if to hurry her response. "Sorry, didn't mean to startle you. I'm Margaret Payne from the *West Prairie Journal*, and I'm doing a story on a recent development in Waunasha. I'll need copies of the agendas and minutes from the county meetings, and if you have them, village meeting reports with Mr. Hopkins."

She pushed her straight black hair behind her ears before meeting me at the counter. I leaned over it, staring at her while she took a step back, whether because she was wary of me or was being shy with a stranger.

"Um . . . are you looking for something specific? Or a particular month?" Her voice made her sound even younger than she looked.

"I'm looking for information about a new project in Waunasha at Dell Landing. I understand the deal isn't quite done yet, so I expect a lot of back and forth there on specifics, agreements, proposals . . . you get the idea."

"Oh, okay then. It'll take me some time to research." Her voice trailed. "Just leave me your name and number, and I can let you know next week."

"Look, Jodie. I'm on a deadline here. I don't mean to be pushy, but it is important that I get my hands on those reports as soon as possible," I used my gentler, kinder voice to match her demeanor. "But I understand." Disappointment was in my tone and on my face.

I moped out of there, down the hall, and to my car, where I sank low. I felt like a hamster on a wheel, gaining speed but getting nowhere. And my time was running out.

Only two days remained in the week, and despite today's push to make up for lost time with having documents in hand, there was a delay in getting them. Since there was nothing more I felt I could do with the day, I drove back home to Waunasha.

Late afternoon clouds released light drizzle when I arrived home, just in time for dinner. I rushed upstairs to change into a pair of old jeans and one of Papa's flannel shirts layered over a shirt of my own before joining Mom in the kitchen.

"Let me help you with that, Mom, I can finish. You go sit with Papa in the front room."

The distraction was welcoming from earlier in the afternoon. Being home, in the kitchen, and helping to prepare a meal was an elixir for my tension.

The supper of chicken in a pot and biscuits had come together well, thanks to Mom's cooking and the fresh vegetables and potatoes. While I puttered with Chip, who danced around the kitchen swishing his tail and waiting for his own dinner, I glanced at those two. When once they were sitting on the couch together, close, they were now in different places, lost in themselves, she knitting and he reading one of his books about Red Cliff. The nights when our home was heavy with conversation had quelled along with Bean's death.

mercy town

We came to the table like any other family, only minus one. I hadn't put out a place setting for Bean.

"Okay, I think we're ready. C'mon, let's sit," I told them as I settled the steamy pot on the table.

A slight grimace on Mom's face told me she noticed the imbalance at the table made without a setting for Bean. Papa caught Mom's expression, and together, they glanced at the open spot, as if remembering when it was filled with Bean's arms resting on the table. She recovered from the moment quickly, starting the supper chat while scooping heaps from the pot onto plates. He held his plate out to take what Mom served.

"And how was your day, dear?" she asked me.

"Good. I saw Mr. Shoots today at Farley's. Actually, he saw me." I looked at Papa. "I didn't know they had a new owner. You never told me that."

"I didn't think it was important," he said, burying his face in the plate. He ate fast, barely getting a word or two out of his mouth before filling it with food.

"It *is* important," I said, setting my fork down. "Seems like the family-owned businesses are being taken over. Just the other morning, I ran into a couple of suited men in the diner who I believed were the developers at Dell Landing. Looks like the changes are underway, with all the markings in the ground there and by the little bridge."

"And how would you know that?" He raised his voice and his head. Mom kept nibbling away on a chicken leg.

"I took the path Bean and I usually walked from the river to the bridge. I think of him a lot, sometimes talking to him. Do you talk to . . .?"

"Don't be going over there, now. That's no longer a place for you. You don't belong there," he said, waving a finger at me. Mom stared blankly ahead at the lazy Susan sitting in the middle of the table.

nancy chadwick

"Oh, but I do belong. Always have since Bean and I were little, and you took us to the river and showed us the path to the bridge. I had a sit spot, and that's where I always wrote. It was where I've always gone for understanding. There's nothing wrong in that."

His heavy brows met in the middle above his narrowed eyes. "He's still over there. You don't want to associate with him." His voice was the clearest it had ever been.

I knew he was talking about Mr. Kipp. I swallowed a mouthful of milk hard to clear my mouth before speaking, choosing my words carefully and remaining calm. "Papa, it was an accident. A horrible one. Moving on is not showing that we are forgetting. Not setting a place at this table for Bean doesn't mean we're forgetting him. We are not to feel guilty because we choose to let the accident go. He'll always be with us, in our memories and in our hearts. It's okay to talk about him, though he is gone from here."

He placed his elbows on the table and brought his hands together as if in prayer, then opened them to cradle his head. His shoulders relaxed. I reached for a hand and one of Mom's too.

"Mr. Kipp is not a bad person. I want to hate him for what he has done. I am angry that he has taken Bean away from us. I've struggled with this since I got here. I've seen how the hate and anger in this town makes us something other than a home I've grown to know. Holding anger all these years sure weakens a soul and closes a loving heart."

I hoped joining them in the middle would create a connection I felt had been missing for a long time. Reaching out to one another had ceased the day after Bean had died, as we all now seemed to flee to various corners for isolation: Papa to the shed, Mom to the kitchen, and I to my sit spot. "And I think deep down in your hearts, you two know it was an accident. The best gift we can give to ourselves and to Bean is to forgive Mr. Kipp. We can't let the hate keep a hold on us. The pain over all these years has crippled both of you." I paused and took a breath. "It took the

mercy town

years being away from here, then coming back, to see how stuck we all are in the tragedy from long ago."

Papa wiped away tears. He slowly got up, put on his jacket hanging by the door, shuffled through the front room, and out the door to sit on the front porch. Mom watched his every move before she sat back in her chair, blotting tears under her eyes with her napkin.

"I didn't know how bad he had gotten," I whispered. "I believed after I left, that the time would heal us all." I felt as if I was carrying the weight of my parents, Mr. Kipp, and all of Waunasha on my shoulders. The chicken pot dinner no longer tasted as delicious as the first bite. I finished eating and let the silence in the room calm the emotions I had stirred. "Mom, why is Papa working more hours?"

"He just wants to, that's all, Ret."

I could always tell when she was lying. She kept her head down and avoided my direct question while fiddling with the front of her blouse, checking to see if all the holes were buttoned and wiping away an imaginary spot.

"No, that's not it, Mom. What's going on? The unopened notices on the counter over there. How bad is it? Please, tell me."

And with that, she broke down, her face becoming red and tears streaming like the river on the first day it was cleared of ice.

She straightened the already flat placemat and pushed away her dinner plate. "I don't want to burden you with the difficulties of our lives when you and Jesse are busy making one of your own."

"Mom, these are not burdens to me. You and Papa are my family, as are Jesse and Bean. You need to tell me so I can help," I pleaded, knowing she needed more urging and assurance that it was okay to talk with her daughter about financial things. All the while Bean and I were growing up, we never thought that we didn't have money because we did. Our lives were always complete, making do with what we had. We never felt as if we needed anything; Papa always provided. And Mom would always have three meals a day, freshly made beds, and clean clothes for her family. Life felt simpler back then, and now, how complicated it had all gotten. Maybe I was understanding things as I had become a grown-up, with adult responsibilities too.

"Developers came by last week, before you got here," she said, turning from me and looking out the window. "They were interested in taking the whole lot, the house and barn and shed. Want to build a subdivision. Said it's a prime location, off Rustic Road, near town, the river, and the woods. This Payne land has been with your father's family for generations on up." Her voice grew stronger. "It has been good to us, providing food and shelter, keeping livestock. At first, of course, we told them no, the Payne homestead wasn't for sale. But then I thought maybe it was time your father and I downsized to something more affordable. We need to look ahead a few years, Ret, as your papa is not getting any younger, and I'm certainly not either." She paused in contemplation. "Your papa has picked up more hours at the store, trying to make ends meet."

"Mom, no decisions have to be made right now. We need to sit with Papa and figure out a plan to get you and him through. In the meantime, I want you to open every piece of mail sitting around here. And grab the register book, too. We'll figure something out. Don't worry, Mom, you and Papa are not selling a thing."

But really, I did worry. What would happen to my parents? Where would they go?

This divided town had not forgiven. Waunashans had been displaced. Financial hardships felt by those who built Waunasha had been pushed to move forward when the past had not yet been settled. I wondered just what I had gotten myself into. But I understood that the assignment I had been given had brought me

mercy town

here for a reason. I, and only I—not Lonnie, not Clarissa—was the one who needed to return here and make things right. It had been wrong for so long.

The hours passed deep into the dark evening, when a chill crept over the landscape like moss to the north side of the maples. Papa came in from the front porch and sat in the tweed chair that, despite heavy use since its first day there, had held its form. I sat on the couch and watched the moths flit around the porch light. Mom's soft steps could be heard moving upstairs in tandem with Chip's thumping tail from his dreaming. The subdued room took me back to when Bean and I were growing up. I remembered conversations when his voice was strong yet gentle, teaching me and Bean a thing or two "never to be found in a book," he said. This got Bean's and my attention, as we considered learning something not in a book to be like knowing something no one else did. "It's about the senses," he'd say. "Listen hard, and you'll recognize the howls of the coyotes. Stretch your eyes far, and you'll spot a deer nibblin' from the blackberry bushes." Then he'd bend over to look us close in the face. "Breathe deep and long to smell the rains coming soon. Hug an oak and give thanks for its protection. Embrace its strength running like an electric current from its roots to its canopy, then out through its limbs." This was when he gestured with his hands, waving them back and forth, and then with a turn of his wrist, he pointed to the sky with his finger. "Study cloud formations and herons' flight patterns, find east by the direction of the sun and what time of day it is by how high it is in the sky. This is home."

I never felt more connected to home, here, than I did those nights sitting next to Bean, close to Papa and Mom. Papa taught us to observe everything. Sometimes you can see things others can't. And that's why I told Bean that if you got to the river at just the right time, when the sun pierced the river, you could see diamonds sparkle.

"You told us some good stories when Bean and I were young," I said, interrupting his concentrated stare out the picture window. I wanted in on an apparent conversation he was having, either with himself or with Mother Nature.

"You two made for a very attentive audience," he said. His voice was gentle.

"Where are you now, Papa? Where are your thoughts taking you?"

He never did answer. I think maybe he was trying to work things out within himself. I think we were all trying to work things out within ourselves.

I shut Bean tight in my thoughts. How we all missed him terribly. I would hope one day we could embrace him not as an absence, but as a ray of light wherever we went as if the whole world was smiling, to remind ourselves of when the sun kissed the river and the glorious sparkle that came of it.

"I'll see you both in the morning. Sleep good now," I said, recalling what Mom used to tell me and Bean when we were little after tucking us in.

My old bedroom looked as if Mom had done some tidying. The clothes once hanging catawampus on the hangers were now sitting straight. Not a shoe was scattered around the bed, but pairs were matched and lined up in the closet.

I thought about how much I once looked forward to Thursday nights with Jesse. They were date nights to Piper Falls, a rustic, down-to-earth hangout with a squeaky wooden door and smudgy, square windows centered above booth tables around three walls. We'd start the evening after work at a café table in a far corner, surrounded by dark wood paneling, with a touch of yellow light from sconces on the wall above our heads. Cornwall Blake, aka "Corny," stood his ground behind the bar. Corny Sr.'s hours had lessened and his years increased, which did not stop him from beginning his pours as soon as the regulars walked

mercy town

through the doors. A slight man with white hair like cotton balls and missing a tooth or two in the front, he knew exactly where each bottle of scotch and tequila and vodka sat behind him and which tap delivered which beer in front of him. This was a good thing as he never relied on his eyes to search for the libations. Then Corny Jr. would seat us at our usual table in the dining room next door to their sister place, Peter Falls; there, it was a relief from the conversational noise and clanging of glassware to sink into the coziness and croon with a band that played folk music. These memories defined our new life as a married couple. We enjoyed ourselves and learned a thing or two about how not to take our lives too seriously and to have fun. But after my conversation earlier in the day with Jesse, I didn't recognize the man I talked to as the one I had had dinners with on Thursday nights at Peter Falls.

My weary body sank into the bed, and just when sleep was about to hand me comfort, the phone rang. I sat up and reached for my phone on the nightstand. It was Jesse.

"Hi."

I paused, wiping my eyes to open them and to bring me to the present.

"Hi."

"I didn't like how our conversation ended earlier in the day. And we've always agreed to never go to bed angry with one another," he said.

"Jesse, I'm not sorry about what I said, but I am sorry about my tone of voice . . . and that I hung up on you. Were you ever going to tell me?"

"Well, I did try, a few times. I didn't push because I didn't want my work to be a problem for you."

"It's kind of a conflict of interest, isn't it?"

"I'm on your side, Margaret, always have and always will be, and I will always do the right thing. You have my word."

"Just tell me that Mr. Kipp won't lose his land and his home. That's all I want to hear."

"Agreements haven't been signed. The markers you saw were the work of the surveyors."

More questions revolved around my head like a roller coaster. "You didn't answer my question."

"I can't. Not right now. It's too early."

"Then we have a problem."

"Margaret, please . . ."

"Jesse, as angry as I am at Mr. Kipp, the reality is it was an accident, a tragic, awful one. Evicting him and the settlement is just not right. I'm standing up for what I know is right, and you said you would do the right thing." My voice tired and so did my will to continue the conversation I believed had no resolution.

"It's late, Margaret, you get some sleep. We'll talk this through tomorrow, and it will all work out. I promise."

I put the phone back down on the nightstand, then let the bed catch the weight of my body. The ceiling fan became a focal point to stare into, as if answers could be found in the surrounding cracks and the mismatched colors of paint. I shut off the light.

friday

New Billy cawed with the dawn as it pushed its way through the window. The aromas of coffee and bacon made their way upstairs to my bedroom. I sprang to my feet and readied myself for the day before hurrying downstairs, with Chip lumbering behind.

"What a beautiful morning it is, Mom. Spring is here, and I can't wait to see more of her." I squeezed her shoulder as she grabbed plates and coffee mugs and settled them on the counter.

"Sure is. How nature's lights can make us hopeful."

I was happy just to see a smile on her face and pink in her cheeks. "Oh, no breakfast for me. I've got to get going."

"Well, before you leave, can you please get your papa? He's out in the barn or the shed or doing whatever," she said, sitting down to eat.

I pulled on my gum boots and swung a jacket around my shoulders, then went out to the barn. On my way, I checked the chicken house, which looked like he had already been there; it was tidy and picked free of eggs.

"Papa? Papa . . . breakfast," I yelled.

I didn't hear a response, so I went back to the kitchen and

looked out the window into the backyard to see if he was there. And sure enough, there he was, trudging through fox sedge and prairie and manna grass—wild land, I called it, as anything and everything seemed to grow there. And that told us how fertile the Payne acreage was, always providing us with land as far as we could see. However, this made the backyard prone to flooding because of its improper drainage. After a good rain, I used to challenge Bean to look out from the front porch and to count the number of footprints settled into the puddling mud from the first step to the driveway. You could count them by seeing each step pooled with water. You could also tell the ones that were Papa's by the large size and deep indent in the mud. Mom had a narrow foot and so did I, so sometimes it was difficult to tell whose foot was whose. Papa usually won as he was the busiest one of all. His many footsteps told us so, going back and forth from the driveway to the front door.

Papa had moved closer to the house, to a worn path that wound around the front. There he was, fitting chunks of flagstone, left over from the tearing down of the old Johnson place, snugly together as if they were pieces of a puzzle. He was constructing a sidewalk that was long and windy, like the curves of our shoes indented in mud.

I tapped on the window and waved. "Breakfast is ready," I yelled as if he could hear me from inside. Mom always told him she wasn't in the habit of holding breakfast for him, but she usually did anyway. For all thirty years of their married life, she always insisted he eat breakfast, as it was sure to start his day with focus and fortitude.

He continued what he had started, checking out a flagstone walkway he put in years ago.

"He checks it often, Ret," she said, attending to fried eggs in a pan at the stove. "Claims the earth is shifting all the time, especially with the freezing, then thawing of it. It's just for his own

mercy town

peace of mind that we remain as stable as we can be." She sighed. I detected a double meaning in her comment—we weren't stable at all.

Papa took emphatic steps, moving his lips as he counted. He was in the distance, stopping every once in a while to hammer a stake into the ground. It reminded me of the markers that were pummeled into the ground on Dell Landing. I couldn't help but think he was indicating the homestead's property lines. I couldn't get into it then as I needed to go to town. I grabbed my laptop, notebook, and files from the desk near the door, then told Mom I'd see her later.

Negotiating the ruts that had embedded in the dirt road, I drove onto the R 32 that led me downtown. I thought back to what I had read last night in the *Nasha News.* Mr. Clem, who was looking pretty good to unseat Mr. Hopkins, had said how much Waunasha needed economic stimuli and that the town required something new, something big, to build upon. The drive to move forward could only happen when and if Waunasha put its unsettled past behind them. It had become a sore that festered; you wanted relief from the pain and mental anguish as you saw how bright and promising it would be when you were relieved of the trauma.

I turned onto Main Street and looked for a parking spot in front of Neena's. Ten years seemed like a long time ago, yet you'd think it was just yesterday I had walked down these streets. Had the businesses here moved on to the next generation? Was it a good thing to pass down a family business, or was it holding Waunasha back from finding better places for itself? Change was a funny thing. Sometimes we loved to see it happening, as we were hopeful about what lay ahead, yet we couldn't let go of what we held so dear. We cherished our past, and we held it in the palms of our hands as if it was a treasure, carrying it home with us and wherever we went.

Before I went inside, I peeked through the slats of the window shades to see if the boys from ECCOSTAR were seated. But all I saw were a couple of bulky men sitting in booths and no one sitting at the counter.

Chimes above the door announced my entrance. I didn't hesitate to slide into my booth, the one I'd been calling my own lately. Amber was behind the counter with her back to me, shifting coffeepots to open burners to make room to drip more coffee. I kept my eyes on her to get her attention. She emptied the last of the coffee into the bulky men's cups, and I gave her a wave.

"Hey there, Ret, how's it goin'? Here the whole week, huh?" She looked crisp and rested.

"Still working it. Hey, by the way, have those suits been in again lately? You know the ones, shirt and ties and shiny shoes and slick briefcases. Not from around here."

"Oh, yeah, once or twice. The last time, Mr. Clem joined them. Quite a trio, laughing and nudging each other. Not sure what was going on there. They had a lot of paper on the table, not much room for their plates, and a lot of coffee refills. Had maps too."

"Have any idea what they were talking about? You *did* eavesdrop, right?"

"Oh, Ret, I'm not as good at that as you are. You're a regular at picking up on so many things. I got a diner to run and people to serve. Sorry 'bout that. But if they're in next time, I'll try my best. Do you know who they are?"

"Yes, I've got an idea."

"Well, then, put your skills to better use and call them up direct."

"Thanks, Amber."

She turned on her white Skechers and glided back to the counter. These men weren't the twins I had previously met but were a different clan.

mercy town

A misty fog made the street damp and slick. I was hoping the delicious spring day would continue, with canary yellow daffodil heads bobbing in large planters along storefronts replacing winter monotones. West Prairie may have had manicured landscaping and abundant foliage, but Waunasha had its own boundless natural beauty in many pockets of town.

Amber delivered my regular breakfast: a bowl of oatmeal with cinnamon and honey and a slice of toast with peanut butter. I dug in as if I hadn't had a meal in days. I took a slurp from the hot bowl and coughed when I was startled by a stout figure standing next to my table with a belly peeking from an overcoat.

"Hey there, Margaret," he said, before sliding into the booth. I recognized his voice before I had a chance to get a good look at him. It was Lonnie.

"Lonnie? What the hell are you doing here?" I sat back in the booth, gaping at him.

He didn't answer right away. His eyes were puffy, and his cheeks lacked their usual rosiness.

"Wait. Don't tell me. It's Mr. Simpson. He told you to check on me, didn't he? Or, wait, that's after maybe Clarissa put the bug in his ear and suggested *she* come."

"Margaret, please don't take this the wrong way. He's worried about you."

"About me?"

"Well, about the feature. You haven't given him anything when he's called, and he's had to call. You haven't exactly kept him in the loop since being here."

"He should know above everyone else that I don't need to be micromanaged. I deliver, Lonnie, every time. You should know that. And Clarissa should know that too."

"Don't be mad. I'm just here as a friend. You're calling the shots all the way. I want to help if I can, but only if you need it."

"This is my piece, Lonnie," I said, raising my voice. I saw Amber glance my way, concerned. She came over with a coffeepot.

"Coffee for the gentleman?" She gave Lonnie the up and down.

"Amber, this is Lonnie Johnson. He's come to . . ."

"To check on his buddy who seems to be a little delinquent in getting the job done?" Amber's eyebrows shot up. Her blue eyes stared as if casting a spell.

"Just a little support, that's all," I said.

"Well, then, I'll let him support you while you finish your breakfast."

I leaned closer to him and lowered my voice. "I don't want even an iota's chance to give Mr. Simpson reason to add your name to the byline. No one is going to muscle in on this one."

He loosened his collar and sat back, taking a breath while looking out on Main Street. I took a breath, too. Our mutual pauses calmed our discussion; I wasn't feeling good about my tone of voice. Though I may have come across as upset that he showed up unannounced to check up on me, it was really that I was feeling the pressure to get my job done.

Gesturing outside to Main Street, he said, "How about you show me around your hometown?" At first, I wondered how he knew I was from here, as I didn't recall ever telling him much of anything personal during the many years we had worked together. And then I remembered Clarissa, who read the article with the photo of Bean and me. I relaxed when I realized my ire wasn't directed at Lonnie; I knew he wouldn't hurt me. It was good to see him. His face was warm and comforting in an impish way, with chubby cheeks, a crooked moustache, and eyeglasses that always needed a shine. His innocence and honesty hung on him like his oversized sport coat.

"Okay, then, let's get going. We're burning daylight, and there's something I need to show you." I packed my things, and as Amber was always on it, she set coffees to-go in front of us.

mercy town

"A real regular here, are ya?" he asked, looking at me with raised eyebrows.

"You could say that."

I didn't tell him where we were headed, as I figured the drive through town to the Plaza and then west along South Hill Road would orient him just enough. We didn't speak during our ride; his head swiveled freely from side to side as he took in the storefronts, both sides of the streets, and the feel of the town. Civilization faded after we turned off Main Street, closing the gap between the woods and the Loch River like a zipper. His eyes were wide and his brows jumped with curiosity when I parked at Fisher Gate, my usual docking station by car.

"Well, we're here," I told him.

He tried to jump out of the car before I even put it in park, but thank goodness, his seat belt got stuck and held him back. I went around to his side of the car. As he stepped out, I looked at his shoes and, of course, he wasn't prepared for a hike through the woods, with nothing on his feet but a pair of loafers. Luckily, I had a spare pair of men's rubber boots in the trunk.

"Here, try these. You'll need 'em," They were Papa's that had never been taken from my hand-me-down car, along with a flannel shirt and pair of Wranglers and socks, should the need arise for clean clothes. I had changed into my boots while he hurriedly prepared his feet for a muddy adventure.

"I'm sorry, Margaret, if you thought I was sent here to check on you. Truth be told, we learned a little something about you that was cause for concern for Mr. Simpson."

His chest heaved. I thought it was because he was out of shape, but maybe it was because of his nerves when disclosing something he didn't think I knew that he knew. I kept on walking, picking up the pace.

"Oh, and what would that be?"

"We know you're known as Ret here, and we know ten years

ago your younger brother Bean died in a tragic shooting near a little bridge. Shot dead by a Mr. Kipp, an Indigenous person living at a place called Dell Landing. You never did mention this to Mr. Simpson when he assigned you the piece, and you know how he doesn't like it when people keep things secret."

"Tell me, Mr. Johnson, how you all came to learn such information."

He slowed. I continued to walk.

"Let me guess: Clarissa," I said, being snarky. "And she just had to tell Mr. Simpson, who, in turn, called you into his office and told you to come out here and track me down to check on how I was getting along. Only he wanted you to be a backup, soaking up from me every bit of information and sources so you could write the feature in case I, well, defaulted? Became distraught with grief? Unable to complete my duties?"

I knew I had hit it all right as Lonnie stopped.

"So, why *are* you here?"

"Well, I thought about asking Mr. Simpson if he'd heard from you. When I tipped my head into his office, he asked me right away, 'Any word from Margaret?' before I could say a word."

"And where was Clarissa? I'm sure she was listening in."

"In the break room, unaware that I was with Mr. Simpson behind closed doors."

"Are you sure? If she was watching you, she'd be waiting for you to open the door so she could fire the five W's—who, what, where, when, why—at him, which had nothing to do with reporting an article and everything to do with the possibility of gossip and things Mr. Simpson wanted kept to himself."

"I'm sure. I told him that I did talk to you but admitted that I was a little concerned that you might be having difficulty with this feature. I told him you asked me to trust you. I was thinking that things were a little more involved than you first thought and that maybe you needed some help."

mercy town

"Oh, Lonnie, really?" I stopped walking. He caught up to me, pushing away errant swinging branches obstructing his path. We held our balance by clutching two basswoods growing between us.

"Mr. Simpson narrowed one eye and stared at me with the other, as if saying, 'Ya know what I mean?' I asked him if he wanted me to drive to Waunasha and check on you."

"I'm fine with working on this article. I've never let him down in all the years I've worked for him."

"Look, I told him I would not make a big deal about it and that I'm not taking over and you're still in charge. . . . And he asked that I not call you to tell you I was on my way to see you."

"Why?"

"Because he thought it would upset you, as you already are just with me being here."

I walked ahead to my sit spot, tramping delicately so as not to discourage the budding bluebells and trillium, to where the old fallen oak log was still holding its own. Lonnie stomped his way to me, weaving in and out through oak saplings and dogwoods, then plopped next to me on the log. His breath was hot, his cheeks red and forehead popping sweat.

"Look, I don't like the position I was put in, but I didn't have a choice. Regardless of the circumstances, you've got an article to write. You're due back in the office next week. Mr. Simpson wants me back on Monday. I know you can make this work."

"Lonnie Johnson, what makes you doubt I haven't made it work?" I scooted over to make some distance between us.

"You haven't given Mr. Simpson anything. He says you cut his call short, the one where *he* had to call *you*."

"Oh, I have something, all right. I've got all I need to complete the feature."

"So, why didn't you tell him?"

"C'mon, let's go. I need to show you more."

nancy chadwick

I grabbed his hand and helped him to his feet. We hit the well-worn trail, the one Bean and I took where I didn't have to worry about him getting lost, as it always led to the little bridge. The wind picked up, shaking the pines that surrounded us. Ominous clouds bloomed against gray skies, dimming what little light we had to follow the trail.

Neither of us said anything for half a mile. I could sense Lonnie was doing some heavy thinking, with his head low and his arms swinging purposefully. For my part, I simply ran out of words to say, at least until we reached that spot.

I kept it to myself that we wouldn't be able to see where the sun kissed the river. The right time had passed, and the sun was still wrapped under cover of traveling clouds. But there would be a time, no doubt, when we would all be able to watch the river sparkle like diamonds once again.

I slowed as we neared the little bridge. The Loch River ambled in a rhythm somewhere between calm and hurried. I homed in on the red-tailed hawks circling in climbs and dives, as if to keep residents of Waunasha company. The scent of sweet pine broke through the earth's warming at the river's banks. Lonnie caught up with me.

"We're stopping here. It's the end of everything." I pointed over the bridge to the Landing, then turned to Lonnie. "What do you see?"

"Well, on the hill on the other side are one . . . two, three . . . four, five . . . six cabins. Just one with a light on. The others look dark and unoccupied."

"What else?"

"Fluorescent orange ribbons flapping from stakes in the ground?"

"Uh-huh. And notice where they're placed?"

"Kind of surrounding the hill."

"They mark the property lines for the new development. A builder wants to knock down those cabins and build big, touristy

mercy town

rentals with fishing and kayaking and tennis, and God knows what else. Indigenous people occupy those cabins. Do you have any idea how far back this land goes—this land that is theirs and no one else's? But Clark County believes it's theirs just because it sidles up to Sugarbush County Forest. Their records don't go as far back as the settlement next door. It's not like they've got their land deeds archived in some sort of modern storage facility smack dab on the reservation; it's more like it's archived in their culture and threaded through the stories they've passed down. When they dig, God only knows what's buried deep in the layers of earth over there. The picture being painted here, Lonnie, is not a rosy one. There's a lot of taking and not much giving back in return."

"Sounds like this piece is turning into an exposé, rather than any kind of model for development of a town that has been shrinking and starving for revitalization."

"That's only half of it," I told him.

"What's the other half?"

"I grew up here, and ten years ago, my then twelve-year-old brother was shot accidentally by Mr. Kipp, who lives in that cabin right over there. The one with the lights on. When I returned here to work on the feature, I could see how divided this town was. Some were so angry they wanted to see him punished, in prison, sent away. Others understood it was a tragic accident and wanted everyone to just get along like we once did. My heart just . . ."

I leaned against the trunk of a hickory, its vertical ridges holding up my slumped body.

"C'mon, let's get out of here and to some place where we can talk more," he said.

He reached out for my hand and held steady while I worked myself upright and called upon my legs for strength. We turned and headed back onto the path along the Loch River in silence, with nothing but the patter of raindrops pinging leaves of oaks and hickories. I watched my steps, wishing for the steady rain to drown my internal cries for my fallen brother.

"No. Lonnie, we've got work to do. You're with me," I said with fire in my belly and a rush through my spirit. "We're going back into town to talk to a few business owners. I want to see if they know about the new development on Dell Landing and how they feel about Indigenous people being displaced."

We made it back to the car before the rain made itself better known. Lonnie fell into the car and slammed the door shut. He looked at me with the strangest expression. His eyes got small, and I thought maybe a little teary. I settled myself, pushing my wet hair away from my face and wiping my wet palms on the tops of my thighs.

"Ya ready? Let's go."

"Wait . . . if you don't mind me saying," he said, "it sounds like the real story here is one you're already working on. It's not about the development of downtown Waunasha, but a town still divided over an accidental shooting. The victim's sister returns and tries to heal those open wounds and unify her hometown . . . and keep the killer of her brother from losing his home."

Rain splattered the windshield, confusing my vision and my mind. I supposed I didn't want to admit what the facts I had gathered meant—that further injustice was being done to Indigenous people who already had such a long history of being treated unfairly. But what was really good for it was healing and moving on. To forgive those who had hurt us so badly. To do it all for Bean.

Lonnie was right. It couldn't have been clearer from when I first saw Amber at the diner. I had lived away for ten years. Every time I'd call Mom, she said how everything was fine, Papa was fine, and it was the same old thing. Well, if everything was fine at home, then nothing had changed elsewhere. While no one

mercy town

would ever forget what had happened, we had moved on in our own time and at our own pace. But now, I knew those wounds had been festering. If gone unworked and unheeded, discomfort only grows. Now that I had returned here and seen Mom's broken heart and heard Papa's angry tone, I realized there were walls within them I wasn't sure could ever be torn down. There were walls around Waunasha, too, and the pending development would force them to come down.

Soon, Lonnie and I were driving along Main Street. I parked midway through town. That way, we could work our way up one side of the street, cross over, down the other, and then go back to the car. We stopped first in the Supervalu. Navigating wayward shopping carts crowding the entrance, we headed straight to the back of the grocery store to the office. With Lonnie at my side, I knocked on the door of Mr. Mason, the owner and manager. Only it wasn't Mr. Mason's name on the door, but Mr. Rhodes's. All I could see through the window was his coal-black head bent over books and registers and the like, with a desk lamp spotlighting his workspace.

"Mr. Rhodes, may I have a word?" I said through the window after gently knocking.

He disappeared for just a moment, then stood in the open doorway. He was a young man, dressed in a white button-down shirt that was neatly tucked into a pair of black slacks. A loose black tie hung from his skinny neck.

"Hi, Mr. Rhodes. I'm Margaret Payne, and this is my colleague, Lonnie Johnson. We're from the *West Prairie Journal*, and we'd like to ask you a few questions about the Supervalu and the new ownership. It won't take long."

Mr. Rhodes checked his watch and pursed his lips. He motioned us inside, where we stood near a desk with the remains of a nibbled breakfast sitting in its grease-stained wrapper. The small office was lit in bright overhead fluorescence and smelled of coffee and hash browns.

"What can I do for you?"

"The *Journal* is doing a feature on new development going on here in downtown Waunasha, and we're just talking with business owners to get their perspective on how they see things happening around here. Can you catch us up on how you came to succeed Mr. Mason?"

Lonnie scrambled to take out his reporter's notebook from a front pocket, an old habit; he really didn't need to because this was my interview.

Turned out Mr. Mason had no one else to pass the store down to, so he sold out to a larger grocery chain. "Interest these days," Mr. Rhodes said, "isn't in small grocers, but in big boxes. Times have changed. Nothing is small and simple anymore, but big and confusing and hard to come by. I'm just here during the transition." Lonnie and I couldn't argue with him there.

"Did you hear about the new development on Dell Landing?"

"Dell Landing? No, why on earth would anyone want to develop that old plot of land and disturb those cabins and the people living in them?"

I filled Mr. Rhodes in as best I could about what was going on. He shook his head and did not respond. I didn't expect him to. But it was what he *did* say that Lonnie and I wrote down word for word. "Isn't that where the shooter lives? And wasn't that shooting somewhere near there? I tell ya, listening to some of these folks' conversations in the aisles and in the checkout, you'd think there was a dividing line."

"How do you mean?" Lonnie piped in. I was just as interested in this answer as I wanted to learn from a business owner's perspective.

"Well, some are still carrying a torch to see the shooter put away forever. Others are sympathetic, wondering if he's been

mercy town

doing all right, as they really see little of him in town. You gotta wonder what would happen to those cabins and that man when the development comes through."

I got this same perspective from Jeri and Jim Long, owners of Long's Hardware. They had been around for as long as I remembered. Long's Hardware was an institution, selling hot dogs every second Saturday of the month, giving away a free bag of birdseed in the spring with the purchase of two flats of pansies, and hosting visits with Santa Claus, which I always did with Bean and my parents before going to Jim Harper's Christmas trees, perched for sale in the south corner of the parking lot. I thought it was more Jeri's idea about clever ways to give away something free, but with a little catch. It was their way of keeping sure that folks would return and to see value in the store and with their customer service.

"Thank you, Mr. Rhodes. And welcome to the neighborhood."

We continued to make our way to Piper's Hair Salon, Mervin's Department Store, and the local pub and restaurant, The Fluffy Raven. Some we spoke with weren't aware of the development proposed on Dell Landing. A handsome fellow sitting in a chair at Major and Marjorie's, getting a shave and a haircut, wondered if there shouldn't be a town meeting about the whole thing. "Don't we have a say any more about what's going on around here?" he complained. He was so agitated about the prospect of any change that Major had to stop clipping his hair, lest there be a slip up with the scissors.

Lonnie and I had completed a circle around town, covering both sides of Main Street, when we returned to our car. The sun's light was tipping the horizon. It was time to end the day. I settled my things in the back seat, and we buckled in. Usually, when we'd come from doing a story, we couldn't stop talking about the facts, reciting them back and forth as if we were lawyers in a courtroom arguing a case. But this time, there was silence, except for the noise in my head replaying conversations with business owners. Lonnie tapped his right knee. It was his way of recounting all that he heard, as if making mental bullet points. I turned on the engine, then wondered what I should do with him. Should I invite him to my house? Out to the Fluffy Raven for a couple of beers? I hadn't planned on entertaining anyone, as my focus had remained on Waunasha.

"I know you need to get on home, Margaret. You need to be with your family. We'll talk tomorrow," he said, as if he read my mind.

"But where are you staying? I can drop you off."

"I'm over at the Carlisle Inn."

"Oh, yes, over on the east side. I heard they expanded, adding a new block of rooms and more parking. Talk about development. You'll have to ask around about their story. See what you can find."

I smirked at giving Lonnie direction. It felt good to take the lead, and he had no problem following. Years ago, a quick ride to the east side found it undefined; now the lots were plotted in blocks with a bookstore, coffee shop, and a pizza parlor with a wood-burning oven. The mini blocks sat like a checkerboard, houses with porches and back yards built as small businesses with outdoor dining.

I pulled into the circular drive to the Carlisle Inn's front door, bending low to see through to the elegant entrance.

"Okay, then. We'll talk tomorrow," he said, stooping to see me through the car's open window.

"Hey, Lonnie. Thanks. You're the best, you know. And I really am glad you're here."

"I'm glad too." His tired face broke into a smile.

Traffic going in the opposite direction cluttered Main Street. Cars turned from Chestnut to the east side of Waunasha, where the evening's entertainment showed itself with bustle and lights. A pocket of young life, like a new shoot from an old tree, had

mercy town

sprouted in this town. I could understand how developers saw an opportunity here as a market for younger folks with disposable income who might be interested in a getaway from West Prairie, for example. But my thoughts remained with Dell Landing, with Mr. Kipp, and his neighbors.

I pulled off from the two-lane onto Rustic Road, where the end of the dirt driveway was home, stopping at the mailbox and flipping its door open to grab the mail. A few envelopes were marked PAST DUE, reminders of the financial burden Mom and Papa were carrying. I pulled ahead to the house and stopped near the barn. The sun had cast it and the house in silhouette. 1060 Woods Mill was a memory of coming home to this whitewashed framed house with Bean after our walks in the early spring. It was home in every way, with our mother's roasted chicken and potatoes, and the oak farmhouse kitchen table Papa had made for his mother, Effie, as soon as Papa Clay trusted him enough with a saw. The setting sun offered just enough light in the background to frame our home, the place where we belonged.

I walked into the kitchen and tossed the mail on the desk, as if there were nothing noteworthy in the stack to call attention to. I figured what lay there didn't need any special announcement. The house was still, with only Chip sauntering to me, giving my ankles a sniff and nuzzling his nose against my hand for attention. "Hello, old boy," I said, "And what kind of day did you have?" How predictable his life was every day. It was something he could always count on.

A lone lamp cast an orange glow in the front room, highlighting Papa sitting comfortably in his chair and reading the newspaper. His face was calm, his hair neatly combed. I plopped next to him on the couch, close enough to smell the earthiness from his eucalyptus Castile soap. I pushed off my shoes and tucked my legs underneath me.

"Hi, Papa. Mom still at the Supervalu?"

"Yes, should be home in an hour or so." He didn't look up from his paper.

"Papa, I'd like to ask . . . I want to say something . . . " I hesitated to disturb him, to break the silence he appeared to be enjoying. But I knew I would find no better time or place. "Do you blame me for Bean's death?"

His eyes shot from reading the local headline to me.

"Papa, we need to talk about this, please," I said, lowering his paper-holding hands to his lap. His posture stiffened.

"Ret, you're here because of an assignment from your boss. Now you must focus on completing it." He resumed reading. I sat back on the couch, staring at him to encourage more conversation, but he was having none of it.

"I'm still working on it. But . . . how you still feel about Bean's death is important too. We never really talked about it. I think you're still so angry. I see it in your face when you're talking to anyone who brings up the subject or mentions Bean's name. Maybe you get a little agitated at the machine shop when Mr. Shoots and his pal . . . what's his name? . . ." He didn't answer though I knew the name of his pal. ". . . starts in with his theories about how Mr. Kipp came to shoot Bean."

Darkness was dropping outside like the final curtain of a play. The world had calmed with neither a cough of wind nor a shadowy moon and I wanted to use the peaceful time to encourage a quiet conversation.

"Papa, I'm finding this town to be really divided. And I think maybe we should be an example of forgiveness." My heart was heavy with the need to be honest with Papa. "You and Mom need to let go of your anger. It's taking much out of you and turning you into the papa I don't recognize. It's time we all let it go."

He put down his paper and jumped up from his seat. "My anger and contempt for the man who killed my son has made me a changed man," he said, stepping into his boots lined up at the

mercy town

front door. "I can't be responsible for how people think in this town." He grabbed his coat.

"But you can, we can. It has to start with us first," I pleaded before he went outside. His outburst startled me, and I shook. His dark figure marched to the shed like a prowler on the hunt. It was the only place where he could escape, losing himself in his tooling work.

The car door slammed. Mom was out front walking to the kitchen side door, balancing two grocery bags in each hand. I went to meet her at the door, but she remained standing at the bottom of the stairs, her arms close to her sides with the weight of groceries pulling her shoulders down. Her mouth moved, but I couldn't understand what she was saying. She dropped the bags, freeing her arms that were now flung up. I remained at a distance at the top of the stairs. Papa stood away from Mom in the light cast from the back porch fixtures. For as much as she appeared angry, he was unaffected by emotion.

"Ruth said her boys would help you with that. You don't have to do this yourself."

Papa stomped around, picking up errant farm tools and setting them inside the shed.

"Did you hear me, Ellis?" She raised her voice. Her annoyance at him doing something that appeared benign puzzled me.

"Those boys aren't worth a darn. If a man wants work done, he needs to do it himself, to make sure it's done the right way." His deep voice rose above Mom's.

"Maybe if you asked them nicely, showed them patience and kindness. It would go a long way, ya know."

"I don't need any help. Not theirs, not yours."

"Why are you being like this, Ellis? You've been punishing me all these years for something that wasn't my fault. It was no one's fault. It was an accident." Her voice cracked to a near breakdown. Her hair, once pulled back into a ponytail, had fallen out of its hold.

I stood silent, holding back from interceding, believing it was their time to work things out between them.

"Then why do we keep living in the past? Tell me, huh?" she pleaded.

He took steps closer to her. "And why does Mr. Shoots stand in my face at the feed store and stir up trouble about Kipp and why I shouldn't be taking it out on the rest of those Natives while I'm at it?"

"Well, you're not the only one here who's suffering, Ellis. What do you think it's like for me at the Supervalu when Mrs. Simon comes in and acts as if her mentioning Bean is unintentional, when she always does it on purpose just to see my reaction? Or when Ret came home and set the table for only three. Don't you think it stabs my heart too? You're being selfish and self-centered and . . ."

I rushed down the stairs when I heard my name, jumping from the landing to the sidewalk in sneakers, hitting the mud with a splat. I stood next to the two of them, looking at Papa's face, red and clenched, and Mom's contorted with crying.

"This is none of your business, Ret," he said, holding out a hand to stop my interference. "You go back inside."

"None of her business?" Mom shouted. "This is all of our business, Ellis. What happened to Bean happened to all of us. Your anger is destroying you and everyone who comes near you. My sadness and loneliness have brought upon a depression like a dense fog that won't lift."

"And stop punishing me for Bean's death," I whispered.

It was as if they stopped breathing then.

Their heads turned to me in unison. New Billy cawed and flapped in the open window in the barn, like he was looking out for us, protecting his human flock. He showed us his wingspan and dove from above, flying past us to the porch railing.

"Yes, that's right. Ever since I got here, I've felt like an outsider, an intruder, instead of your daughter, instead of your son's

mercy town

sister. The emotional distance you have inflicted on me has been my burden, but not as big a burden as you two are still carrying. Aren't you tired of holding tight this weight? The guilt that has eaten you from the inside out?"

I took their hands. We were a threesome surrounding the memory of Bean, who stood among us in the middle. And New Billy hopped madly on the railing as if to say, "Me too."

"You have got to stop punishing yourselves. And punishing me, too. No one did anything wrong," I said.

Then Papa reached for Mom's hand first. A circle formed. She grabbed it as if it were a lifeline. He had tears in his eyes; she stepped closer to him. She touched his face, his tears, and he hugged her as if holding on to life itself.

"It's time, Ellis. Bean wouldn't want it this way," she whispered. "I want Bean to know that his death will no longer tear us apart in grief and anger."

"Carolyn, I hurt . . . The pain. I miss our Bean every minute of the day."

"He will always be with us, Ellis, warming our hearts and comforting our pained souls."

My parents embraced like they had found each other after being lost.

We trudged up the stairs and into the kitchen with the weight of every thought and word and emotion to be contemplated in every heavy step. We took our usual positions in the house: Mom in the kitchen, pulling groceries from the bags and setting them on the counter; Papa by the front window, rocking in his chair; and I went upstairs to the familiar setting of my room. We retreated to places and routines that brought comfort to our still raw emotions. We needed to think about things, confront our fears, and welcome unity in a family that had been led astray and lost for so long. Though now apart, the distance between us no longer measured in emotion, we respected each other's need for space.

Once upstairs, I refocused on wrapping up my job. I was tired, yet relieved that it was all out in the open. We had peeled away the many layers of protection that had grown around us over the years. No more did we have guilt and blame as crutches that kept us from walking strong. I remembered what Lonnie had told me in the car. My story was not about Waunasha expanding but about how divided it had become because of an accident ten years earlier.

I confirmed I was the only one who could write this piece.

And then I typed my first thoughts at my desk:

"On the outside, Waunasha is just another small town that has moved forward with the opening of small businesses, remodeled storefronts, and an expanded downtown. On the inside, my hometown has been divided since I left it after a tragic accident that broke it apart and shattered my family. My brother, Bean, was accidentally shot in Waunasha ten years ago by a man named Mr. Kipp, who lives on the north side of the Loch River on Dell Landing. Like a dais, a small bridge hung over the Loch River where one early morning, I discovered it sparkled like diamonds. I shared my vision with Bean that morning; however, he never made it to the bridge so he could see the light for himself. Instead, it became the site of his death. Mr. Kipp has been living in hiding because of unforgiveness. This story is not about Waunasha's development, but about a town and family that have shown mercy to the man who killed my brother."

I thought of Bean and heard his voice telling me, *"If you want something to come true, you've just got to believe."* I whispered to him, "I do, Bean. I believe. And you'll show us the way, right?"

I moved to my favorite chair between my desk and a window. Prickles of sleet and wind gusts battered the glass. It sounded like I felt.

I thought about this morning and how it started out to be a lovely morning of spring sun and the return of hungry robins.

mercy town

And then Lonnie showed up. I may have appeared to be angry with him, but really, I was pleased he was there. I could show him my story instead of him reading it in the newspaper and then talking about it after. Jesse and I had talked yesterday, although I realized what could happen with a failure to communicate. But sometimes I just needed space to figure things out, separate from being a wife to a man working on a project that would remove a generation of Indigenous people from their homes. Though I still worried about what would happen to Mr. Kipp, I trusted Jesse when he told me he would always do the right thing. Maybe there was a way to help bring my hometown community together. Waunasha wasn't all about its revitalization, but it was also an unforgiving town that could find mercy.

It was late into the night when the sleet turned to rain, and sleep brought dreams of a united town. Waunashans stood together at the plaza, hooting and hollering as we always did when we gathered for any social occasion. I envisioned these once-tired people letting their anger go, dropping it into the Loch River to be carried downstream and away forever.

Keep close to Nature's heart . . . and break clear away, once in a while, and climb a mountain or spend a week in the woods. Wash your spirit clean.

—John Muir

saturday

The refrigerator's churning hum was all that could be heard in the house. Chip, lying next to me, hadn't stirred yet. And even New Billy was hushed, as he was assuredly nestled in his hay bed in the loft in the barn.

I got out of bed and took a shower, letting the hot steam warm me to my bones, then dressed in jeans and a bulky sweater. Standing in front of the full-length mirror that hung from the inside of my bedroom door, I saw a pale face and worn eyes reflected back to me. I gathered my bag, then peeked out the window; I would need rain gear. And then my phone rang. It was Lonnie, asking me to meet him at Neena's.

"I'm meeting Lonnie at Neena's," I said, greeting Mom in the kitchen. She moved effortlessly, as if she didn't have a care in the world. Her eyes were clear and rested. "I'll be back later." She was the mother I had missed seeing. Whenever Bean or I would enter a room, Mom would always stop what she was doing to acknowledge us with a smile, as if she was glad to see us. Or perhaps that look in her eyes now indicated a moment of clarity. She had let go all that she had held inside, no longer pushing the emotion down.

mercy town

She shared her feelings with Papa and showed him that it was okay for him to share his, too.

"By the way, you look great this morning, Mom." The sides of her mouth curled upward. I thought she'd consider the evening such an emotional, difficult one that she'd give me a frown instead.

"I'm now seeing what's right about a few things that I once saw as so wrong. I remember last week at the Supervalu, when I couldn't see life as having anything right with it. I was working late to close the store. I didn't mind being the last one to check each department and make sure managers did their own shutdowns. It was the last few dawdlers that stole my patience, like Mrs. Simons, who could never decide between French vanilla ice cream or orange sherbet. She was an ice cream regular, and her husband, Judd, was a sherbet man. I always suggested she just get both to satisfy each other's needs. I wasn't much interested in solving marital discrepancies but was more motivated to get everyone out so I could close and get home. Finally, Mrs. Simons checked out, and sure enough, Ginny was right behind her, Mr. Shoots's wife. She asked me how it was to have you home. 'Must feel kind of strange, having one without the other. I mean, just that Bean and Ret were inseparable, going on their walks in the spring and . . . ,' she said. I ignored her talk, knowing it would only lead to more fodder for Ginny and an unsettled mind for me, but she went on: 'I think it was around this time, wasn't it? We'll remember Bean as a strong, smart young man, though taken from us too soon. That shooter should have been jailed and forgotten and here he is, still living.' Well, I took her $12.52 and slid it into the cash register and closed it with a swing of my hip, then handed Ginny her grocery bag without saying a word."

Mom dropped her head and twisted the dish towel tightly around her hand.

She continued, "I could be reminded not only of Bean's death, but of the voice of public opinion in the town. I had carried this burden like a ball and chain. It was difficult for me to ever rid myself of the weight when people like Mrs. Simons and Ginny kept reminding me. After the two checked out, I walked all the aisles to make sure no one was in the store. I left an errant Snickers wrapper on the floor, along with a split-open sack of white sugar, since I knew I was opening the store in the morning and could clean up the mess then. With the front doors locked, blinds drawn, and the cash register emptied, I grabbed my coat and dashed out the back door after turning the locks behind me."

"Mom, I'm so sorry you had to deal with all this at the store." Her voice quieted. I stepped closer to her.

"I tried to drown out the repeated conversation from my head with the turning of the radio dial in the car on the way home, but no music or talk radio calmed my troubles. When I pulled onto Rustic Road toward the house, I saw a dark figure walking back and forth. The distant figure was unfamiliar, walking a little bent, a little thin, clothes a little baggy. Then I remembered how he once walked tall and assured, with lean limbs gliding in a confident stride and big hands tinkering with farm equipment. It was your father. I had a good cry, feeling broken and seeing your papa so changed."

Mom's hands on my shoulders were reassuring that everything was going to be okay. "And all three of us had our moments, didn't we?" she said.

It wasn't a bad thing that happened among us last night, but a good thing that we owned our emotions and showed one another our vulnerabilities.

"We've taken a step toward healing, Mom. Now, I've got to get going." We hugged tightly.

I let the screen door slam—a habit that must have started when Bean and I were young. Every time we let the door bang, the sound alerted Mom that the Payne kids were on the move.

mercy town

Dark clouds hung heavy in the sky, pressing down like a looming shadow. Papa, dressed in a rain poncho with his head tucked under a hood, was out in the field with Bolt, our oldest black gelding. I could see in the distance the horse's ebony body soaked from the downpour, looking like an ink spot on a canvas. There was no other place that Papa and Bolt wanted to be than treading grass together. Watching them, I couldn't help but think the scene was one of contradiction for Papa. When he would take Bolt for a walkabout, that meant he wanted to be alone to think things through, from how to fix Mr. Max's seeder to how he could earn extra money. Yet, I think this time he didn't want to be alone. I swore I could see his lips moving. I think he was talking things through with Bolt as he rubbed him between the eyes down to his nose, then stroked his face, his own emotions seeming to relax in the act. He hugged Bolt around the neck. It had been a long time since I'd seen Papa like this with him. Maybe after last night, he was finding the man he used to be and the connections he used to have.

I hustled into the car.

The rain was letting up when I tossed my bag on the passenger seat and pulled out for downtown. The drive was quiet after the noise of the windy storm. Neither an animal nor another human being could be seen during my drive there.

By the time I entered Main Street, the squall had moved on to let in strips of light. Regulars were filing into Neena's, and I chuckled at how I felt like one of them.

I had just slid into my usual booth when the door jingled, announcing Lonnie's entrance.

"Come here often?" he said breathily and winked, squeezing into the booth.

"Did you run over from Carlisle Inn, or what? And why exactly did you need to see me? Wait. You got a call from Mr. Simpson, didn't you? He's looking for an update."

"Um, no. I didn't." Lonnie bounced the back of his spoon against the shiny tabletop.

"So, why did you get here earlier than you needed to be?"

"Well, I got to thinking . . ." Lonnie stared out at Main Street, where the pavement was losing its wet shine to dryness. He looked like any other Waunasha father and Little League coach, wearing roomy jeans, a sweatshirt, and a Green Bay Packers baseball cap. I had never seen him dressed like this before, looking younger and so unlike a newspaper guy.

"Well, hello there, again, you two," said Amber. Her dimples deepened with her toothy smile. "Working on a hot story?" She giggled, and I ignored her words. I wasn't in the mood for light-heartedness, but for more serious business.

"Hi, Amber. Um, a pair of black coffees, and Neena's Saturday's special, please," I told her.

"Same here," he said, giving Amber one of his sweet grins.

"I'm on it," she said, scooping up the menus, giving him a wink.

I leaned in after the two appeared to have a moment, then set my elbows wide on the table and cocked my head. "And what exactly is all your thinking about?"

"This is it, Margaret, your chance to make things right. And I know you can do it."

"What are you talking about?"

"The shooter."

"You mean Mr. Kipp."

"Yes." Amber slid a pair of full coffee cups along the table. Lonnie dumped a couple of packets of sugar into his cup and stirred hurriedly. I sipped my black coffee slowly.

"And what about him?"

"Look, I've always been one for confronting the elephant in the room, only this time, it's a bull in a ring surrounded by an agitated audience. After I read the clips about the aftermath of the accident, I realized human nature dictates that such things

mercy town

are not easily forgettable. I don't pretend to know what's going on with the Paynes, but I've had an ear to the buzz and an eye to the locals, and what I've seen is a whole lot of tension. I've heard chatter about the new development on Dell Landing, and that that's where Mr. Kipp lives. Some welcome his displacement. Others want to leave him alone as he hasn't bothered anyone all these years and he is where he belongs—on the other side of the river."

It wasn't unusual for Lonnie to say what I was already thinking. There would eventually be a time to confront Mr. Kipp. Questions about that night revolved like a Ferris wheel, perhaps some never to be answered. But I believed he had some answers.

"You need to sit with old Mr. Kipp. Talk to him." I remembered Jesse urging me to do this too. "We need to hear from him, Margaret. For too long, Waunasha residents have been talking among themselves. Put a voice behind that face, and let's hear directly from him . . . so he can be forgiven."

I told Lonnie that he was right. But for now, I had to wait for the documents. They would be the backup I needed about Waunasha's landownership and about the deal made by the developer and the county. Proof was needed about any claims that the developers had made before I could talk to him.

"So, how long are you going to stay around and babysit me? Will Mr. Simpson be satisfied with your update on me? Because he is expecting an update from *you*; *I* don't have to give him one. I want to make sure you'll make him feel that I'm still competent to deliver the feature."

"Now, you don't have to get all sassy on me, Margaret. He was worried . . . I was worried. We didn't know how, or if, being back in your hometown would have an effect on how you'd do the assignment. I'm sticking around until Monday, just in case you might need me." He paused, slurped coffee, and wiped a spill from the table. "He was expecting you to only be here a week, ya know."

I could always use Lonnie's help. We were a team, and although I might get defensive about my work—okay, maybe a little territorial, too—in the end, he was a shrewd journalist with sharp instincts and a way to get to the heart of any story.

I asked Amber for a coffee to go, and jotted an affirmation in my notebook, *I must meet Mr. Kipp*, while we waited. The sun shone on all the right spots of Main Street, the spring flowers, front doors, and window shoppers as all came alive just in time for the opening of businesses. I remembered when no one was in a hurry, when meandering was a way of life and conversation with strangers was part of the rhythm of one's day.

Suddenly, a loud pop rattled the window and me. It gave me such a good jostle that I spilled coffee. A pickup coughed, accelerating just enough to catch an empty parking spot. The noise like a firecracker brought me back to the reverberating gunshot that had sliced through chilled air, the one that once broke our hearts and silenced this town.

Yes. It was time I visited Mr. Kipp.

Lonnie urged me to get back home and spend the remaining day with my parents. "They need you," he said. "I'm going to spend the day as a tourist. This town is kinda growing on me."

I was glad to see him more relaxed and enjoying his time away from the office. He deserved it, though his visit was really all business.

Lonnie and I went our separate ways, for the rest of the day, anyway, as I was sure it wasn't the last time I'd be seeing him before he went back to West Prairie.

sunday

When I went out the door first thing in the morning, it was warmer than I had expected. Perhaps later in the day, I could shed this sweater and push up my long sleeves. I stopped in the shed to scoop up corn and oats to refill New Billy's tray, then waited for him, searching above. In my eagerness, I called for him with a two-fingered whistle. He wasn't far, as he appeared from the small window in the loft above. Apparently, he was sleeping in, the warming sun keeping him in a comfy slumber. He had been spending time in the barn lately, and I could only hope he wasn't badgering Ace and Geneva, the barn cats most adept at keeping the place mouse free in exchange for nuzzles and back strokes.

With hops and flapping wings, New Billy followed me to the porch railing, where he settled in for breakfast; I settled on the old wicker chair with a foot up on the railing. Delicate breezes whispered cotton clouds along. I thought of Bean, as I usually did when I wasn't occupied with other important matters. I played our route to the walking path along the river in my mind and remembered again, too well, as if my heart had been struck by lightning when Bean never answered my calls. I thought him to be lost but then disagreed with that conclusion, as I knew he could walk that path in the blackest of night.

"I thought you'd be inside, working on your article. What brings you out here?" Mom said. She sat in my chair's mate and had a good look at me. I continued to stare into the distance at the apple tree grove in the far west corner, hesitant to bring up what had popped into my mind.

"You used to tell me to never come back without my brother. And I came back without Bean."

She sharply sucked in air.

"Maybe I'm blaming myself. Maybe if I was with him all the way, I could have protected him. We always walked together, until that day . . . when he started walking ahead of me."

"No use in thinking through all the maybes, Ret. It wasn't your fault, or my fault, or your papa's. It was an accident."

"I considered him not to be a little boy anymore. He was growing up, and his fearless ways of knowing the world kept him taking one step after another. He followed the trail, chasing the sun as it led him to where it kissed the river. Oh, the joy in his face! Every step he took was deliberate in pleasure. He knew he was going to see something no one else would ever notice. Bean would want us to enjoy life as much as he did." I put my feet flat on the porch floor and faced her. "He showed us what it meant to hold wonders of Mother Nature, to be happy, and to find joy in our lives. We will never forget him. He'll always be with us."

And with those words, New Billy hopped and waddled as if dancing, fluttering his wings in delight of himself. Mom and I laughed as he appeared determined to find peace and mirth among us once again.

She unwrapped her arms from around her folded knees. In the deep distance, Papa trod the earth, making squares and angles. I grabbed her hand and held it tight.

mercy town

"It's time to heal now, Mom, to let it all go and let Bean live on in our dreams."

Well, she looked as if she did let it all go, right then and there, as if the plug had just been pulled from a horse's water trough. Her shoulders fell, and her head dropped heavily to her knees. She became small and deflated. "Bean taught me how to live, and to love life," I whispered. "And we need to accept that gift from him."

We sat for a while, staring at the black oak, and the pair of swings, and New Billy, then letting our eyes wander into the forest beyond.

I thought of Jesse. It was Sunday. He'd be home, puttering around the house while watching the Masters golf tournament on television. I hurried upstairs to my bedroom to call him, making myself comfortable in my chair by the window.

We first exchanged pleasantries about the weather and what our plans were for the rest of the day.

"Yes, I'm fine. It's been an emotional time here. Um . . . by the way, I want to ask you . . ." My stomach tightened, and my heart picked up speed. "Did you realize that it's not only Mr. Kipp living on Dell Landing, but living in all those cabins are Indigenous people?"

He didn't answer.

"Jesse, what did you think would happen to them? Those people on Dell Landing who would be displaced. Where did you think they would go, and how would they make their living?"

"Um, I thought they would be given plenty of time and personal attention from the county in finding housing, and as has usually been the case, there really hasn't been . . ."

"Well, this is not a usual case." I tried to keep my voice calm. "That's their land. And it has been theirs for generations, and the county has always left them alone."

"I'm . . . I'm sorry this has become a problem for you and for us. I never thought my job would interfere with yours."

"Squatters' rights. Do you know that Mr. Kipp and his neighbors have them? They also qualify for an adverse possession claim. Unless a deal is made that allows the Indigenous people to stay where they belong, on the only land they have known as home, they will make this claim." I took a deep breath and let it out. "And I will see to it that it is made."

"You do what you have to, Margaret. I'm not about to stop you. But the deal is pretty close to being done."

I sat up taller and placed my feet flat on the floor. "I am also a reporter for a major metro newspaper who has the power of the written word and media attention to fight against the development, unless these people are given acceptable alternative housing."

He sighed. "It's getting late, Margaret. Let's leave it here, for now. We'll talk more about this, but not over the phone. I love you, Margaret Reed."

"People round here call me Ret."

I didn't know why I told him that, as I was sure he couldn't understand. I had been Margaret Reed from West Prairie when I first got here, until recently, when I had started introducing myself as Ret Payne of Waunasha. But it didn't really matter, did it? "I love you too, Jesse Reed," I said before we disconnected. I thought about how Jesse and I had never been apart this long. We rarely talked on the phone unless it was a timely thing, like he was telling me he needed to work late, or I was stopping by O'Henry's, the new fancy grocery store, to pick up a special something for dinner. Otherwise, things could wait until we saw each other at home.

I lingered in the chair for a while, staring out into the emerging color of a spring afternoon. I stayed in my room with Chip as my companion until it was time for supper.

monday

My phone rang at 8:00 a.m. sharp. It was Jodie from the records department at the county building. She said she had my copies ready for pickup. I flew down the stairs through the kitchen, telling Mom I had to get to the county building. She didn't look up but gave me a wave.

Warmer temperatures were forecasted for later in the day as the sun marched higher in the sky. I was already warm with anticipation, hopeful of collecting from Jodie the crumbs that would lead me to complete the article.

While driving to the county building, I thought back in the days before Waunasha became incorporated, most millers worked where the masonry building now stood and the townspeople were employed by the county and lived in gated communities of one-story homes made of wood siding. You didn't go into Haven Mill unless you had to, unless business was calling. And, in my case, I was calling on Jodie and Mr. Jennings.

I made it to the records office, a closet-like room, in good time. In only two steps, I was at the counter. The lighting was eerily incandescent, as if science experiments were taking place there.

nancy chadwick

"Hi, Jodie. Margaret Reed. Here to pick up what you've got for me."

Jodie jumped at the disturbance while appearing mesmerized, sitting in front of a very large computer screen behind the counter. She shook her head to clear her eyes of her long bangs.

"Oh, yes. Right here. I've got it." In all her efficiency, she swept up the top folder from a short stack of others next to her and walked to the counter.

"Thank you, Jodie. I appreciate your working to put this together for me."

She handed over the bulging folder with a curt smile and a nod, then retreated to her workstation.

I left the room and stood outside, searching for a place to sit. Finding an open bench near a coffee kiosk, I sat, itching to see what was inside. I reached in and pulled out the stack of papers, then got busy reading. But it didn't take long for me to skim through the documents, as there weren't enough of them. I expected to find a paper trail of minutes of meetings, maybe contract terms, dealings between the county and the developer, stacked pages of stapled packets of paper. I had expected to find what Mr. Jennings and Mr. Hopkins wouldn't tell me. But there wasn't much recorded about the deal or, even more importantly, what would happen to Mr. Kipp and his neighbors on Dell Landing. This project was a big deal for the county and for Waunasha, and it should have warranted a lot of paperwork, covering an even longer period.

I stuffed the wad into the folder and marched to the elevator, then stabbed the number 4 button, and waited for the door to open to Mr. Jennings's floor. I raced down the hall, a woman on a mission, and entered his office without knocking. There he sat behind his desk; or reclining was more like it. He was shuffling papers, not acknowledging the intrusion.

187

mercy town

"Well, Mr. Jennings, I certainly can say there are a whole lot of changes going on in this county, and Waunasha is no exception," I bellowed.

He looked as if my interruption was of no disturbance to him. "Well, Ms. Reed. Nice to see you again, too." He smiled curtly, stood, and extended his hand. "Do have a seat, please."

I started in, shaking the folder in the air and my head along with it.

"Well, then, what can I do for you?" he said, sitting with folded hands in front of him.

I spoke louder than I intended to. "I won't be staying long. I received copies of what was available, which wasn't much, on the new development at Dell Landing. I expected more here.

"I'm referring to what you have signed off on, to rezone property that was granted free and clear to the Indigenous people living on Dell Landing. You do realize their settlement goes back generations, before the county even decided to draw its map. We should be indebted to them for much of the establishment of Waunasha, instead of forcing them off their land with no place to go. And it *is* their land, always has been. What did they say when you notified them? You *did* talk to them about this, right? And what it would mean for them? I didn't see any notes about it in here." I waved the folder at him as if asking him to produce the evidence.

"Miss Reed, those folks on Dell Landing have essentially been squatters, living unlawfully as residents. Times are changing. The county has a financial opportunity to develop that land and to bring Waunasha into modern times. Our research tells us that old Waunasha is not serving its taxpayers as it should. Developers came to us with an offer we just couldn't refuse."

"Research? What research? That appears to have been missing from the file." I shook my head. "Never mind. I'm not here to debate whether Waunasha could use the economic benefit of development. I am here to see to it that the people living on Dell Landing stay on Dell Landing." I moved closer to him, not giving him a moment to reply. "Dell Landing has been the home for generations of Indigenous people. They have built their way of life there, giving back what has been given to them. Their respect for their provider, the natural world, will never waver."

I waited for a response, but I was sure none would follow. And it didn't. Mr. Jennings stayed silent. Mr. Kipp and his neighbors would be displaced with no county help to find a new place to live or a means to make a living.

I tucked strands of hair that had fallen in my face behind my ears and continued to wait. The longer I held out without talking, the more Mr. Jennings's face reddened. He shifted in his seat, eliciting piercing squeaks from the chair.

"So, the county considers them squatters?" I asked.

"Well, yes. They may be settlers with no legal title to the land they occupy—"

"Adverse possession, Mr. Jennings. Are you familiar with the term?"

I had him now. My voice became defiant. His eyebrows lifted. Fear and curiosity held them in place.

"If not, let me remind you. Adverse possession allows a squatter to file a legal claim on a property they have occupied for a certain period. And that time here has been generations. If the claim succeeds, the squatter can become the actual property owner. Now, it could so happen that they may soon become aware of these rights, in which case they would be there to stay, and your builders would have a difficult time building on an occupied site." I let my words sink in for Mr. Jennings. "Litigation could be avoided here if the county meets their needs. You have no right to displace them. It *is* their land."

He pushed his chair back, creating some distance, then licked his lips to combat a dry mouth. A beam of bright sun pushed

mercy town

through the dirty window behind him, silhouetting his frame. I couldn't see his face, but I could hear his words. I remembered when I last stood near the little bridge and heard Mr. Kipp's voice but couldn't see his face.

"Well, Miss Reed, the deal is—"

"Done, you say? I checked. No signatures have been executed, or at least none of these copies prove it." I fanned a pack of paper I held in front of his face. "You're an influential player in this deal. Right? You and Mr. Hopkins? And as I understand, Mr. Hopkins, Waunasha's longest-running mayor, is up for reelection, and wouldn't this deal for a money-making Waunasha put a feather in his cap? You've been around a long time and have called many shots over the years. Surely you can talk with them about making an amendment. Just call it an incentive package."

He rubbed his unshaven face. "I can't promise you anything . . ."

"Oh, but you must, as I *can* promise *you* that you will see a claim filed faster than you'd arrive home tonight for dinner." I took a deep breath. "How about I check back with you at the end of today? That should give you plenty of time to work it out and do what you need to do with whomever."

I shoved the papers back into the folder and then into my bag. I straightened my jacket, standing tall and assured.

"Good day, Mr. Jennings."

Standing up for the people on Dell Landing marked a turning point in forgiveness. Choosing kindness was an act to be carried out in the name of mercy, an act of grace, of doing the right thing.

I turned and left his office. I believed I had some leverage to call attention to the ramifications of the development. Yet I couldn't help but consider how some in Waunasha wouldn't mind displacing an offender who had killed an innocent child. It didn't matter to them if it was an accident. As far as they were concerned, it was high time Mr. Kipp was run out of town. But I felt differently. I believed Waunasha could have it both ways, by keeping him where he belonged and moving forward with the development. Only one thing was left: I knew I should be the one to talk to Mr. Kipp about what was happening. No doubt he understood something was going on at Dell Landing, as the placement of stakes outside his front door and the congregation of men wearing hard hats told him so.

Driving home, I thought about how I would talk to Mr. Kipp. This wound has been open too long. Meeting with him, face to face, would be the right time to begin the healing and close the wound shared by the Paynes, Mr. Kipp, and the town of Waunasha.

When I got home, I started right in helping Mom with lunch while Dad was out in the yard, trying to repair the lawn mower. He could easily fix any piece of outdoor equipment that had a motor, but a lawn mower seemed to take more of his time than one would think. As I went out the door to yell to Papa that lunch was ready, I noticed the table was set for three this time, with Bean's placemat covering the seat of his chair pulled close under the table. Mom placed the tureen of beer cheese soup where Bean's plate would ordinarily go. I acknowledged her attempt at slowly introducing the present with a shared bowl of food on the table while still marking the empty setting. She was trying. After pulling off his chore boots and placing them on the boot mat, Dad sat quickly and dug right in, ladling generous amounts of soup into a bowl. He grabbed a hard roll and tore it apart, slathering butter on it before popping it into his mouth, but not before saving a scrap for Chip. Papa paid no attention to me or to Mom but remained occupied with sating his appetite. Mom watched her husband with a grin, and I watched him in relief as he ate with abandon; it was as if he hadn't eaten in days. I supposed there was some truth to that saying about a man's heart and his stomach. His look of satisfaction and contentment appeared to go beyond a full stomach and all the way into his heart.

mercy town

"I've got some news for you two," she said.

"Do tell us, Mom. What's up?" I said.

"Well, you know how I've been needing a change, away from the Supervalu—"

"Away from nosy, no-good Ginny Shoots, you mean," he chuckled, giving her a hard look.

"Go on, Mom."

"I applied for a teaching job at the elementary school in Crystal Springs, and, well, I got it!"

"Oh, Mom, that's great news!"

"Before I met your papa, I thought I'd be a schoolteacher, educating Wisconsin's young people to be the best and brightest. I was Miss Carter back then, and teaching young ones how to read and write was all I ever wanted to do. And then I met your papa. We bought this place and started a family, and for a while, *that* was all I wanted to do. And now with Bean gone, and you married and off on your own, it's time to find my place again."

"I'm so glad for you! You deserve it. Papa, what do you think about that? There's now a schoolteacher among us." I made the declaration with pride. It was a blessing to see her looking out for herself and finding happiness and joy again.

"Did you negotiate the salary, Carolyne? Ya know to never take what's first offered but to let them know you are worth more than what they're offering."

"Not everything is about money, Papa. She's just starting out. Plenty of time for raises."

Or maybe it *was* about the money.

We finished lunch quickly, a sure sign that Mom and Papa's routine was finding its rhythm again. "Burning daylight," was his cue to keep the hours moving along.

Mom and I stood side by side at the kitchen sink, cleaning plates, and I asked her if it really was about the money and if Dad was pressuring her to get a better-paying job.

"Not in the least, Ret."

She answered me while looking into the sink. I knew she was not telling me the truth. It wasn't the time or place to talk to her about the Payne finances, as I had to continue with my day. I let it go for now.

We finished cleaning up. Papa was sitting out on the front porch in his rocking chair, setting a back-and-forth rhythm that seemed to pacify him. Seemed these time-outs had become part of his schedule, as his endurance during a long day beckoned for a break to rest. He stared at the heavens and the sun, and the tree-tops. I wished he was seeing in them hope in the future for him, Mom, and the farm, but I decided not to join him as his thoughts were his own as he succumbed to the hazy afternoon sky. I could only think that I'd be back at the paper by now, and that my work in Waunasha would be completed with ease. I considered my assignment clear-cut, but it had proven to be a rough one.

Mom was getting ready to leave for her afternoon shift at the Supervalu, and I sensed her dread about having to go there and deal with the customers. A few days of work remained, and I admired her for sticking it out as long as she had, given the whispers between neighbors in the aisles and outright statement of opinions in the checkout. She couldn't escape the remembrances of that day and the loss of Bean. You could tell a lot about someone by how they run at the mouth, she often said. I respected her thick skin and her ability to take insults just so she could pay bills and contribute to the Payne household. "It's the big picture you need to keep your eye on," she once told me.

"I know it hasn't been easy, Mom," I said, "working at the Supervalu and taking all that flak from the customers. I'm sorry our friends disappointed you and fell short of supporting you after Bean's death. But you've got a new job now, one where I

mercy town

know you'll shine. You can put the store and those difficult years behind you and start down your own path to living a happier life."

"Things always, always work out, Ret. And don't you forget it," she said, taking my hand in hers. Pink bloomed in her cheeks, and her eyes were reflective like glass. She inspired me to take the next step. A dose of confidence and resilience, courtesy of the Payne way of life, shot through me.

"I think today's the day, Mom, and also the right time of morning. I'm going for a walk, a very long walk." I didn't need to explain. She understood I was ready to venture over to the path along the Loch River, to sit in my favorite spot, and then trace Bean's steps to where he saw the sun kiss the river. "It's time I talk to Mr. Kipp. And knowing that Bean would be with me, I believe we can all be healed."

"You do what you have to do, honey."

"Funny, that's what Jesse told me after I reminded him of squatters' rights."

"Just don't tell your papa."

"And why not? I don't want us to keep hiding things from one another. How can this town move forward if we don't talk about what happened and share our hurt and anger and reconcile our differences? This accident happened to everyone here, not just the Paynes at 1060 Woods Mill Road. It has eaten us alive for over ten years now: the gossip, the false rumors, all of which you and Papa have been caught up in. They've turned Mr. Kipp into a monster, which he's not."

"Ret, just take it easy. This is all going to take time. You can't expect everyone in this town to feel the way you do," Dad said, standing just inside the kitchen doorway. His denim hems were caked with mud; his work gloves stuck out from a front pocket. "Your mother and I, though we're on a better path, are still working on a few things when it comes to Mr. Kipp."

194

nancy chadwick

"At least you can now say his name," I said under my breath.

Papa came in, squeezed my shoulder, and then poured himself a cup of coffee. I set my dishes in the sink and looked outside to the back acres. The sun was peeking over the canopies of the firs and pines fanning in winds like brushes on a canvas. Only in his own due time would he find the strength and courage to face his demons.

It was my turn to look beyond the trees that dissected our property along the banks of the Loch River; to be with Bean, and then to let him go; to find the truth, and then set it free.

I outfitted myself with a warm coat and made sure I had my boots. I was prepared in mind, heart, and feet for a chilly start to my early morning walk in the woods.

Fact-finding had always run through the marrow of my bones, clear back to that day when I saw the diamonds in the sky. I traversed the backyard, making footsteps in the dew of the emerging grass. Bolt's ears pricked when I came closer and stopped to have a chat with him, offering a heavy-handed rub along his flanks. The sun rose quickly, and I hurried into the boughs of the pines and firs, speaking to them in gratitude for their protection and asking for continued safety as I ventured into the unknown. Bluebells dotted the forest floor as I made my way along the path, following an indent of endless footsteps made over the years by Bean and me. Downy woodpeckers created a noisy echo, and the chickadees a soft stirring. My old sit spot was up ahead. I would not stop a while now, sit, and pour emotions and thoughts onto pages in a journal like I once did. I continued my journey, trudging over downed branches and beds of decayed leaves until I came to the little bridge. In the steady pace of the river's run, I heard Bean's voice. It was reassuring and full of life. "You'll be all right, Ret. Everything will work out," he whispered to me through the trees.

mercy town

I walked farther to the foot of the bridge where its frosty wood planks were not yet warmed by a higher sun. The crooked railing, engraved with betrothed lovers' names and primitive shapes, was rough when I grabbed onto it. The air shifted and brought warmth as the sun's rays reached through nearby willows, piercing the sedate river. The sunbeams pulled me to the highest point on the bridge; I knew it was the right time to see them kiss the river. The resting river appeared to explode like sparkling diamonds. My eyes filled with tears. The guilt I had held tight for sending Bean at just the right time to witness this, putting him in the wrong place where his life had ended, had disintegrated into a million starlights. My heart became full of Bean.

Over the bridge on the other side of the river, a golden light burned in Mr. Kipp's front window. I thought of this land that his people had settled hundreds of years ago and held tight through the generations. Bean and I had once considered Indigenous people somewhat of a mystery. We'd spy on them from our side of the river, watching one man working inside a big barn busy with millwork, and catching him chatting at the river's edge with his neighbors while fishing. We never saw Mr. Kipp up close but would see him in the distance. He was a large man with an arm span the length of an eagle's wings and wore his jet black hair straight and shoulder length and topped his head with a red baseball cap. We rarely saw him passing through town, and never sitting in Neena's or walking the aisles in the Supervalu.

I crossed the bridge and walked warily toward Mr. Kipp's cabin. The whack of an ax splitting wood startled me, and I stopped. He was settling a log onto a tree stump with sharp hand-eye coordination and bursts of power, every motion coming from a now aged man. He was so focused on the rhythm of his work that he didn't see me standing but a few yards from his front door. Mr. Kipp, who had once loomed larger than life, had softened and become lost inside his suede jacket and denim trousers.

nancy chadwick

His formerly broad shoulders leaned over the toes of his boots. He still worked as hard, but with more effort. I thought how he had made his life here appear easy, playing the natural world like drawing a silken bow over a violin, making music with Mother Nature.

"Can I help you with something?" He belted out strong words that echoed bigger than his body. I remembered his once deep, bellowing voice could be heard from across the river, as Bean and I worked the path.

"Mr. Kipp. I'm Mar . . . Ret Payne. I don't know if you remember . . ." I yelled, staying strong in my stance.

He stopped chopping and looked my way with a squint, not from the sun but maybe from poor vision.

"Yes. I do. You're Bean's sister. And I've been waiting for you." He stuck the ax in the stump and straightened.

"Oh . . . I . . .Yes. I'd like to talk to you if you don't mind. I'd really like to talk."

"Well, it's 'bout time now, isn't it?"

I moved toward him, my heart pounding with every step. It wasn't that I was afraid of this man. It was the confrontation with a man of the past who did great harm to our family, the man who had killed my brother.

"C'mon in. I'll put a pot on for some tea." He waved me through with a calloused hand peeking from a frayed coat sleeve. I followed his lead. Standing just inside the doorway, I waited, while he lumbered a few feet ahead and to the right, where there appeared to be a kitchen. The rudimentary space was identifiable by a rectangular wooden table and two chairs, and cabinets above storing mismatched plates and bowls, all handmade, no doubt. The wood-burning stove off to the side looked like something out of the mid-twentieth century.

"You don't have to stand there, Miss Ret. Please have a seat by the fire. I'll be round in just a moment."

mercy town

His cabin was welcoming and warm. I had never been this close to Mr. Kipp, nor had I ever gotten this personal, standing among his things, his life. A striped blanket covered the seat and back of a threadbare couch that faced the fireplace. I recognized the glimmering from the oil lamp, sitting in the center of a square table under the window, as the light I'd seen when walking the path from the other side of the river. An old, scraped leather chair and ottoman, with an evergreen wool blanket folded over the arm, was his seat. He scooched it up to the fireplace.

While I sat on the end of the two-seat couch and waited for him, I glanced at artwork tacked to the walls on either side of the fireplace: sketches in charcoal of a young girl and boy, and the river, black strokes against cream newsprint paper. Though the outlines were simple, the coming together of shapes told of a depth, a vision, a story.

"Here we go, Miss Ret," he said, setting a couple of copper mugs on a carved wood table between his chair and the couch. I pushed aside the blanket and felt how its once-rough wool fibers had softened to warm comfort. "How you have grown up now," he said in a raspy voice, eyeing me closely before pouring simmering water from the kettle. His once-chiseled face was sunken and weathered, a scar predominant across his forehead. He took a couple steps backward, feeling for his leather chair, then sat slowly as if every ache in his bones had found relief.

"Yes, I am. Mr. Kipp, I came here to talk to you about what happened . . . ten years ago this week, as a matter of fact."

I watched how his hand trembled when he brought the teacup to his lips.

"How Bean had been waiting for spring to turn a corner, when the rains ceased, and the sun pulled us outside." I took a sip of comforting tea, sat back, and succumbed to the couch's soft cushions. "That morning seemed to be the perfect time. Bean finished his chores and begged for a walk into the woods along the river. I couldn't tell him it wasn't time yet, as I believed there was no better time than then. We ambled along the path, noting the springing of green things and the icing over that was still holding strong. I stopped to sit on a log for a while, telling Bean to be careful as he pressed on to the little bridge. The ice was weakening, and the mud was softening."

"That was your favorite spot, where you usually stop to write," he said softly.

"Yes. But how do you . . .?"

"I walk along the river to check on things. I've seen you."

He was right—Bean and I had walked along the river many times once spring was in the air. We usually paid more attention to our side of the river than to what or who was on the other side.

"I didn't need to mind Bean. I trusted he knew the way. He was a good walker and would never get lost. He'd learned to read the forest floor and sky and how to mark his tracks." I sipped more tea and stared out the window. Maybe I hoped to see Bean in the distance, walking along on the other side of the river, knowing Mr. Kipp and I were having a sit-down. But there was nothing there but the old trees yet to bud and the dull brown of defrosting earth. "I went looking for him after a while. And then I heard . . . I heard the shot." I turned and glared at him.

I had never told the full story to anyone before, and when I recited the story of the accident to the man who had caused it, I was letting out anger I never thought I had.

"I yelled for Bean, Mr. Kipp, but he didn't answer. I yelled, again, and again. There was no movement in the trees or a shiver along the ground. I couldn't find him. Where was he?"

I cried, or wailed was more like it in front of Mr. Kipp. I was losing Bean all over again.

"The moans got louder. I ran toward them. And there he was, whimpering my name. And there you were. Standing over him, with your shotgun still tucked under your arm. You had that

mercy town

stance, looking upon the earth and checking your downed prey. How could you, Mr. Kipp? How could you?"

I yelled at Mr. Kipp and dug my hands into my knees, holding them tight. I wanted answers, but I knew none would come.

"Ret, that was the worst day of my life. I make no excuses. I have lived with seeing Bean lying on that ground, bleeding, every day since. And I am sorry for causing such pain for you and your mother and your papa." He covered his bowed head with his open palms then wiped with his sleeve tears running down his ruddy cheeks. "I-I thought it was one of Mr. Shoot's pals, or even Mr. Shoots himself, tiptoeing around here again, being nosy. Once I found the barn door wide open and some of the woodworking tools out of order. I just grew furious that it was happening again. I lost my sense. It was supposed to be just a warning. It's no excuse, though."

"I'm sorry too. I'm sorry for what the accident did to the people of Waunasha. Some think you should be sent to the county jail and the key thrown away. Others realize it was an accident and that we all need to move on with our lives. We're so divided," I told him.

My head dropped in defeat, as if there was no simple answer to the healing that was being called for.

"I forgive you," I whispered. "It was a tragic accident."

"Ya know, Bean and I used to visit," he said. "He'd come knock on the door whenever he was at the little bridge. I could see him standing at the top of it, looking over and spotting the turtles on the banks and following the fish swimming under the bridge as he moved from one side to the other. I could tell he was always listening in on nature's calls, the tree limbs swaying, leaves upset in strong winds, the birds' conversations, even the deer pulling and nibbling at the saplings. Yes, we got to know each other real well."

nancy chadwick

Mr. Kipp stared long into the crackling fire.

I never knew that was where Bean had gone. After I sat down on the tree stump at my spot, I knew he trailed west on the path along the river, but I never knew how far or where he went. I just figured he was on an adventure. Sometimes the places we visit should be kept to ourselves.

He stood and refilled our cups. "We told stories. Bean made up some good ones. I told him some of my own, of our ancestors, and how our very existence was once threatened."

Mr. Kipp had a good look at the drawings on the wall. I studied them, too. He seemed to be connected to those images of a young boy wearing a red knit cap, frolicking in the woods, squatting by the river's bank, the water flowing through his fingers, looking skyward, mesmerized by . . . nothing. And then it occurred to me.

"Mr. Kipp, is that . . . Is that Bean in those pictures? The red cap . . ."

"Yes, Ret, that's Bean. He liked to draw so very much. I'd tell him about our connections to the natural world, that we find an understanding with ourselves by connecting to the talk of the bird, and the meeting of the wind, and the grace of the tree. I showed him through my drawings of sun and clouds, of trees inhaling and exhaling, the sacredness of the clean air and trees we depend on for our survival. We drew together, of our love for Mother Nature, and shared a kindred spirit."

Sadness pulsed where my heart beat and in gratitude for Mr. Kipp's friendship with Bean. Any remaining hard feelings that had lingered for so long, while living with the loss of my brother and being in the man's company who took it, had been freed. Mr. Kipp taught Bean about the earth, and about the life of the river, and the trees, and the stories found among those who are all connected.

mercy town

Suddenly, three bangs sounded at the front door. The windows rattled in tandem. Again, another two thunks of what sounded like pounding fists. It took a moment for him to get out of the sunken seat of his chair, even with the help of a cane, and open the door.

"Papa! What are you doing here?"

Papa stomped over the threshold and stood between me and Mr. Kipp. "And what exactly are *you* doing here, Ret?" He pointed a stiff finger near my nose. "I told you never to pay him any attention, let alone come face-to-face with him."

"Papa, I'm not a child. And 'him' is Mr. Kipp," I shouted.

My reminder didn't alter Papa's demanding stance and taut face.

"What's going on here? Someone tell me, and tell me now," Papa said.

"Papa, it's time we forgive Mr. Kipp and let it all go. We need to be at peace." I sidled next to Papa and put a hand on his chest. "And this is where we start. The heavy heart you have been carrying all these years has turned you into someone I don't recognize. You have lost your spirit, your joy in discovering the simplest of things, your way about you that was once such a strong model for me and Bean."

"Please, sit, Mr. Payne," Mr. Kipp said, offering Papa a spot on the couch next to me. Instead of sitting, Papa eyed the paper sheets on the wall. Turning his head this way, then that, he examined the drawings as if trying to figure out a puzzle. He inched closer to the pictures as if with each step, they would be made clearer. His eyes locked on the one of the little boy who was bent over at the river's edge, his hand in the water, watching the tiny ripples weave through his fingers. Papa's face relaxed, his eyes filling with tears as he appeared to recognize the picture. He used to show us how to squat by the water, put our hands in and feel the water's temperature, emotion, and energy.

202

He gave Mr. Kipp a hard stare.

"That one's of Bean. That's mine. But the one below it, Bean drew," Mr. Kipp said.

I tensed, not knowing if Papa, now within striking distance, would get physical with him.

I moved to Papa's other side. "Bean came here, Papa. Mr. Kipp showed him how to draw stories from memories," I said, leaning into his chest and looking up. "Bean learned from Mr. Kipp. He learned about Mother Earth, and the river, and the trees, and how dependent we are on each other. Papa, we are all connected. Not only out there, but in here too, with each other." I said, tapping softly on his heart.

"But that was *my* job. I was his papa," he yelled. I took a step back. "It was my job to show him the value and the care we must take with . . . with . . ."

His face was streaked with tears. How hard he tried to hold them in. His shoulders slumped. I think he and I realized at the very same moment the friendship between Bean and Mr. Kipp. The bond created over the years between the two of them was reflected in the drawings.

I put my arms around Papa and cried with him while telling him about forgiveness. "It has to start with the Paynes. We must show Waunasha that we have forgiven and lead by example. We can show how to remember Bean as a curious, happy, and smart little man, and not dwell on the tragedy that happened to him or the ill will we have for Mr. Kipp."

I looked over at Mr. Kipp, who was sitting on the seat's edge. His hands, one on top of the other, rested on his cane's crown, a wooden carving of a bear, with his forehead atop them. I remembered Bean once told me that the bear is a symbol of strength and survival. I didn't know how he knew this, but because Bean liked to read books about indigenous cultures, I assumed this knowledge came from his reading.

mercy town

With tears running like the flow of the Loch River after a heavy rain, Mr. Kipp broke down, his voice weak and halting.

"It was an accident. And I am so very sorry for your loss." How small he looked, succumbing to his contrition.

"Mr. Kipp," I said in a soft voice, kneeling on the floor in front of him, "you lost him, too. You were a part of his life, and now I understand the extra spark he had in his stride once he left me at my spot and headed on down the trail. He was excited to see you. And I have no doubt that after he saw the sun kissing the river, he was on his way to tell you how he saw diamonds in the sky."

I put my hands on Mr. Kipp's hunched shoulders. The once-formidable figure was now a shrunken old man. He had faced the father of the boy he killed, and the only words, the most important, most valuable words he had the strength to say were, "I'm sorry."

Those words went a long way. "Sorry" is a validation that the person saying it is still someone, even someone good, who has just made a grave mistake.

"I know you had no intention of killing Bean," I said, looking straight at him with a side eye on Papa to see if he was listening too. "Bean would want nothing more than for Waunashans to forgive and move forward with our lives. There's still time for peace, for hope. And Bean is lighting the way."

He struggled to get to his feet. His wobbly legs led him to the wall of pictures, where he carefully unstuck the half dozen drawings. He patted them into a tidy stack, rolled them, and handed them to Papa, not saying a word. Neither of them needed to speak. Papa gently took the drawings into his own shaky hands, big tears still dropping. He took a step closer to Mr. Kipp, who stood using his cane for support. Mr. Kipp cowered as Papa moved toward him. I thought Papa was going to take a swing at him. But he didn't. He bent to meet Mr. Kipp's eyes, then wrapped his frame in a bear hug with Bean's pictures clutched in his hand. The force of their two bodies together plowed through any remaining fear in the room.

The fireplace wall was now empty of the stories Mr. Kipp and Bean shared. But the stories could never truly be removed from Mr. Kipp's home.

Sitting small on the mantel, but looming large in identity, was a plaque of solid wood with an inscription:

We, the Anishinabeg, the people of Odaawaa-Zaaga'ig-aniing, the Lac Courte Oreilles Tribe, will sustain our heritage, preserving our past, strengthening our present, and embracing our future. We will defend our inherent sovereign rights and safeguard Mother Earth. We will provide for the educational, health, social welfare, and economic stability of the present and future generations.
—Band of Lake Superior Chippewa Indians.

Mr. Kipp reached for the plaque, touched the words as if in prayer, then steadied himself with a hold of the mantel.

I helped Mr. Kipp back to his favorite chair. Papa put another log on the fire. We left him alone, for now, but we knew we would see him again soon.

Papa slid the drawings into his jacket pocket. Together, we left Mr. Kipp's cabin and ambled to the river. We walked until we met the foot of the bridge, then crossed over to the other side and continued for home.

It was well after noon when Papa and I walked through the door. And we knew Mom wouldn't be home, as she was working her last shift at the Supervalu. The skies had turned to Wedgwood blue, a sure sign that spring was here to stay. The air had warmed enough for us to eat lunch out on the back porch. Papa and I sat

mercy town

next to each other, he comfy in his rocking chair, and I settled in Mom's seat. We ate our ham sandwiches among the quiet of the back acres and the black oak, recalling memories of my youth and Bean's. When he was finished, he set the empty plate on the wood table between us and rocked in a familiar rhythm. Only this time, he wasn't getting ready to tell Bean and me a story; he was getting ready to revel in all the stories rolled up in his jacket pocket. Papa studied each drawing as if watching Bean and the Loch River come alive that very instant. I think he heard Bean's every curious step as he got closer to the river's banks, and his laughter at discovering new growing things. He felt Bean was with him. Our hearts filled with love for Bean and where he had taken us.

tuesday

The next morning, while we ate breakfast, I told Mom that I had something important to tell her. She looked up from the crossword puzzle and narrowed her eyes to study me, trying to discern if it was something truly important or just something I had on my mind.

"I need to tell you what happened yesterday at Mr. Kipp's cabin."

She put down her fork. I put down a half-eaten slice of peanut-buttered toast on a plate.

"This is the first day of a new beginning for the Paynes and for all Waunasha," I began. "It's time now to forgive and let Bean's memory live on in the good of our hearts. I sat with Mr. Kipp in his cabin, where drawings were posted on the wall next to the fireplace. The image of a boy, who was wearing a tight-knit cap in one picture, looked familiar. That boy was Bean. Mr. Kipp and Bean had been friends all along. Bean would visit him, and Mr. Kipp taught him how to draw pictures of the outside world to make memories of our connections to it. Papa has those pictures now."

I told her that when Papa banged on Mr. Kipp's door, he was mad to see me there and even madder that he had to stand in front of Mr. Kipp. But his anger soon broke, and the barrier

mercy town

between us was defeated. Papa could see the good in Mr. Kipp. The drawings told him so.

As Mom cried happy tears, she bowed her head and clasped her hands as if saying a little prayer. We were both relieved for Papa's sake. He had been holding in his pain all those years, never giving a voice to his grief, to all the emotions stirring inside him.

"Mr. Kipp deserves our forgiveness and friendship. Bean wouldn't want it any other way. He was an important man to Bean. There's one picture Bean drew of Mr. Kipp standing in front of his cabin. He appeared large, with a long wingspan and solid frame. He looked like an eagle had landed and was showing his might—"

Just then, my ringing phone interrupted us and I answered. I recognized the voice.

"Mr. Jennings. How good to hear from you. I'm assuming you're calling because the county and ECCOSTAR developers have worked out a resolution?"

"Well, that's why I'm calling. I'm out here now on Dell Landing, and someone I think you might know has brought me here."

I first bristled at the thought that there was action going on at Dell Landing, that Mr. Jennings was onsite, and I was left out, unaware. What was he doing there, and why?

"Oh, please tell me, who could that be, Mr. Jennings?"

"It's your husband, Jesse."

"What? Jesse?"

"Perhaps you could find time in your schedule to drive over so we could all have a talk?"

"I'll be right there." I stashed the phone in my pocket and grabbed a jacket hanging by the door. "Mom, I've got to go. Jesse is out at Dell Landing with the county. There's something going on there. I'm sorry. We'll talk more later," I assured her.

I pulled on my boots and ran across the front yard to meet the trail. I reasoned I could get there faster on foot than by driving.

208

nancy chadwick

While following the path Bean and I had taken so often, I listened to what the natural world was saying. I prayed to Bean. I stirred right along with all the universe's energy, asking it for strength and grace to meet whatever was to come my way.

The thought of soon seeing Jesse made my strides longer and my adrenaline stronger. The last time we talked, I remembered him saying how we needed to not talk further about things on the phone. I smiled to think he might have thought this was a good time for a personal visit to the place that was causing a stir with me and between us. There would be a time and a place, and it seemed as if everything had come together at the right time now. I knew this would all work out for Mr. Kipp and his neighbors. It just had to.

By the time I neared Dell Landing, I was sticky with sweat from my hurried pace and nervous anticipation. Misty fog blurred the cabins' outline and obscured the identity of two men standing near them. Darkness filled Mr. Kipp's window like a black checkerboard square. I kept my eyes on his cabin, even while walking over the bridge, until I stopped to survey the other cabins. My eyes jumped from one to the next. There was no smoke coming out of any cabin chimney. Fear shot through me like a lightning strike. And then I was angry. Mr. Jennings had evicted all of them already? How could Jesse let this happen?

"Hey, we're over here," a voice hollered. It was Mr. Jennings, dressed in khaki pants and a fluorescent yellow vest over a navy shirt not quite wrapping around his rounded torso. Jesse stood several feet from him, hunched over a makeshift drafting board where large white pages hung from the board's ends. I waved, then trudged through the thick floor of springing foliage to meet them.

"Well, hello to the both of you," I said.

"Honey, hello. It's so good to see you. I missed you," Jesse said.

I wrapped my arms around his neck and gave him a kiss and a hard stare into his eyes. He hugged me around the waist for

mercy town

just a little longer. He was dressed like Mr. Jennings, only his vest was zipped. Both men wore white hard hats with "ECCOSTAR" printed in gold on the front. "I tried to get here as quickly as I could. I trust no noteworthy conversation has transpired that I should be privy to," I said to Mr. Jennings, shaking his hand.

"Uh, well, no, Mrs. Reed. Jesse and I were just having a chat about Waunasha and how far it has come from the once-docile community of just a few thousand to a now-healthy five figure census—"

I looked first at Mr. Jennings, then back to Jesse, then back and forth between the two of them until someone piped up to start the conversation. "So, what have you two concluded? I'm listening."

Mr. Jennings broke the silence. "Mr. Reed drives a hard bargain here."

"C'mon over here, Margaret," Jesse said, taking my hand to have a look at the project plans spread out on the makeshift table.

Jesse showed me a "before" rendering, a road map of where all the new cabins would be plotted, and then an "after" picture showing not much difference between the two.

"Look, you're going to have to spell this out for me in lay terms. I don't understand what I'm seeing."

"Ms. Reed, the county will annex additional land that is next to this project. The land essentially will be a buffer, like a privacy zone. That land over there," Mr. Jennings said, pointing to the other side of the river, near the little bridge, "will be the new home of Mr. Kipp and his Indigenous people."

"But that's where the accident was," I piped up. My heart fluttered.

Jesse put his arm around me and pulled me close.

"We talked to them, Margaret. We offered them the same opportunities as they have now. They will have a brand-new woodworking mill and an arts center to teach their craft to

nancy chadwick

others, all as a means of income for Mr. Kipp and his neighbors. In Bean's honor and memory, Mr. Kipp would like to teach drawing lessons to tell his stories and the value of the natural world. The settlement's new cabins will be upgraded, providing an easier and more comfortable way of life."

"So, what about the expansive redevelopment with all the touristy attractions on the Landing?"

"The redevelopment has been scaled down to preserve the land here and the old growth."

"There will be a cabin right where we're standing, as a heritage center for visitors to come and to learn about the history of the settlements here. All Dell Landing residents will manage the place; it will be all theirs," Mr. Jennings added.

For a time, I didn't know what to say. I was skeptical, thinking that there must be a catch about the whole thing. But after Jesse walked me through the plans with Mr. Jennings at our sides, I was reassured.

Sometimes you have to fight not only for what you believe in, but also for what you know is the right thing to do. Sometimes it may not work out in your favor, but sometimes it does. And when it does, you are filled with a sense of purpose. You have made a difference. You have done the right thing.

"I need to go talk to Mr. Kipp right now," I said, looking into Jesse's eyes with urgency.

"Do what you have to, Margaret," Jesse said. "I'm driving back to West Prairie as soon as I wrap things up here."

We hugged for a long time before I thanked Mr. Jennings for his attention.

When I knocked on Mr. Kipp's door, it squeaked ajar. "Hello," I said, taking a couple steps inside. He was seated in his usual chair near the fireplace, with his head resting against its back. He was staring into the dimming fire and watching the embers glow, then fade. Though appearing tired, with small eyes sunk

mercy town

into a pallid face, he managed a slight upward curve of the sides of his mouth. I knelt beside him. Though his enthusiasm for the project's resolution did not appear to match mine, he appeared content.

"You and your neighbors will be staying on Dell Landing." I spoke softly, placing my hand on his knee. "I know having a new development nearby will be a big change, and I'm the first to tell you how change can be traumatic, but you are not being displaced. You will be okay. And all is forgiven." I patted his hand, which rested on the chair's tattered arm. His other hand rested on mine.

"I knew something was going on," Mr. Kipp said. "But I just couldn't fight the county. After the accident, I had no voice. " Mr. Kipp sunk lower. He tried to speak, but the words were difficult in coming. "I deserved to be run out of here after what I did." Mr. Kipp had a cry, burying his shame and remorse in his hands. "Thank you, Ret, for all you have done for me and for Dell Landing. Without you, I daresay we could have been homeless. " Mr. Kipp smiled, and a bit of color returned to his face.

A newfound spirit traveled home with me, but not before I stopped at the little bridge, hung over its railing, and looked deep into the river's bottom. I looked east, then west, then up to the skies, watching nature's way of spending her day and the details of an otherwise ordinary spring vista. Tulips had opened their red faces wide, and anemones tilted their white heads to receive a brighter sun, splashing a landscape of virginal green. And then I thought about how today was not like any other. This was the first day that Waunasha would be united again. The Paynes no longer wore their anger on their faces or in their dispositions. We were free to talk among our neighbors about the bonds of human vulnerability.

The Dell Landing project would go on as scheduled, with the newly agreed-upon amendments. With a new outlook and a lighter step, Papa looked into the eyes of those who harbored anger and showed them what the power of forgiveness looked like. It was only by our words and deeds that we could become an example for others.

We ate outside on the porch that night, with warmth and comfort in the air. The white lights strung from the railing and up around the posts offered peace and hope while we enjoyed ourselves in the twilight. My head rested in the crook of my arm while I peered up into the heavens. The stars were bright that night against an inky blue sky. In all the years I had grown up here, I never realized until now how dark a sky could get and how a bright star could beg for wishes. Papa grabbed a book to tell us a story, rocking in his chair as I sat opposite him and Mom. When he was finished, it was my turn to tell a story.

I told of how when spring came, Ma couldn't wait to get out her gardening toolbox from its winter spot in the shed. She'd pluck her gloves from the box and knee pad from her armpit and start planting her favorite red geraniums in clay pots, then line them up so evenly on the floor of the front porch that if you took a ruler to their spacing, you'd see the same measurement every time. As soon as Mom pulled out that box, Bean would announce, as he did every year, "It must be time now, huh, Ret?" And finally, when I'd tell him, "It is, Bean. Shall we go out and welcome earth's rebirth?" I thought every seam on Bean's clothing would bust from excitement. After being cooped up in hibernation, he was ready to greet a new life cycle of growing things. And here we were in another new cycle of growth, where we had learned about ourselves and each other.

wednesday

I was awake even before New Billy crowed to announce the new day. The excitement about finishing my article and getting back home to Jesse jump-started my typing fingers. The air outside was as warm as the clear air inside this house. I hadn't known such a brightness before, until now, when clouds that seemed to hang over us had moved on.

I tucked my journal in a jacket pocket and set out for a walk, a one-last-time kind of thing. I made tracks through the backyard to the open field, then slithered through the woods, noticing that the undergrowth was greener today than even yesterday. Tree limbs had exploded in verdant tips, a green never to be seen again until this time next year. I followed the path that Bean and I typically took, knowing he was with me. I caught a first glimpse of deer nibbling a patch of spring buds, then a robin flitting from tree to tree and ravenous squirrels filling their empty bellies after a long winter. Soon, I could hear the morning rituals of nature, water splashes, and the honking of Canadian geese. The little bridge was in sight. I hadn't lost my timing as I stepped upon the wooden planks and walked uphill to the center of the footbridge. I was neither too early, nor too late, as the sun shone bright. The river sparkled like diamonds. I smiled and laughed and cried all at the same time. My heart was no longer heavy but lifted with love from Bean.

"It's a good story tonight, Ret, isn't it?" Bean had whispered to me, as I helped to put his bleeding body into Papa's truck. "I found out what happens next . . . I saw the diamonds. They were real sparkly, Ret."

I believed it was God who led Bean to the river with the allure of promise, of happiness. Bean stepped into a halo of bright sun reflecting off the river and back to him in explosions of diamonds. He understood what Mom had been telling us when we sat under the black oak. He used his senses, just like how Papa had told us. He saw the web of connections from the heavens to the earth.

My little brother was a wanderer in those days, and I was a walker. There's a difference. Bean's goal was to explore as much ground as he could. Mine was to get to the bridge to see stars explode on the river. And I couldn't wait to share my discovery with my brother.

Bean was a walker that day with a destination in mind.

That was what mattered to Bean. He was now at home, and so were we.

I returned home and grabbed the car keys to drive to Neena's and say goodbye to Amber. As I drove slowly out to Rustic Road, it felt as if I had been here forever. Moments of the previous day still whirled. I slowed when I reached the sign that read, "Welcome to downtown Waunasha," recalling when I first saw it, smiling at how a small downtown was made to be dressed up so fancy.

Main Street was filling quickly, and so were the parking spaces. Chimes jingled as I opened Neena's door, and I quickly took my usual spot. I had a full view of the heart of downtown, a

mercy town

place where good things were planned. It was a snapshot I'd take with me back to West Prairie. Mesmerized by the view, at first, I didn't notice Amber standing at my table. With neither a coffeepot in hand nor a smile on her face, she looked as if she had been fired. I dismissed my impression because Amber basically ran the place. People came to see *her*.

"What's up? Coffee still dripping, or what?"

"Um, Ret, I've got some . . . some not-so-good news."

She slid into the booth opposite me and leaned over the table, close, as if about to tell a secret. I thought it mysterious and unlike Amber, who was more likely to just blurt something out.

"Well, what? Don't tell me. Grainger Jr. sold the place."

"No, no, nothing like that." She hesitated, pulling a rag from her apron and wiping errant smudges from the table. "It seems a couple of county folks went over to Mr. Kipp's place yesterday afternoon to let him know they could move into their cabins as soon as their new ones were built, sometime next spring. But he didn't answer the door. They looked all around, and there was just a skinny trail of smoke coming from the chimney. They knocked harder on the door, but when they got no answer, they pushed it open. . . ." Amber's voice weakened. "Mr. Kipp was slumped in his chair. He . . . died, Ret. I'm sorry, dear."

I gaped at her. "But . . . I just saw him yesterday in that chair. He was okay; he smiled when I told him . . . How? What happened? Does anyone know what happened?" I searched her blank face for an answer, but she didn't have one. Her hair fell around her face as she lowered her eyes.

"No one knows, Ret. Sometimes things just can't be explained. His heart had been broken for so long. Maybe it just finally quit on him."

The weight of the news came tumbling like an untethered stack of pine logs, heavy and quick. How I wanted Mr. Kipp to see the project completed and to see the success of all who lived on the Landing. But I understood he must have been tired, so very tired; a heavy toll was taken on him over the many months. There could be no other place to call home like the one he already had. Maybe the thought of unearthing the roots of his ancestors, of disturbing a Native nation that was his tribe, was too much to bear.

But perhaps the greatest reason he had let go was knowing he was forgiven—This was the greatest gift. He could leave this earth and rest in peace.

"They said he was clutching some drawing. A sketch of a little boy crouched at the river, touching . . . something. It looked like stars or diamonds, something sparkly."

I clutched the side of the table with one hand and felt with the other my heavily beating heart. And then I cried, the grief unbearable. I wanted to run away into the woods, to see Mr. Kipp one last time, to tell him again and again that I was sorry, and to tell him that I loved him for giving Bean such precious gifts.

I was numb, walking out of Neena's door and to my car. At first, I didn't remember where I had parked it. I wandered Main Street, taking in as much of Waunasha as I could hold. I imagined Mr. Kipp and Bean together, sitting in Mr. Kipp's cabin by the fire, drawing pictures at his wood table. I imagined their conversation to be simple and limited as Mr. Kipp relied more on showing through his pictures than through the telling of their stories. Now he and Bean were of this earth, connected in spirit, woven into the tapestry of earth and sky. They just had to be together now, standing by the river, where many suns would kiss the water.

When I pulled in at home, I didn't get out of the car. I cried puddles of tears, pouring out gratitude for knowing Mr. Kipp, for befriending the very person who had accidentally shot Bean, for his teaching us that forgiveness, in the wake of sorrow, heals the heart, bonds us together.

mercy town

I found Papa in the barn and told him about Mr. Kipp's passing. We hugged as we shared emotions; we exchanged no words. I went to find Mom. She was in the front room, sitting and reading. When I told her about Mr. Kipp, she laid down her book and looked out through the picture window, then got up and went into the kitchen to stare out the window at the black oak in the distance. I joined her, and together, we bowed our heads in gratitude and prayer for Mr. Kipp.

My journal got a heavy dose of reflection that day.

I didn't want to leave Waunasha. But I had an obligation to my job, and a greater one to the people of my hometown. I had a story to tell, one that seemed to have already been written and an ending made.

That night, after I helped Mom with supper dishes, I told Papa I wouldn't be sitting for one of his best stories; I had my own to write. Fear in my ability to tell the story just as it should be slowed my steps upstairs to my bedroom. I considered my assignment from Mr. Simpson. Would he accept a different piece, or reject the lesson the people of Waunasha, and anyone who lived in a small town burdened with any accidental loss of life, had come to realize? I knew of only one way to write the story: with mercy and compassion, reflecting on what we could all learn from a tragic accident.

Before I wrote, I called Jesse. I told him what had happened. And then I spilled more. I told him how when I first got here, I had moved on and forgiven Mr. Kipp. And then I saw the rage and hurt eating up Mom and Papa, and how the people of Waunasha had shown their prejudices by talking around town about him and the accident. I saw what grief looked like, and I saw how the bonds of friendships and the connections with nature brought us close to each other. I saw how Mom had kept it all inside, and how Papa was ready to explode, sometimes seething with pain. And then that day in Mr. Kipp's cabin, I think he understood what

nancy chadwick

Mr. Kipp had done for Bean, and what Bean had done for him. A child's innocence and an old man's wisdom. They had learned from one another. Their stories played out in the drawings they shared.

Jesse had learned of Mr. Kipp's passing just before I called. The county commissioner's office had notified ECCOSTAR. A temporary hold was placed on the project until the residents of Waunasha had their time. "It seems the Dell Landing project will take on a new meaning," I told him.

"There have been a few motions to rename the hill project in honor of Mr. Kipp," Jesse told me. "ECCOSTAR won't stand in the way. Write your story, Margaret, the way it's supposed to be written, and then c'mon home."

I wrote through the night. My fingers rushed along the keyboard, keeping up with my firing thoughts.

Some say you can never go back home after a tragic accident. But I had to. And when I did, I quickly learned that a story about the revitalization of downtown Waunasha wasn't the real story to tell. . .

thursday

I woke up early Friday with New Billy calling for the sun to hurry and rise, and his favorite dish to be filled with dried worms. I ran out the front door with Chip at my heels, the screen door slapping behind me, which was sure to wake Mom and Papa. The new day was full of promise, and light, and new beginnings. I stared at the sun above the horizon, playing peekaboo among the pines deep into the front yard. I let the chickens out and fed them. And I led Bolt and Quincy out to pasture, watching their deep breaths pushing through their nostrils. They galloped in freedom, stretching their limbs and shaking their heads in delight. Tree canopies deep into the backyard held still as neither a breeze nor a hawk stirred.

Mom and Papa wove around one another in the kitchen as they made pancakes and fried bacon, while I fired up my laptop in my bedroom and opened the article to give it one last read. I smiled at its conclusion, knowing Bean was with me all the way.

After breakfast, I packed the car and returned to the front room to find Mom and Papa in their seats. "I left an envelope for you two on the desk," I told them. "I'm off for home." All three of us stood in the middle of the room, with the sun blazing through the picture window and shining on the family Payne. We gave each other hugs that we felt in our bones, and pecks on each other's cheeks. Our faces glowed with smiles, with life, with spending each day as if it was our last, with taking each moment as if there would never be one like it.

I got myself situated in the car and waved to them standing in the window. They were a reconciled pair who had weathered an emotional storm and come through it all with lessons learned. I smiled through my tears, knowing they were all right now. As the car rolled away from the house and down the dirt road, they became mere figures in my rearview mirror. Chip chased the car, and New Billy circled the front of the house. They became smaller, but I had a wide view through the windshield of what was ahead.

With every mile driven and moment passed, I thought of Mr. Kipp and Bean and the Waunasha I left behind. But my thoughts were good ones this time as I recalled when I first arrived, when trepidation reared in surprise. I chided myself for being this way as I thought ten years was plenty of time for me to work through the anger and grieving and loss.

Receiving the assignment that had called for me to come here had not happened because of luck—it had happened because of destiny. With pride and in memory of Bean, my work was done here. "You got yourself a good story there, Bean," I told him, remembering when he answered Papa, "A good story is one where you want to know what happens next."

I also thought of the note and check I had left them in the envelope to pay off all their outstanding bills. I told them they didn't need to sell any part of the Payne home, as it was my home too. I'd talk to Jesse about the house on Woods Mill Drive becoming part of our home.

By early evening, I passed the WELCOME TO WEST PRAIRIE sign, where I reacquainted myself with the familiar. I felt as

mercy town

if I had been away for a long time, measured in the rising and blooming of tulips, the clusters of daffodils bopping their yellow heads in agreement, the smell of the first cut of grass, Kenny's boy sweeping the front walkway of shedding catkins from the oaks, and the twill of robins' calls.

I turned the corner onto Fairfax and had my familiar corner in sight, the one I passed twice a day, to and from work. The one where I saw Mr. and Mrs. Davies walking hand in hand to the bus stop that would take them to the strip mall, where they would buy toilet paper, milk, eggs, and pumpernickel bread and make a last stop at the pharmacy to pick up Mr. Davies's prescription. A pair of young girls rode their bikes, the wind taking their long hair behind them like wings. A new For Sale sign suddenly popped from the ground where the old inhabitants had moved on, and a new family would plant roots. The routine would no longer be mundane as I had a new vision of my landscape. This was where we tried our best every day. I wasn't driving down Fairfax to home; I was seeing deep inside everyday life.

The Reed house was the fourth one in on Arbor. This was the older part of West Prairie, and Jesse and I were drawn to its charm, the sloping roofs and shutters of the Cape Cods, the ranches, the farmhouses. My attention was not necessarily drawn to the houses, but to the homes that were made in them.

I pulled into the driveway and sat, letting the tiredness of the past two weeks find a settling place in my mind. Shadows stretched across the kitchen; the sun had just fallen below the horizon, yet its glow was still seen in the periwinkle sky. I dropped with a thunk in the middle of the kitchen floor all that weighed me down. "Hello . . . Jess? . . . I'm home," I yelled, but there was no response. I peered into the refrigerator and rummaged for a beverage or snack, but there was nothing to satisfy my thirst or my hunger. When I turned on the light, the kitchen was as clean and tidy as when I had left it.

"Well, aren't you a sight for my longing eyes," Jesse uttered from the sliding door. He looked cozy and warm, dressed in sweatpants and a long-sleeved shirt.

"Jesse . . . don't just stand there watching me," I said, going to him with outstretched arms. I stood holding onto him as if I never wanted to let go. I had missed us, this place, our home.

"C'mon out here. I've got us set up outside on the back porch."

And he sure did. He had set a table for two with a fancy table-cloth, flowers, votive candles, and a glass each of prosecco. We sat and plucked at a charcuterie board of meats and cheeses and fruits while talking and gazing at the horizon. I was immersed in the moment's goodness and in the satisfaction of knowing I had done a good job with my article.

We talked for hours about what we had learned from our jobs, and from each other, and about doing the right thing. As the day slowly drew her shades, Jesse cleared the table while I went upstairs and showered away all the emotions of the past two weeks. I unpacked my suitcase and backpack, redistributing what I had gathered just weeks ago. When I emptied my tote bag, something tumbled from it onto the floor. I chased the tube-like paper roll and held the unfamiliar in my hands. I wiggled the rubber band to one end and freed the papers of their roll shape. Once they were unspooled, I laid the curled papers flat on the floor. A note was clipped to the upper left corner.

> *These are yours. You showed Bean love and awe of the natural world. And you showed me the power of mercy and forgiveness. When the sun kissed the river.*

It was a note from Papa. He had given me Bean's drawings, the ones that Mr. Kipp had given to him. I held Bean in my hands and Mr. Kipp in my heart.

mercy town

That night and for all the nights thereafter, I never had another awful dream about Bean, about hearing gunshots, about seeing Bean down on the ground bleeding. Waunasha would move on, and Mr. Kipp would be remembered as his spirit lived among the ancient trees on what would be called Kipp's Landing.

I would be ready to get back to work on Monday, to jostle with Clarissa about a new feature, and grab real coffee at The Drip with Lonnie at a break or give Mr. Simpson a new angle for a story he had in mind at the weekly morning meeting. I would get ready for work as I usually did, Jesse in the kitchen making sure I had something to eat, me counting the number of items in my bag. Jesse and I would walk out together to our cars, each of us waving to Beth and Bob across the street, who always seemed to retrieve their newspaper at the same time that Jesse and I were leaving. And the routine of my day would flow more lightly because I carried a better Waunasha in my heart.

friday

I settled well into my first night back in West Prairie. The familiar echoes of air pushing into the attic crevices above and the popping and creaking of the house contracting below told me I had never been gone, though it sure felt like it. My breath rose and fell in sync with Jesse's as I chased moon shadows on the ceiling. I thought of Waunasha. It would take some time for a community once lost to restore itself to the place I had always known it to be: a place where people worked hard and raised families and learned a thing or two about the values of home and belonging. But at least I had left, knowing Waunasha was off to a good start.

The Loch River would always run through my veins, pulsing blood through my heart and soul. It was where I had experienced death and life. I had learned about the woods from Papa, and stories about them from Mr. Kipp—how they could be cruel yet also offer kindness. The forest would forever continue its cycle from old-growth trees to the sturdy saplings just finding their footing.

When I opened the doors of the *West Prairie Journal* on Monday, everything was the same—the positioning of the desks, the organization of papers on them, even the placement of the coffeepot in the break room—yet I felt I had changed. I had made

mercy town

peace with the tragedy of my past: my family that could not forgive, and a town that wouldn't let me forget what happened. The first thing I did when I sat at my desk was to pull the photo of Bean and me out from underneath the desk blotter. I dug for a small frame buried in my desk drawer and slid the photo into it, then settled it in front of me.

With the newspaper folded and tucked under his arm, Mr. Simpson was the first to walk in. He treaded the worn carpeted aisle with deliberate steps into his office. I thought this early start to be unusual.

"Good morning, Margaret," he said, without so much as a glance my way.

"Welcome back, Margaret," Lonnie said with a smile, following behind Mr. Simpson.

Lonnie and I assumed our routine, firing up computers, pulling out new files, and pushing aside old ones. I watched Mr. Simpson in his office doing the same practice. Only this time, he remained standing, which was out of the ordinary for him; he hadn't yet filled his coffee mug or adjusted the window's shade behind him. He stood behind his desk, put on his eyeglasses, and then unfolded the paper, shaking the pages open. I stood, breathed deeply, and walked to his office, watching the look on his face for a reaction. My presence outside the door made him look from the paper at me. We held our stares for what seemed like forever until he lowered his hands. His face had reddened, and his eyes were shiny. He waved me inside.

"You know I approved this last night after you sent it to me, without looking at it. I've never done that before with anything written by anyone here. Because I believe in you, Margaret. And this, this," he said, waving the paper as if it were a winning lottery ticket, "is your best piece. On behalf of the *West Prairie Journal*, thank you for an outstanding feature."

We shook hands and walked out of his office together, with Mr. Simpson holding up the full page of the feature for all to see. Lonnie and Clarissa stood, clapping with big smiles, and Rae Ann and Calvin and Jimmy stood too, and even Kirby had stopped with his mail cart. There was a large card sitting on my desk when I returned. It read, "Congratulations, Ret, on a job well done."

And then I looked at the photo of Bean and me and smiled.

If you enjoyed reading *Mercy Town*,
consider these books also by Nancy Chadwick:

The Wisdom of the Willow, a novel – A metaphorically rich and reflective tale of sisterhood and strength, *The Wisdom of the Willow* is a story of hope and healing, of the choices that shape our lives, and the challenges we all face as we seek to find our places in the world.

Under the Birch Tree, A Memoir of Discovering Connections and Finding Home – An exploration of what it means to belong, this is Nancy's success story of survival and triumph over adversity.

Books are available by scanning this QR code:

acknowledgments

While my first novel, *The Wisdom of the Willow*, was winding its way to a conclusion, I knew I had one more story in me. And I also knew this one did not involve trees. Well, not as characters, anyway.

This story was born from a short story, "When the Sun Kissed the River." I wanted to know what happened to Margaret "Ret" Payne, then twelve, and I wondered just how the Paynes and their hometown had survived the accidental shooting of Bean, the youngest Payne. Was the town still angry, or had they forgiven the killer? Could family and town even move on from such a tragic accident?

Soul searching followed. I thought about when the time is, if any, that we can forgive those who might have caused us pain. I thought about what it means to make mistakes, and then I thought to be human was to find mercy and forgiveness.

Thank you, She Writes Press. I am grateful for your continued excellence in publishing and the commitment of the entire SWP team to not only the books but also to the authors behind the books.

mercy town

Mercy Town would not have gotten to its ready-to-publish stage without the diligence of developmental editing by Annie Tucker. She has been my guide and support for all my book projects, calling out where my writing was deficient and where it shined in abundance. And thank you to Marcia Trahan, who is not only the editor of all my writing projects, but is also a published writer of memoir and poetry. I'm grateful you have helped guide *Mercy Town* to the finish line.

And last, I acknowledge you, the readers and supporters and followers of my writing work. It is you I speak to and write of the simple things in our complicated world.

For a Book Club Discussion guide, please visit the author's website at nancychadwickauthor.com.

about the author

Photo credit: Cassandra Rodgers

Nancy Chadwick is an essayist, memoirist, and fiction writer. After a decade in advertising, another decade in corporate banking, she quit and began to write full time. She is the author of *Under the Birch Tree: A Memoir of Discovering Connections and Finding Home* and *The Wisdom of the Willow*, and her essays have appeared in *The Magic of Memoir: Inspiration for the Writing Journey, Adelaide Literary Magazine, Meaningful Conflicts – The Art of Friction, Writer's Digest,* and other outlets. Nancy and her husband reside in Glenview, Illinois.

Looking for your next great read?

We can help!

Visit www.shewritespress.com/next-read
or scan the QR code below for a list
of our recommended titles.

She Writes Press is an award-winning
independent publishing company founded to
serve women writers everywhere.